"I'm sorry I kissed you last night."

"I'm not." His response sent chills racing down the arm he still held in his strong fingers.

"I didn't mean to—"

"I spent most of the night wishing I didn't have a guest room."

Her lips twitched and hope flared.

"The thing is..."

"Right." She sank back against the seat, and this time her sigh couldn't be stopped. "Of course there's a thing."

"I don't do well mixing business with pleasure. You're part of a case, however indirectly, and honestly, I'm worried I can't do my job if I'm distracted by...you. And if I don't do my job, people get hurt. I definitely don't want one of those people to be you."

She blinked. Then frowned. His words soaked in, but she didn't quite accept them. "I distract you?" She broke her promise to herself and looked at him, unable to hide her disbelief. No one, certainly no man, had ever said that to her before.

Dear Reader,

Writing a Colton book has become one of my favorite things to do as an author. Being a part of this series always feels like a bonus of sorts. The puzzling together of the stories and characters, bringing yet another branch of this family tree to readers? It just makes me happy.

Hunting Colton's Witness features Nathan Colton, an honorable police detective faced with a lot of unexpected family drama. His life's been turned upside down with the death of his father and the secrets that death has exposed. Of course that makes it the not-so-perfect time to fall in love, but that's what happens almost from the moment he sees Vivian Maylor from across a crowded restaurant and bar. Before they even speak a word to one another, sparks fly. And then, so do bullets.

Vivian's been talked into taking some chances with her social life. She had no idea accepting a date with an online match could result in every aspect of her life being upended. She barely leaves the house! What is she doing in the middle of a dangerous mystery? She's so far out of her comfort zone and experience, and yet...Nathan Colton seems the perfect hero to see her through.

I hope you enjoy Nathan and Vivian's journey to happily-ever-after. They've got a lot of work to do to get there, but by the end, it'll be the perfect holiday romance that I hope warms your heart.

Happy reading,

Anna J.

HUNTING COLTON'S WITNESS

ANNA J. STEWART

ROMANTIC SUSPENSE

Special thanks and acknowledgment are given to Anna J. Stewart for her contribution to The Coltons of Owl Creek miniseries.

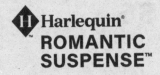

H Harlequin®
ROMANTIC SUSPENSE™

ISBN-13: 978-1-335-50245-2

Hunting Colton's Witness

Harlequin Enterprises ULC
22 Adelaide St. West, 41st Floor
Toronto, Ontario M5H 4E3, Canada
www.Harlequin.com

Printed in U.S.A.

Recycling programs for this product may not exist in your area.

Bestselling author **Anna J. Stewart** honestly believes she was born with a book in her hand. After growing up devouring every story she could get her hands on, now she gets to make her living making up stories and fulfilling happily-ever-afters of her own. Her dreams have most definitely come true. Anna lives in Northern California (only a ninety-minute flight from Disneyland, her favorite place on earth) with two monstrous, devious, adorable cats named Sherlock and Rosie.

Books by Anna J. Stewart

Harlequin Romantic Suspense

The Coltons of Owl Creek

Hunting Colton's Witness

Honor Bound

More Than a Lawman
Reunited with the P.I.
Gone in the Night
Guarding His Midnight Witness
Prison Break Hostage
The PI's Deadly Charade
Deadly Vegas Escapade
A Detective's Deadly Secrets

The Coltons of Roaring Springs

Colton on the Run

Colton 911: Chicago

Undercover Heat

Visit the Author Profile page
at Harlequin.com for more titles.

For the legions of Colton fans.
This one's for you.

Chapter 1

"Can I get you another drink, Nate?"

Detective Nate Colton stifled a disheartened sigh and glanced at his club soda with lime. "No, thanks, Seb." He flashed a tight smile at the bartender/co-owner of Madariaga's before casting an even quicker glance into the mirror. Leave it to scam artist Dean Wexler to turn his free Friday night into one of alcohol-free surveillance duty. "I'm still nursing this one."

"Working, huh?" Seb's sympathetic expression did nothing to ease Nate's irritation.

"Afraid so." Nate paused, considered. He glanced around, trying to take some pleasure in the plethora of Christmas lights strung around, through and over the crisscrossing beams covering the ceiling. "Question, Seb."

"Shoot." The middle-aged man whipped a hand towel over the shoulder of his festive red vest. "Sorry." He grinned and had Nate chuckling. "Not a lot of cops come in here. Don't get many opportunities to use my well-honed humor. What's up?"

"This guy." Nate inclined his head toward the table at his left. The thirtysomething man wore simple jeans and a dark T-shirt beneath a black leather jacket. His hands flexed and relaxed in a kind of rhythm that had him alternating between grasping his half-filled beer glass and slicking back his straw-blond hair. "You see him in here before?"

"Don't think so." The gray in Seb's hair and full beard shimmered beneath the dim recessed lighting when he shook his head. "Why?"

Telling Seb the man in question was a convicted scammer and con artist probably wasn't the way to go. Instead, Nate shrugged. "He looks jittery."

"My guess? First date. Probably a blind one." Seb reached for a glass on the drying rack and set it aside. "Ever since we implemented our safe dating protocol, we get a lot of them."

"Safe...?" Nate shook his head.

"We put up a notice in the ladies' room," Seb told him. "They order a certain drink, we know they need help." Seb inclined his chin down the hall on the other side of the room that led to an emergency exit. "We call for a car, and they get picked up at the back of the building. Date's none the wiser, and the lady gets home safe and sound."

"Nice." Nate grabbed a pair of olives and tossed them in his mouth. "More restaurants need that kind of policy."

"It's definitely upped our business," Seb said. "Speaking of business, haven't seen you in here in a while."

"Been busy. Work and, you know..." Nate paused, ate another olive, this one stuffed with an almond. "Family."

He was still adjusting to the fallout of recent Colton family events and revelations. While he and his sister had always known of their too-close-for-comfort connection to the Colton line branching out of Owl Creek, that part of the family hadn't known either he or Sarah existed at all. Until recently, that is. The emotional fallout on both sides was still being assessed. It was one thing to know he had other siblings living not too far away. It was another to have to deal with them. And the role his mother played in the situation.

That needle-sharp prick of disdain caught as it always did and lodged like a bullet in his chest. Leave it to his mother to set off a familial bomb that resulted in near cataclysmic repercussions. Jessie Colton's calculated actions, as usual, bordered on cruel. But what bothered Nate most was that she never, ever did something like this without a bigger agenda in mind.

His mother was up to something. Something big enough to warrant blowing up a near thirty-year-old family secret.

Part of him didn't want to think about what was coming next. But he needed to do just that, if for no other reason than to protect his sister. He swallowed hard. Plus all ten of the half-brothers and sisters he now openly counted as family.

"Let me know when you're ready for another." Seb offered a sympathetic smile before he moved off to serve a pair of newcomers waiting at the bar for their table.

Pinning his gaze on the mirror to keep track of his target, Nate's stomach rumbled around the teasing promise of food. He'd made a mistake skipping lunch, but he'd been neck deep in planning how to deal with Dean Wexler, the aforementioned table dweller who seemed to grow increasingly fidgety as time passed. Well, Nate thought, he'd followed worse leads and trusted sketchier sources.

He took a deep breath and filled his senses with the familiar and intoxicating aroma of garlic, smoky paprika and saffron, which carried the sweetest hint of honey. The combination increased his crankiness and his hunger.

No one cooked a rib eye like the chefs at Madariaga's, but he couldn't count on Wexler sticking around long enough for him to finish eating. He'd have to make do with the selection of spiced olives and… He raised off his stool enough to grab a dish of mixed nuts farther down the counter. Judging by the way Wexler kept checking his phone for what Nate assumed was the time—or a message from his soon-to-arrive date—it was either going to be a quick wrap-up or a long, long evening. Either way, Nate was in it to the end.

Wexler was the closest thing he had to a lead when it came to his extortion and racketeering case against Marty DeBaccian. Since his release from prison two years ago, DeBaccian had been making his way up the criminal-element food chain here in Boise. Nate, along with a number of his fellow detectives, were determined to stop him before he got anywhere close to the top. Which was where Wexler—a smaller, less careful fish—came in. Nate had been working this case for going on six months. He was getting as antsy as Wexler appeared to be. He wanted this case closed. Now.

"Totally explains how you're spending your Friday night," Nate muttered to himself.

Friday nights on the Basque Block, an area of downtown Boise dedicated to the mix of French and Spanish culture, were notoriously crowded and energetic. The brisk December cold blowing through the city triggered temptations of warm, comforting food and drinks within the welcoming confines of the community. The streets were lined with countless lights and lanterns, windows displayed various images of the seasons, holiday sale signs were abundant and welcoming.

Add in extended Happy Hour at Madariaga's, a restaurant known for their clams Portuguese and in-house brews, and there were numerous festivities in which to partake. The snow had been somewhat gentle on his way in, but he could smell a storm coming.

As he lived a short distance away, Nate often found himself sitting right in this very spot, listening to various musicians performing on the small circular stage in the center of the dining room. Tonight, the usual weekend percussive sounds of drums, tambourines and flutes had been replaced by a solitary guitarist, who, if Nate was honest with himself, conjured a deep-seated envy as she plucked out familiar Christmas music with a finger-flying Spanish-inspired flair.

His lips twitched in unexpected humor. Growing up, he'd loved the idea of becoming a musician, but it soon became obvious the only talent he possessed where a guitar was concerned was stashing it in the back of his closet.

As entertaining as the place was, Nate bit back a self-pitying sigh as he rotated his glass. He'd really been looking forward to a night in, slugging down more than a few bottles of beer and binge-watching the latest in a series of ridiculous, over-the-top, high-speed vehicular action movies.

Seated on a corner stool at the bar, Nate ran through Wexler's rap sheet in his head to keep himself occupied and, more importantly, focused. There wasn't much Wexler hadn't been accused of in his thirty-three years. His first adult arrest had come two days after he'd turned eighteen.

Wexler's juvie record was sealed, but Nate would bet a year's salary the guy spent a significant amount of time locked down from a very early age. Now the guy had a tendency to mix things up and expand into whatever worked best for him. These days, burglaries seemed to be his preferred method of income. After going over numerous victim statements and reports, Nate strongly suspected Wexler was behind the rash of thefts that had relieved nearly a dozen single women of a significant amount of cash and property.

A streak like that had to have caught DeBaccian's attention, which gave Nate some solid leverage. Wexler's spine was as solid as straw. He'd bend over and kiss whatever backside he needed to keep himself out of prison. Or off DeBaccian's hit list. Nate planned on being the person who could make both those things happen. For a price.

Exhaustion crept up his spine. He hadn't had a good night's sleep since he'd gotten back from Owl Creek. Whatever switch that turned his brain off had been overridden by stress, circumstance and what probably amounted to an unhealthy amount of professional obsession.

"Heads up." Seb crouched to retrieve a trayful of clean glasses. When he popped back up, he jutted his chin toward the front door. "Your boy just went on full alert."

Nate's gaze shifted not so subtly to Wexler, who had indeed straightened up and was looking toward the door, which clicked shut.

Wexler's nerves didn't abate, Nate noticed. Instead, they intensified to the point of vibration. Like a cheetah poised to pounce on unsuspecting prey. Wexler stood, lifted an arm, and only then did Nate see the gleam of relief—or was it calculation?—on the man's face. Whatever it was, Wexler definitely had Nate's full attention.

Or at least he did until Nate looked to the door and saw her.

Her back was to him at first as she hung her coat on a hook. She wore a knee-skimming black dress and matching short-sleeved sweater. Her long, dark brown hair draped beautifully down her back. The knee-high boots spoke of practicality where an Idaho winter was concerned. She had curves where he preferred them and not an angle in sight. She was, Nate thought as she turned around and displayed a face worthy of a classical sculptor, the kind of woman who conjured carnal thoughts of endless nights spent in front of a fire while a winter storm raged outside their door.

"Beautiful," he murmured in a way that had him glancing around to confirm he hadn't been overheard. Impulse had his hands curled into fists before reality knocked him back down. He wasn't here for her.

But he wanted to be.

The woman paused, ran her hands down the front of her dress in a motion that spoke to her own bout of nerves. A thin gold chain around her neck displayed a solitary charm that, from a distance, Nate couldn't decipher. Rather than makeup, it was the cold that tinted her cheeks. Her full lips pressed together until they disappeared. Nate could all but hear the pep talk she was giving herself before she stepped shakily over to the hostess desk.

It seemed a cruel trick, or maybe it was a stroke of luck, when she was escorted to Dean Wexler's table.

Nate inclined his head, unable to pull his attention away. She stood beside her chair and offered her hand to Wexler, who immediately grasped it. He could see her mouth move, but couldn't, with the music and conversation bouncing around the restaurant, hear what she said. Her smile seemed strained when she pulled her chair back to sit. Polite. Reserved.

Nate gave Wexler's chances of a second date a whole one out of ten when the idiot neglected to play the chivalry card and pull out her chair for her. *Typical*, Nate thought with a silent snort. Why would Wexler act on something he probably couldn't spell?

Nate was so caught up in that observation he didn't realize she was looking directly at him.

Their gazes locked, and he couldn't, for what seemed like a full minute, find his breath. His smile came without thought, and he felt a chill of accomplishment when she offered him one in return. Maybe he was fooling himself, but this smile, unlike the one she'd offered Wexler, appeared genuine. A flash of uncertainty illuminated her candlelit hazel eyes before she turned her attention to Wexler and the menu he handed her. Reaching into her purse, she pulled out a pair of round glasses.

Nate glanced away, cursing himself for being tempted

to forget about the case and keep her in his sights. Darn if those glasses didn't add to her appeal. He'd never been into the librarian look. Oh, how wrong he'd been.

Focus, Nate told himself. If Wexler's pattern held, this woman could very well be his next burglary victim. Nate's hand tightened around his glass at the thought of anyone—Wexler in particular—taking advantage of her. Of eroding the trust and shadowy optimism he saw in those amazing eyes of hers.

"Seb!" As if taken over by someone else, Nate signaled for another drink. He couldn't risk surrendering to temptation and instead fixed his gaze on the mirror image of her.

Guilt had him shifting uncomfortably on his stool. He hoped he didn't look as pathetic as he felt. He needed to think about someone, anyone else, another woman he'd dated, met, talked with who had intrigued him more than this woman did. But it was a no-go. It was as if this woman, simply by walking into view, had erased every other woman from his memory.

"So?" Seb said. "What do you think?"

Nate took a too large sip of his club soda. "About what?" he choked out.

"Them." Seb tilted his head. "You think they'll make it to a second date?"

"No." Nate lifted his glass, toasted Seb with it. "I do not."

If only because Nate planned on having Wexler behind bars in the next few hours.

Vivian Maylor's head was spinning, and not in a good way. Why, oh why, had she let Lizzy talk her into online dating? Because Lizzy was her best friend and had rarely steered her wrong. Clearly there was a first time for everything.

Vivian's vision blurred as she tried to focus on the open menu in her trembling hands. Anxiety had grabbed hold, not when she climbed into her car or even when she'd parked a few blocks away. Oh, no, her old heart-stuttering friend had locked its twisty, suffocating bands around her back when she'd first clicked Accept on the online dating profile.

"Just jump in and rip the Band-Aid off," Lizzy Colton had told her a few weeks ago when Vivian made the mistake of lamenting feeling lonely out loud. "Just go out on one date and see what happens!" This from the woman who less than a month ago had been trapped in a blizzard only to be rescued by a man who may as well have stepped right out of one of Vivian's romance novels.

Of course, Lizzy's headline-making kidnapping around the same time had no doubt left her searching for an outlet for the residual trauma. As happy as Vivian was to serve as a support for her friend, she hadn't anticipated having to agree to a date in order to make Lizzy smile again. But she had. And Lizzy seemed relieved. About that at least.

"Leaving you to rip off the Band-Aid," Vivian muttered then suddenly realized she'd spoken out loud. She peeked over the top edge of her menu and smiled at her date. "Sorry." She forced a smile before reaching for the ice water their server had delivered. "I live alone, so I talk to myself." She took a big swallow. "A lot."

"Who doesn't?" her date teased. But the glint in his brown eyes didn't lessen her unease. She had the feeling he was trying too hard. "Have you been here before, Vivian?"

"Ah, kind of?" She set the menu down and did her best to ignore the tingling racing down her spine. There was this—she didn't know how else to describe it—this force, pulsing out at her from the bar. Not the bar, she corrected quickly and glanced to her left and saw him looking at her again. But the man sitting there. She pushed her glasses higher up her nose, a nervous habit she had when uncertainty descended. He looked familiar, but she couldn't for the life of her figure out why. "I live a little ways away, but I've ordered from their delivery menu." She needed to focus on her date. He was, after all, why she'd made the white-knuckle drive into town. "So. Sam." She needed to give this an authentic chance. "Is that short for Samuel?"

"Nope." His eyes flashed. "Just Sam. Sam Gabriel."

"Right." She shook her head. "Sam Gabriel." Truth be told, she'd only retained a modicum of the information that had been listed on his profile. While she was at the top of her game in the PR department, socializing outside of work wasn't her thing. She wasn't…outgoing. Or adventurous. But loneliness was a surefire trigger to pushing someone outside their comfort zone.

She supposed it was a good idea to leave the house for something other than getting her mail. Since her cat Toby died last month, she'd spent an inordinate amount of time feeding the strays in her neighborhood, an activity that was quickly earning her loony cat-lady status. All that was missing was the bumper sticker on her car declaring herself a cat mom. Best to get out in the world before that became a reality.

She'd have thought all the cheery holiday decor lining the downtown Boise streets would have elevated her mood, but instead, it only reminded her of how alone she truly was. "You're a teacher, aren't you, Sam? What was it? Third grade?"

"Second." He leaned his arms on the table and grinned so wide she could see the fillings in his molars. He was good-looking enough, she supposed, but that smile. She couldn't help but suspect there was something else lurking behind it. "I just love kids, don't you?"

"I haven't spent enough time around them to say, honestly." She looked back at the dinner offerings, telling herself not to be paranoid. His questions were normal for a first date. Her instincts were out of practice and headed into overdrive. It was a simple dinner date. Nothing more. She was the fish out of water here, not Sam. "I think I'm just going to get the panzanella." Her stomach rumbled at the very idea. She'd been so nervous all day she hadn't had much to eat. The idea of a bread salad hit all the right notes. "How about you?"

"Haven't decided yet." He reached over and pulled her menu down with one crooked finger. "You don't have to be nervous, Vivian."

"It's my natural state." Her smile felt stiff this time, and that voice in the back of her head was definitely crying out more loudly to be listened to. She shouldn't have done this. Taking chances, doing the unexpected—that was Lizzy's way of doing things, not hers. Vivian shoved her hands under her legs and scrunched her fingers, felt the wood against her nails. "So, um." She glanced around, did her best not to let her gaze drift anywhere near the man at the bar. Even as her mind raced to place him. Thankfully, their server arrived and took their orders. The few minutes gave her enough time to get at least some questions lined up in her overactive brain.

The guitarist had taken a break, and to be honest, Vivian welcomed the silence. Or at least as much silence as the crowded restaurant allowed. A solitary votive candle flickered in a deep vessel, sprigs of rosemary pressed up against the glass, casting wintery shadows on the red tablecloth. "So, how long have you been using the dating app?" she asked when they were alone again.

"Not long." He was back to leaning on the table, a semi-smirking expression on his face now. "I like how it gets all the tedious stuff out of the way. I saw on your profile you're in PR. You own your own business, don't you?"

"Yes." She tucked her hair behind her ear. "PR Perfection. I represent a number of clients from various industries. I focus a lot on authors and entertainment figures."

"Sounds interesting."

It must, given the sudden spark in his eyes. "Social media is a big part of what I do," she said. "I guess a dating app didn't seem out of the norm by comparison." If only she was as good at talking about herself as she was discussing her clients. So far, the only word that came to mind regarding this date was *excruciating*. "It can be pretty long hours, unexpected work hours sometimes." A few of her clients had run into some rather scandalous situations as of late. How she'd handled them had earned her a few more clients in return. "But I like the challenge of staying on top of things for my clients and helping them expand their reach."

"I bet that pays pretty well."

The man at the bar coughed and shifted on his stool. Vivian couldn't help it. She glanced over and found him looking at her again. This time, the pretty blue eyes carried a bit of a warning. Vivian straightened in her chair. Was he... Was he listening to them? Her stomach knotted to the point of pain.

"I do okay," she said. "What made you go into teaching?"

Sam's smile widened. "I liked the idea of helping shape the minds of the future."

Vivian frowned. That sounded so rehearsed she could almost see a script sticking out of his pocket. "Second grade is, what, ten years old?"

"Thereabouts." Sam leaned back as his second beer was delivered. "So, this place is a favorite of yours, then?" He looked around. "It has a nice vibe."

"It has good food." It was one thing she indulged in. Some people had a weakness for aged whiskey or bookstores. Vivian held an affinity for cuisine. It was a safe way to be adventurous, especially these days with so many restaurants offering delivery service. "How long have you been teaching?"

"A few years." He picked up his beer. "Do you travel much?"

"No. Do you?"

"When I can. Gets a bit costly on a teacher's salary."

Vivian nodded, making note of the fact that that was the second time he'd mentioned money. Was it her imagination or was this guy digging for something? It didn't feel like a normal date. Not that she knew what that felt like. She couldn't recall the last actual date she'd gone on. She had to be overthinking this. She looked to the man at the bar, who offered an encouraging smile before he looked away again.

She silently sighed and tried to return her focus to Sam. He was currently talking up a storm, about what she couldn't really say, but the man at the bar? He hadn't said a word, yet she had this unsettling desire to sit beside him and strike up a conversation.

Vivian slid her gaze to the mirror behind the bar, found him watching her again. But instead of making her feel uncomfortable or targeted, that *whoomph* of a force field seemed to pulse in tempting rhythm.

Those eyes of his were so bright against the light brown of his hair. She'd never been one to like messy hair before, but on him it worked. She couldn't see much more than his face, hunched over his drink the way he was. He had wide shoulders, though. Strong shoulders, she imagined, and a broad chest to match. Beneath the long sleeves of his navy shirt, muscles bunched and tightened in a way that left her feeling a bit foggy-headed. She liked his smile. A lot.

"Vivian?" Sam caught her hand in his and gave her fingers a gentle squeeze. "You still with me?"

"Um, yes, of course." She waited for a spark, for some kind of confirmation that there was something between her and Sam. Instead, she had the sudden urge to retreat and pull back into her town house of a shell. Whatever she might have said next was scrapped when their dinner was delivered.

Relieved, she picked up her fork and quickly filled her mouth in order to avoid any other comment. Or any temptation to look back at the stranger who made her feel things she honestly hadn't thought possible.

Despite her intention to speed things up, dinner passed at an excruciatingly slow rate. She had to give Sam points for trying. Her date was nothing if not persistent with the questions and attempts to discover common ground. But there wasn't any. And there certainly wasn't heat between them, not even a spark.

They both reached for the check at the same time.

"I insist," Sam said with a bit of an edge in his voice.

So did she. "We'll split it." Vivian kept her voice light. "I think we can both admit this isn't going anywhere."

"Maybe we just haven't hit the right moment yet." His smile was tight as he reached into his back pocket for his wallet. He flagged down their server and waved off her determined offer to add cash to cover her meal. "Tell you what," Sam said. "There's a great little dessert café a couple blocks away. Let's take a walk, get some fresh air and you can treat. They have a great chocolate peanut-butter lava cake."

Proof he'd read her profile. She'd mentioned a weakness for anything chocolate. She did the calculations in her head. Twenty or thirty minutes more in exchange for lava cake? She shrugged, her sweet tooth activated. Seemed an appropriate price to pay for dessert. "All right."

She clutched her hands in her lap, her knees bouncing as she watched him fill out the tip amount on the credit card receipt. He clicked the pen shut and stood up.

"I'm just going to visit the ladies' room before we head out." She pointed toward the back of the restaurant. "I'll meet you out front?"

"You aren't going to go scampering out the back door, are you?" Sam teased.

She'd be lying if she said the thought hadn't crossed her mind. "I'll meet you out front." When he moved off, she dug into her purse, pulled out a couple of twenty-dollar bills and slid them into the bill folder just as their server reappeared to retrieve it. "Thank you for lovely service," she told him. "Sorry about his tip."

"I'm sorry about your date," the young man said with an understanding smile.

"Thanks." When she stood, she couldn't help but give in to temptation one last time.

The corner barstool was empty.

The man with the blue eyes was gone.

"Of course he is." On a scale of one to ten, she was hovering at about a minus two at this point where tonight was concerned.

Since the ladies' room was just an excuse to make up for the anemic tip Sam left—clearly her date had never worked in the service industry—it wasn't long before Vivian retrieved her jacket from the hook by the door and shrugged into it.

Regret over having agreed to dessert surged as she joined Sam outside. She really just wanted to go home and forget tonight had ever happened.

Sam was standing by the valet parking stand, looking at his cell, when she emerged. He straightened when he saw her, shoved it into his pocket in a motion that had her earlier suspicions resurfacing. She did a quick scan of the street in both directions and noticed a number of people around. The windows of other restaurants displayed plenty of customers amidst the holiday decor of garlands, lights and glistening, colorful ornaments.

Sam's smile was back in place, but his eyes were a

bit jumpy, looking over his shoulder before he stepped closer. "All set?"

"Sure." Worst case, she'd head back to Madariaga's and use the escape hatch she'd seen posted in the bathroom. "How far is it?" She pointed behind her as he led her down the street at a rather hurried pace. "I'm parked in the other direction."

"Two, maybe three blocks?" He didn't sound nearly as sure of himself as he had inside the restaurant. He dropped a hand to her back to hurry her along. "I promise this cake is totally worth it."

"Mmm." It would have to be a pretty fantastic dessert to get her to put tonight behind her. Snow drifted gently to the ground. Her lined boots kept her suddenly scrunching toes warm, and she grabbed the lapels of her brown down jacket. She'd forgotten to wear gloves, but the coffee she planned to order should take the chill off her fingers. Her boots clicked against the sidewalk as they walked. "I hope your next date goes better than this one," she said as a peace offering.

"This one isn't over yet." Sam, hands shoved into the front pockets of his jacket, gave her an encouraging smile. "But if you're looking for sparks, yeah." He sighed. "Looks like we're out of luck in that department."

Sparks like what she'd felt when she'd looked at the man at the bar? "I'm afraid so. Is that the place?" She pointed ahead to the lighted café sign two blocks on the left. At nearly nine on a Friday night, traffic was still humming alongside them. The rumble of engines cut through that winter silence she'd been longing for. If she never answered another question in her life, it would be too soon.

"Look, Vivian."

Sam stopped and reached out, caught her arm and brought her to a halt. The display cases in the jewelry store beside them showed off a modicum of offerings that glinted under spotlight bulbs. Sprays of holly and tinsel decorated the windows, along with spray-on snow creating a framed effect.

In the street, a beige car occupied by two men drove by at a crawl. The passenger in front slid down, almost in slow motion as she glanced over her shoulder.

"Maybe we should give this another try?" Sam suggested. "This could have just been first-date jitters, and, well—" His eyes went wide as a pop sounded in the air. She jumped, looked toward the car. Something gold glinted in the back seat. The sound of breaking glass tinkled in the air followed by another pop. And another.

Sam caught her around the waist and knocked her to the ground, driving the air out of her lungs. She hit shoulder first. Her head bounced against the cement. Her glasses snapped, the jagged edge cutting into her face. Whatever scream she might have offered was caught by the whoosh of Sam's body landing heavily on top of her. Now that she could, she couldn't form the thought to cry out.

The weight of Sam's body pushed down on her to the point she could feel the ground pressing against her side.

More glass tinkled, another pop echoed. An alarm went off, blaring into the night as people cried out and tires screeched. Footsteps raced past and around her. Unintelligible conversation picked up speed to the point it became white noise.

Vivian lay there, frozen, the cold of the ground soaking through her jacket and making her shiver. A sob caught in her throat as she tried to move and got one hand up to her shoulder in order to shove Sam away. She kicked her legs in an attempt to extricate herself. "Sam, get up. Get off." She shoved again, only he didn't move. She felt an odd warmth trickle down her neck and spread beneath her jacket. "Sam?" She pushed harder.

The growing crowd didn't seem to know what to do any more than she did. "Help, please," she cried, her voice muffled by Sam's shoulder. "Someone…help!"

"Back! Everyone stand back!" The male voice that exploded through the crowd brought her an unexpected moment of relief before Sam was rolled off her.

Suddenly feeling as if she could breathe again, Vivian tried to sit up. When she did, she saw the man from the bar, crouched behind her, that handsome face of his marred with controlled fear and concern. She lifted a hand to where her glasses had been, where her face hurt. "You." It was the only word that came to mind. The only thing she could think to say. Her ears were ringing, and her head throbbed. She lifted her fingers to her temple. "What are you—?"

"Are you all right?" The man shifted slightly, reached into his pocket for his cell. "Don't move too much."

"I'm—fine." Her mind raced, trying to catch up with whatever had just happened. She looked around. The parked car didn't have windows anymore. Shattered glass littered the sidewalk. She clutched her hands to her chest, took comfort in the hand resting on her shoulder.

"That's not your blood?" The man asked in such an urgent way he left her blinking.

"Blood?" She looked down, saw the glistening red liquid coating her jacket and her neck. She touched a hand to her skin, drew away sticky red fingers. "N-no. It's not mine." Realization shot through her, and she felt her face grow cold. "Sam." She scrambled onto her knees, but the man from the bar shifted to keep her where she was. "Is he hurt? Why isn't he—?"

"Yeah, this is Detective Nate Colton, Boise Police." The man spoke into his phone. He clicked the speaker feature on, placed the phone on the ground beside him. "Stay right there," he ordered Vivian, who could only nod and stare. He turned his back on her, but the second she could move, she was on her knees beside him.

"You're a policeman?" she asked the detective as he pulled open Sam's jacket, pressed two fingers against the side of Sam's blood-spattered neck.

"Dispatch," Nate continued as if she hadn't spoken. "Requesting backup and patrol. And an ambulance to…" He glanced around and recited the address. "I've got a gunshot victim, at least two to the chest. Rapid pulse, but he's alive. I need to keep him that way. Over."

"Request received, Detective Colton. Assistance is on the way. Over."

"Great." He reached out a bloodied hand and clicked off the speaker. A number of people raced out of a nearby restaurant. "You!" Nate yelled over the heads of the crowd creeping closer. "I need towels or tablecloths or napkins, something to help stanch the bleeding."

"I can—" Vivian started to stand, but her knees folded immediately.

"You stay right there," Detective Colton ordered. "And you all, turn those stupid phones off," he snapped at the crowd, who all but ignored his order. "This isn't anything that needs to be shared."

Vivian shivered and tried to breathe regularly. Her head spun. Her stomach churned. For a moment, she feared she might throw up. She pressed a hand against her mouth and tasted bile in the back of her throat.

"Hey." Detective Colton nudged her knee with his foot. "You're okay, right? You still with me?"

"Yes." She nodded, feeling both useless and helpless, which only irritated her. "I don't know what happened. One thing we're walking down the street, and the next thing I know he knocked me down."

The detective gave her a blank look, but if he was going to ask her anything, he was prevented by the restaurant employees returning with a stack of towels and napkins.

"Great, thanks." Detective Colton inclined his head. "Grab some of those will you?" he told Vivian. "And keep one for yourself." He nodded to her face. "You're cut. From your glasses probably."

Her glasses. She looked around but couldn't focus enough to see where they might have ended up. She'd have to get her spare pair from home. Her hands shook as she accepted the offerings and quickly handed the detective one so he could slip it between his blood-soaked hands and Sam's open wounds. "Don't you die on me, Wexler."

"His name is Sam," Vivian corrected. "Sam Gabriel."

The detective leaned forward, pressed down so hard with his hands Vivian winced. "I need you to stay quiet right now," he told her, looking as if he didn't want to be saying what he had. "Just…trust me, okay? I'll explain everything I can soon, but not now."

It was a request Vivian often had trouble with. Trust was a big reason why she lived alone. Why she worked alone. But with this man… She couldn't explain it. "Okay." She said it in a whisper and reached for another towel. "Yeah." She swallowed hard. "I trust you."

Chapter 2

Nate had long ago lost track of the number of nights he'd spent in a Boise emergency room.

His years as a uniformed officer had made visits an almost daily occurrence, from getting unhoused people looked after to overseeing the transport of accident victims, or overdose victims in a sometimes futile effort to get them help before they succumbed to their addictions. Early on, he'd developed that necessary emotional detachment that kicked in every time he stepped through the swinging doors, whether trailing behind a gurney or having hauled someone out of the back of his patrol car. Nate had always been able to keep himself detached and logical in a crisis.

Tonight, however? Tonight was a very different, not to mention unnerving, story.

He'd left the restaurant the second Wexler's date reached for the check. Seemed an apt signal of the end of his target's dinner, and Nate hadn't bothered to dismiss the relief he felt at the encounter tanking. He needed his focus on what Wexler could do for his case, not what plans the scam artist might have for his date.

After signaling good-night to Seb, he'd made his way

outside and waited in the alley between Madariaga's and the dry-cleaning business next door. Out of sight. But close enough to pick Wexler up as soon as he was on his own, once his suspect finished the cell call he accepted.

Only Wexler wasn't on his own. Somehow, he'd managed to convince her to join him for coffee and dessert.

That odd, primal wave of protection surged as Wexler and his date walked past. There had been enough distance between the two that Nate could take comfort in the knowledge there wasn't anything close to a love match. Not that that mattered. That wasn't any of his business.

He needed Wexler to talk, which meant Nate needed to keep his target in sight, approach when he could be assured of privacy. He'd stepped out from the alley, waited until they'd crossed the first street before following.

Even now, Nate was kicking himself for not noticing the beige sedan creeping slowly up the street just behind the pair. He'd increased his pace, was only a little ways behind when the passenger window rolled down and the gun appeared.

What was happening should have dawned on him sooner and not after the first shot shattered the parked car's driver's-side window.

He was running as the second shot sounded and the jewelry store window exploded. Wexler dived forward as glass rained down like a deafening winter snowstorm. More shots. Tires screeched, and Nate leaped into the street to try to catch a glimpse of the plate number as the car raced around the corner and disappeared from sight.

Shouts of shock and terror reverberated before Nate gave up and shoved his way through the instantly forming crowd. He couldn't hear anything other than a low, dull buzzing in his ears. He thought for sure she was dead. She had to be, his mind screamed at him as he'd dropped beside them. For an instant, he let himself feel the fear and the dread, accepting, however reluctantly, the truth of what had happened.

Wexler was on top of her, unmoving. Blood seeped out and spread across the glistening frozen pavement.

His heart stopped. She'd moved. Only a little at first, then with enough of a determined cry he dared to hope…

He rolled Wexler off her. Seeing her blink up at him settled the unfamiliar panic that had surged inside him. She was covered in Wexler's blood as she pushed herself up. Her eyes were glassy with shock, and she was shaking so hard he was afraid her bones might snap, but she was alive.

And so, miraculously, was Wexler.

Now, standing outside the second pair of double swinging doors in the ER, Nate stared through the glass window. He flexed his tight, blood-stained hands. It felt as if he were wearing gloves. His heart pounded. He should have drawn his gun. He should have fired at the car, but there were so many people around and the car had been speeding so fast, it was just as well he hadn't.

"Detective?" A nurse from the registration desk approached. She was older, her silver-streaked hair worn in a long braid down her back. The badge she wore identified her as the duty nurse. "Are you all right?"

"I'm fine." The statement didn't sound like it came from him. "What's his status?"

"We won't know for a while. Why don't you come with me?" She took him by the shoulder and led him behind the desk. "You can use the locker room to clean up. I'll let you know when the doctor's available to speak with you."

Nate stopped outside the door as if he'd hit a wall. "There's a woman who was brought in. Pretty. Dark hair, brown jacket. She's being checked for injuries."

"I'll see what I can find out. Please." She motioned to the door. "Take your time. I'll make sure there's some coffee waiting for you."

Nate almost laughed at the idea of adding caffeine to the situation.

It was only when he was standing at the sink looking at himself in the mirror that he realized why the nurse was so intent on getting him out of sight. His hands, the front of his shirt, even part of his face were covered in blood. At least the dark fabric would hide most of it, once it was dry anyway, but the clothes and probably his jacket were toast after today.

He gave his hands a quick scrub, dried off, then cleaned off his phone and the wallet he'd dragged free to show his badge when the ambulance and other cops had arrived.

By the time he thought himself presentable, his anxiety over Wexler surged afresh. As selfish as it sounded, he really needed the guy to pull through. He needed him. His case against DeBaccian couldn't be made without him.

The nurse was back at the station when he walked past.

"Detective." She held up a large paper cup. "Dr. Billings can speak with you in a few minutes. In the meantime, the woman you asked about, she's being examined right now." She inclined her head toward the hall. "Third room, second bed on the right."

"Thanks. Can you…" He paused. "Did you happen to get her name?"

"Vivian Maylor." The nurse smiled as if understanding something he didn't. "And just so you know…" She leaned forward and lowered her voice, a soft smile on her lips. "She asked about you, too."

He moved away, ducking his head before she or anyone else saw the heat in his cheeks. Just what his evening needed, a matchmaking nurse.

Rehearsing what he was going to say to her would be a lesson in futility. There wasn't anything he could utter that would make any kind of sense, at least not yet. Right now, all he cared about was seeing that she was all right.

He stood outside the drawn curtain, heard her soft murmur of a voice. It was the same murmur he'd listened intently to and for at the restaurant. He closed his eyes, blotting out the words she spoke but listening to the tone. It was a tone that comforted him in a way he'd never quite experienced before.

The curtain was ripped open, and a woman stepped out. She wore blue scrubs and her blond hair up in a messy knot on the top of her head. "Ah. Hello. Dr. Preston." She held out her hand. "You must be Detective Colton."

"I must be." The sooner he got his sense of humor back on track the better. "Is she okay?"

"Near as we can tell." Dr. Preston nodded. "She has a bruised shoulder, so we're waiting on X-rays, and she got a pretty good knock on the side of her head, but no signs of a concussion. We took care of the cut near her eye." She reached up and grabbed hold of the stethoscope hanging around her neck. She'd clipped a sparkly harp-playing angel to the metal center. "She'll be sore for a couple of days and probably have a headache, but other than that, she's okay. I'm going to get her discharge paperwork started for once we see the X-ray's clear." She stepped aside. "Go on in."

"Thanks." Nate didn't know what was more embarrassing—the nurse's romantic coddling earlier or the fact he felt like a teenager picking up his first date.

He peeked around the edge of the curtain. She sat there, sitting up in the mechanical bed, her gaze pinned on him the second he stepped clear of the fabric. They'd put a small butterfly bandage on the cut by her right eye. Dried blood coated part of her face and the side of her neck. Her eyes seemed slightly dazed, the shock no doubt. Even with all that and very pale skin, she still struck him as beautiful. He felt like he could breathe again and yet...not. "Hey."

"Hey, yourself." Her smile was quick and more than a little confused. "Detective." She eyed the cup in his hand with the ferocity and longing of a fellow caffeine addict. "Is that coffee?"

"Supposedly." His first sip hadn't been promising. He removed the plastic lid and handed it to her.

"My hero." She accepted the cup with both hands and drank nearly half of it down. "For the second time tonight." With a sigh, she sat back. "How's Sam?" Nate hesitated long enough for her to roll her eyes. "His name isn't Sam, is it?" The calm acceptance had him frowning. "That might be one thing about tonight that actually makes sense."

"Bad date?" He blinked in feigned innocence, but that only earned him a judgmental glare.

"You know it was." She eyed him dubiously. "You called him Wexler back on the street. Who is he really?"

"Not anyone you need to be concerned with from here on." Nate came into the cubicle and reached for the metal-frame chair in the corner. "Is it okay if I sit?"

"Sure." She shifted on the squeaking mattress. "Trust me, you're getting the better end of the comfort deal." She tugged at the collar of the pale hospital gown. The monitor in the corner beeped out her vitals, which, in Nate's limited experience, still seemed a little high. "My butt's already asleep. You didn't answer my question. Is what's-his-name okay?"

"I'm waiting to hear." From his vantage point, he could see the hallway and the thin bits of tinsel strung in the hall. "Your doctor says you're fine."

"Oh, I'm just great," Vivian said with more sass than he expected. "But I think I'm officially off online dating." She laughed, but it sounded more pained than amused. Her hands were shaking, just enough to signal the shock hadn't yet fully set in. "As if I wasn't already inclined to swear it off completely. I don't think there's ever been a bigger first-date disaster on record."

He sat back and chuckled in an effort to put her at ease. "I once had a date that ended with me mistaking her brother for a burglar. Planted the guy face-first into her refrigerator. Broke his nose," he admitted. "And about a dozen butterfly magnets."

She looked doubtful, but there was a glimmer of amusement in her hazel eyes. "You're making that up."

"Oh, how I wish I was." Funny. For the life of him, he could not recall that woman's name.

"Verbal first aid for the heart. Who knew that was a thing?" She took another drink of coffee before handing it back to him. "Thanks. That jolt should be enough to get me home." Her eyes went wide. "Eventually. My glasses." Her sigh was heavy and resigned. "They broke back on the street." And she hadn't had the wherewithal to attempt to locate them.

"Where is home?"

"Here we go with questions again," she muttered. "Must be inquisition Friday and no one told me. I live about halfway between here and Owl Creek. Am I supposed to give a statement or something? That always happens on cop shows."

"One of the few things they get right," Nate observed wryly. Oh, if he could only list his pet peeves on that front. "There will be another detective to take yours."

"Not you?"

Maybe it was his exhaustion talking, but she sounded disappointed. "I was there, so no, not me." He would, however, have to give his own account.

"Well, I'm not going anywhere for a while, so." She pointed to a sign that listed how long various tests took to complete. X-rays averaged two hours. Vivian sighed in evident frustration. "Let's have it. Tell me exactly who it was I had dinner with tonight. How bad is he?"

"I don't think—"

"You can follow that tidbit of information with why you were running surveillance on my date," she said as if he hadn't spoken.

"I wasn't running surveillance on your date. Exactly," he added at his own doubt. "I didn't intend to, anyway."

"Yeah, well, lucky for me your intentions changed." She was getting fidgety, plucking at imaginary threads on her sweater and trying to keep her hands occupied.

Nate often played fast and loose with the truth. Faking out suspects, questioning witnesses and putting them at ease was necessary in his job. So was assuring people who had witnessed something borderline horrific that there was nothing for them to worry about. He possessed a talent for skirting that thin line of truth that most people only crossed in desperate times.

But there was something about the way Vivian Maylor looked at him that snuffed out that natural tendency and left him uttering the truth. "Long story short?"

"Don't shorten it on my account." She looked completely resigned to hearing the absolute worst. "Going to be here awhile."

"Your date's real name is Dean Wexler. He's a convicted con artist. His last stretch in prison was eighteen months for stealing an elderly woman's life savings shortly after she was put into a nursing home."

Vivian sat up, wide eyes filling with something akin to rage. "Nu-uh."

"Afraid so." He cringed. "He's currently a suspect in a string of burglaries targeting successful single women using various dating apps."

"Of course he is." She leaned her head back and sighed. "So that's why you were following him? To get an eye on his next victim?"

"No, actually." He looked down at his almost empty coffee cup. "That's not my case, unfortunately. But I've got a few leads that link him to another one I've been working on." He might be feeling chatty, but he wasn't about to add to her already overburdened and bruised shoulders by telling her about Marty DeBaccian. "Suffice it to say, I have reason to believe he's connected to a much nastier individual." He spotted the nurse from earlier standing in the doorway. She leaned over, caught his eye and waved him out. "I'll be back in just a minute."

"Sure. Gives me some time to absorb all that." Her tone was completely indecipherable as Nate left to meet the nurse in the hall.

"Dr. Billings has an update for you." She led him back to the nurse's station, where a rather rotund, middle-aged man tapped his finger on a tablet computer. "Dr. Billings?"

The doctor looked up, shifted his gaze from the nurse to Nate. "Detective Colton. Dr. David Billings. I'm a trauma specialist here in the ER." He set his tablet down and held out a hand. "Thanks, Lorna."

"You bet." Nurse Lorna shot them both a smile before ducking around the desk.

"Is Wexler alive?" Nate forewent any pretense. It was the only question that mattered at the moment.

"He is." Dr. Billings nodded slowly. "There's no guarantee he'll stay that way, however. Two bullets caught him in the chest. One went straight through, the other's lodged so close to his heart it's a miracle he's still breathing."

"Any chance I can question him?"

"Not for a good while. We've had to put him in a medically induced coma. Could be days or even weeks before it's safe to bring him out of it. He's semi-stable for now. He won't wake up again until after we get that bullet out. And for that, we need to wait."

"Right." Nate scrubbed a tired hand across his forehead. "Okay. I'd like to be kept apprised of his condition. And I'm going to see about assigning an officer to his room."

Dr. Billings frowned. "Is that really necessary?"

"Someone drove by and opened fire on him in the middle of a crowd," Nate said as he pulled out one of his cards and passed it across the counter to Lorna. "It's a miracle no one else was seriously injured." Last he'd heard, there were some minor injuries, bumps, bruises, scrapes and cuts from flying glass. "That tells me they hit their target. If word gets out he's still alive—"

"Say no more." Dr. Billings held up both hands. "We'll cooperate however we can."

"Is there a room you can put him, away from emergency exits? How's your security system?" Nate took a quick look in both directions. The round rotating cameras gave him some peace of mind. "Recent update?"

"Last year," Dr. Billings confirmed. "I'll alert our security office to pay close attention to the area around Mr. Wexler's room. One last question, Detective."

"Sure."

"Other than an ID for Sam Gabriel, we didn't find any other information or ID on him. Regarding his next of kin, do you happen to know—"

"He doesn't have any that I know of," Nate said. "I'll double check the file we have on him once I'm back at the station." Criminal or not, Wexler deserved someone to be responsible for him. "In the meantime, put me down as a contact."

* * *

Vivian really, really needed to stop watching so many cop shows. Obviously, they'd implanted shockingly unrealistic expectations in her psyche. Or dulled her to the realities of actual crime. Was that even possible?

It had been a shooting. Had to have been. All the broken glass and panicked racing about, not to mention the gunshot wounds in Sam—Dean's chest; there wasn't any other explanation.

"Wait until I tell Lizzy about this," she whispered and heard the growing hysteria in her ragged voice. "One date in four years and *bam!* I get shot at." She shook her head, thinking of her childhood friend. Well, her *only* friend. "She'll probably think I'm making it up to get out of trying again. Who doesn't pretend to be shot at to get out of dating?"

Was she ever not going to feel as if she wanted to jump out of her own skin?

Vivian's mind raced like a broken-down sports car, speeding up one minute, stuttering and stalling the next. Thoughts didn't seem to be completing themselves before another started, and they all sent her down winding, dead-end roads of panic and fear.

The coffee had probably been a mistake. She looked down at her trembling hands, feeling as if somehow, she was hovering above her own body, unwilling to retake possession in order to cope with the fact she'd nearly been killed. She squeezed her fingers into fists, tried to focus on the sensation of her nails digging into her palms.

How funny was it that the only thing that seemed to be holding her together was the thought Detective Nate Colton would be returning to her bedside?

Detective Colton, who had been the first person she'd beheld after the shooting. Handsome, messy-haired, blue-eyed Detective Nate Colton, who, when he'd peeked around that ER curtain, had acted as an instant balm and a kind of unexpected refuge.

Refuge. She squeezed her eyes shut, shook her head. What on earth was going on in her head that she even thought to use that word where he was—?

"Ms. Maylor?"

She nearly sighed at the sound of his voice. In that instant, the jagged edges of her thoughts smoothed, and she opened her eyes, unclenched her fists. "Vivian, please. Detective."

"Nate." His smile was easy.

"Nate." She must have knocked her head harder than even the doctors thought. Just saying his name made her feel better.

His hands were now devoid of the coffee cup. Probably a good thing with the way her heart was racing. Not that she could hide that, given the monitors that kept *beep-beep-beeping* overhead. And the good-looking detective wasn't helping. "Did you find out anything about…" She nearly got his name wrong again. "Dean Wexler?"

"He's alive," Nate said. "They've put him in a coma until he's strong enough for surgery. It could go either way."

"Oh." She didn't know how to feel about that. As off as the date had been, as suspicious as she'd been about Sam, Dean, whatever his name was, she certainly didn't wish anything like this on him. Or on anyone. "That's just…horrible. Do you know who—"

"Not yet," Nate said, then stepped back and motioned

to someone behind him. "Vivian, this is Detective Jim Sullivan. We work together in the Boise PD. He's been assigned to the case."

"Ms. Maylor." Detective Sullivan gave her a friendly nod. He was on the short and stocky side—nowhere near as tall or fit as Nate—and had ginger red hair. She figured him to be about forty years old with a cool, almost jaded awareness in his eyes. "I'd like to ask you a few questions about the incident tonight if you don't mind?"

Incident? So that was what they were calling a drive-by shooting? "Yeah, sure." She pushed her hair behind her ear and managed a flickering smile. That headache the doctor had warned her about was beginning to pound, dully, loudly, on both sides of her head. "I want to help however I can."

"I'll just leave you two—"

"No, stay," Vivian said, cutting Nate off and reaching out a hand that she immediately tugged back and held against her chest. "Please. If it's okay?" she asked the other detective. "He was there. He probably saw a lot of things I didn't." It made her feel slightly less dependent to make an excuse for him to be there. Other than her just wanting him to stay.

Sullivan didn't look particularly pleased at the request. "Sure." He motioned to the chair, but Nate urged him to take it while he leaned back against the cabinet of medical supplies beside the bed. After Sullivan took down her information—full name, phone number, address, occupation—he started in. "How do you know Dean Wexler, Ms. Maylor?"

"Vivian's fine," she said. "And I don't really know him. We connected on a dating app. We messaged a couple of times. A friend of mine told me to take a chance and say yes to a date. So I did." She smoothed her hands across the strangely rough and heavy blanket. "I don't think I'll be taking her dating advice again."

"Detective Colton said you know him under a different name?"

"Sam Gabriel." She rattled off the name of the dating app they'd used. "I'm thinking their vetting process isn't as secure as they state in their ads." How stupid could she have been, putting her faith in anything connected to the internet? Stupid, naive. Her mouth twisted. Lonely. She'd just become a statistic in the lonely to desperate ratio. "We agreed to meet for dinner at Madariaga's. He'd never been there, but I order from them occasionally when I want to treat myself. And I knew it would be crowded."

"Smart thinking," Detective Sullivan said as he scribbled in his small notepad.

"I was thinking it was a good test for temper," she said. "You know, how irritated someone gets around noise and chaos. I wanted to see if he was quick to trigger."

"Never would have thought of that," Nate said.

"You're not a single woman," Vivian said, but rather than the comment sounding or feeling snarky, it felt more conversational. "You've never had to. I'm not a big dater. Honestly, tonight was a complete fluke." One she was probably never going to forget. "Felt more like a game of truth or dare, and I stupidly chose dare."

"There's nothing stupid about going out on a date," Nate said.

"Seriously?" Vivian arched a brow and looked at Nate. "You're a cop, and you're going to say that, in this day and age? I let myself forget the world is full of psychopathic whackadoodles."

"Sneaking past defenses is what people like Wexler do," Detective Sullivan said. "An attitude like yours tends to be a pretty good shield these days."

"Always the exception to the rule. Anyway." She took a deep breath and sighed. "He let me choose the restaurant, which I took as a good sign. I arrived on time—"

"Did you see anything out of the ordinary before you went into Madariaga's?" Sullivan asked. "Anyone lurking or a strange car parked somewhere?"

"No." She shook her head and thought back. "But then I wouldn't have known if they were strange, would I? I parked in the lot across the street. I remember thinking it looked like it was going to storm and that I hoped to get home before it got going." She hesitated. "I don't like driving, especially at night. Add in the weather, and…" She was already dreading the drive once she got out of the hospital. "Honestly, it was just a simple, no-go date."

"Any particular reason it failed?"

"He didn't pull her chair out for her," Nate muttered.

Vivian's gaze flew back to his, and she saw in the way his cheeks tinted pink that he hadn't meant to say that out loud. "No, he didn't. I don't know that I expected him to, but…" She lost her train of thought. "You noticed that?"

"I noticed a lot of things," Nate said, then, after a look from Sullivan, he shrugged. "Sorry. I'll keep quiet."

"He lied to me. S— Dean," Vivian told Sullivan. "Almost from the start. About his job. He told me he taught second grade, but then said his students were ten years old."

Sullivan's brow arched. "Second graders are seven or eight. Good catch."

"It was a little thing," Vivian said. "But it was so strange. If you lie about small things—"

"What's to stop him from lying about bigger things?" Nate held up both hands. "Sorry. Last time."

Sullivan frowned, as if he didn't quite understand Nate's behavior. "Anything else strike you as odd?"

"He kept mentioning money in different ways," Vivian said. "That I must make a really good living with my business. That he liked to travel, but it costs too much. And a lot of what he said just felt rehearsed. Like he had a script."

Sullivan nodded, made another note. "You aren't the first woman we've heard this from about him. Looks like your instincts about Wexler were right, Nate." He poked his pen into the paper and glanced up at Nate. "I'm going to recommend we look deeper into Wexler in connection with those burglaries."

"As long as I get first shot at him for my case." Nate winced. "Wow. Sorry. Really bad choice of word."

"Walk me through after you left the restaurant, if you can," Sullivan prodded Vivian.

She shrugged. "He talked me into going down for a dessert at a café," Vivian said, wanting to get this over and done with. "A few blocks from the restaurant. Proof I'll do just about anything for chocolate," she admitted quietly. "We were maybe two blocks from Madariaga's when he stopped me. I heard what I thought was a kind of pop." She narrowed her eyes, tried to recall exactly what had happened. "I heard the glass in the car break before I realized what it was. I remember looking over my shoulder in the direction it came from and seeing this car. Light brown, like beige maybe? I remember thinking that the headlights were strange. The shape of them. More angular than round. And there was this face—"

"Face? You saw the shooter's face?"

She squeezed her eyes shut. "I'm not sure if it was the shooter or the driver? Sorry." She shrugged. "I didn't realize that was what I was seeing at the time. I remember seeing something bright, shiny. Something that glinted. Then there was another pop, and another. The next thing I knew, Sam, I mean Dean, knocked me to the ground. I remember being irritated because my glasses broke." She lifted a hand to her temple and rubbed it with her fingers.

Nate cursed, and Sullivan shot him a look of irritation.

"How about a description of the man you remember seeing?" Sullivan asked.

"Dark hair, weird…something." Vivian considered. "I feel like there's something odd about him? But it's not there. Not yet anyway. Maybe it'll come back."

"You said Wexler knocked you to the ground," Nate said. "Are you sure about that?"

"Absolutely." She nodded, a chill racing down her spine. "At the time, I was asking myself what he thought he was doing, then I realized…" She looked back to Nate. "The full weight of him landed on me. He was so still. I tried to shove him off of me, and then he was gone, and I was all…wet." She swiped her hand across her neck, which one of the nurses had scrubbed clean. "Oh." Her stomach rolled. "This was his blood."

Nate reached out and pulled her hand down. "It's gone now. Worry about that later."

"Easy for you to say." Vivian shuddered. She'd never wanted a shower more urgently in her life.

"Sounds like Wexler might have saved your life," Sullivan said.

"Yeah," she whispered in fear and awe. "I think maybe he did."

"And you?" Sullivan turned his attention to Nate. "How much of this did you see?"

"After the date? Beige car, late model." He almost snapped out the words. "No plates on the back. The quick look I got at the gun, I'd say 9 mm."

"Techs recovered a 9 mm bullet from the broken glass of the jewelry store window," Sullivan confirmed. "It had blood on it."

"Probably hit Wexler," Nate said. "The doctor said one shot was a through and through."

"We'll get it tested at the lab to be sure. If I put you in touch with our department sketch artist," Sullivan said to Vivian, "would you be willing to come in and work with her? Get an image together? She's good at helping people remember details they think they can't."

"Oh." She blinked, processing. "Sure, yeah. I could do that." Was it wrong to think that was kind of cool? She'd seen artists used before on TV, of course. And read about the process in books. What did that mean about her that she was anxious to see how it worked in real life?

"You don't have to do that," Nate said cautiously.

Sullivan cleared his throat and glared.

"I'm just saying—" Nate tried again.

"I know what you're saying," Sullivan said sharply. "Vivian? You up for it?"

"Yes." While she appreciated Nate's attempt to protect

her, she was going to do everything she could to catch the person responsible for such a brazen act. "I want to help find whoever did this."

"Okay, then. I'll give you a call in the morning." Sullivan stood and set the chair aside. "Nate? Can I have a word before I leave?"

"Sure."

Vivian didn't know anything about Detective Nate Colton, but that one-word answer, to her at least, seemed to convey both dread and irritation. The combination fascinated her. "Could you get me some more coffee?" she asked Nate when he started to follow Sullivan.

"If you can wait," he said, "how about I get you one once you're released?"

"Oh. I thought maybe you'd be—"

"I'm off duty. Kind of. Unless there's someone you'd like me to call?"

She shook her head and thought of all the people he might be considering. Parents, siblings, friends… "There's no one."

"Well, someone needs to get you to your car. That lucky person is me." That smile was back, and she wondered if he was aware of the power it held. "Don't go anywhere."

"Okay." She nodded and breathed easier. Not so long ago, heck, even yesterday, the idea of sitting back and letting a man show even the slightest amount of care for her would have left her laughing in dismay. Instead, she found herself counting the seconds until Detective Nate Colton returned to her.

Chapter 3

"Here you go, Detective."

Nate, keeping one hand at the small of Vivian's back as he escorted her out of the ER, caught the keys the patrol officer standing at the sliding glass doors tossed to him.

"Thanks, Coop." The younger officer, with only two years on the job so far, was one he'd met during a training seminar at the academy. Since then, Nate had found himself as his unofficial on-the-job mentor. Cooper was definitely in the breaking-in stages. The job hadn't tarnished that one-time debate team captain shine yet. Sometimes the kid smiled so brightly it was like he was made of sunshine.

"Your car's in drop-off parking," Coop said. "Thanks for recommending me for guard duty."

"Don't thank me yet," Nate told him as they passed by. "Cool it on the coffee, or you'll spend most of your time in the bathroom. No one but doctors or nurses with ID get in to see Wexler, okay? Learn their faces and their names. Anyone unfamiliar, don't hesitate to question. And remember to look at their shoes."

Cooper's light blond hair fell over his eyes when he nodded. "Got it."

"Shoes?" Vivian asked once they stepped outside.

"Doctors and nurses wear certain kinds of shoes. Soft soled. Practical."

"And someone coming in off the street probably would wear something different." Vivian nodded. "Interesting." She wrapped her arms around her torso and shivered.

"Here." Nate shrugged out of his jacket and draped it over her shoulders. He felt the need to remind her that chivalry did still exist in the world. Besides, he could practically hear her teeth chattering. "Sorry we took yours for evidence."

"Not like I wanted it after tonight." She touched fingertips to her chest and the edge of her dress. "I guess I should be grateful you didn't take everything. I'd hate to have to drive home in my underwear."

Nate felt that comment all the way to his toes. "Yeah," he managed on a slightly strangled note. "Wouldn't want that." The second they stepped clear of the ambulance bay, Nate cringed. "Looks like you were right about that storm." The snow was coming down in steady curtains now. Not blizzard conditions, not yet at least, but that could change on a dime.

"The perfect end to the perfect night. Even without the storm, I'd have been stuck. Can't drive at night without my glasses." She drew the lapels of his jacket close. Something about the way she turned her face into the lining, as if she were breathing him in, had parts of him tightening into complete discomfort. "I think there's a motel near the restaurant. I'll grab a room—"

"You can stay with me." The offer came out of nowhere and apparently surprised both of them. He inclined his chin toward the dark SUV parked in the second space over. "We can talk about it inside. Come on."

"Ohhh…kay…" Her drawn-out response indicated both reluctance and curiosity. He could definitely push back on one of those emotions.

Sullivan had made it clear he believed Nate had a bit of a conflict of interest with this case. Nate couldn't blame him. He'd been vocally protective of Vivian—without really thinking about it. It had just been… instinctual. Arguing would have only made the situation more difficult, so he'd silently agreed to disagree if only to be kept in the loop moving forward.

Once inside, Nate turned on the engine so he could raise the heat up to full blast. At least with the snow the temperatures would calm a bit and the cold wouldn't feel quite so biting. "I've got a guest room," he said without preamble. "Nothing fancy, but it has its own bathroom. You can shower and get some sleep. Sullivan's going to try to get the sketch artist in tomorrow. Might as well get it all over and done with before you head home."

She leaned back in her seat and slid her arms into his jacket. When she flipped her hair free of the collar, he had to stop himself from reaching out to see if her hair was as soft as he imagined. "Part of me is thinking this could be an extension of my bad decision-making tendencies for the evening," she said and looked out his snow-covered windshield.

"Or it's the chance to start making good ones," he suggested. "I promise, you'll be in safe hands. That I can keep to myself—"

She leaned across the console and pressed her mouth to his.

Nate wasn't a man prone to surprises. He prided himself on being able to expect just about anything that could possibly come flying at him. But Vivian Maylor proved yet again she was capable of sneaking past his defenses and straight into his heart.

Her lips trembled against his, as if she hadn't quite thought things through. When he angled his head and moved to deepen the kiss, he felt her hesitancy. Right before her hand slid up the front of his chest and grabbed hold of his shirt.

With the engine rumbling, he slipped his hand up to grasp the back of her neck, held her against him as he dipped his tongue in to taste her, tempt her. Tease her. The curving of her lips had him almost cheering in triumph, but that would mean releasing her, and as he continued the kiss, he couldn't imagine a time he would want to stop.

When he did pull back, it was only far enough to press his forehead against hers. She was breathing heavier than before. She licked her lips, pressed them together as if trying to capture the taste of him.

"Well." He slipped his hand to her face, stroked a finger down her cheek as something unfamiliar and strangely welcomed bloomed inside him.

"I've spent a good part of the night trying to remember where I've seen you before."

"Oh?" Panic swirled, but he kept his gaze steady and even. He could only imagine where she'd seen his name, or even his picture over the past few months. Being outed as one of Robert Colton's illegitimate heirs was something no one would want on their bingo card. "Figured it out yet?"

"No. But then I'm having trouble deciding if kissing you was another bad decision," she murmured, her brow knitting slightly in confusion. "Or a good one. Maybe my brain was a bit scrambled tonight."

"You can think on it for a while." It would be easy, he thought, so easy to make one gentle push that would probably topple her right into his bed. But tonight wasn't the night. For either of them.

She was going to experience the emotional upheaval that always followed a traumatic event, and he had no doubt it would hit with both barrels. While he… He took a deep breath and inhaled the faint fragrance of flowers drifting off her skin. When the time came for him to partake in what he had no doubt was the wonder of Vivian Maylor, he wanted to be fully present, awake, and…prepared.

"So, my place or would you like me to find a hotel for you for the night?"

"So long as I can get home in time tomorrow for an online meeting with one of my clients." Her smile curved her swollen lips and almost reached her eyes.

"What time would that be?" he teased.

"After lunch. One thirty."

"That should be doable," he assured her.

"Then I will accept your offer of the guest room. If that's really o—"

He kissed her this time. A quick one, just fast enough to convince her he understood but also give her a hint of what a promise between them might hold. "That's perfectly fine. And before you ask…" He hit the windshield wipers and cleared the view. "I have more than enough coffee to get both of us through to tomorrow."

"How did you know, Detective?"

He chuckled and shifted the car into Reverse. "Lucky guess."

As Nate pulled his SUV into the driveway of a darling little cottage of a house on the very edge of Boise, Vivian realized she might be attempting to deal with the evening's events by diving into something even more outrageous than a blind date.

But there was no need to rationalize Nate's invitation to use his guest room for the remainder of the night. It was closing in on one in the morning. The first dose of OTC painkillers the nurse had given her before she had been discharged was already wearing off. She'd felt a bit of a buzz the second she'd stepped outside into the cold December air. Almost as if she'd been given a second lease on life. Whatever else had happened, she'd literally dodged a bullet, and for the next few hours at least, she was giving herself permission to go with impulse.

Impulse had worked well so far and helped her to answer the one question that had been floating around in her mind since she'd first seen Nate Colton sitting at that bar: what would it be like to kiss him?

She pressed her lips together again. Well, she had her answer.

The only problem was she wanted to ask the question again. And again.

Some inquiries took multiple investigations to come to the correct and accurate conclusion, she decided and had to cover her mouth to stop herself from giggling. Man, she was really out of it.

"Well, here we are." Nate turned off the engine and

rested his hands on the steering wheel. "Ready to make a mad dash?" He leaned forward to examine the snow that had consistently fallen during their drive. "No," he said when she started to shrug out of his jacket. "Wait until we get inside. I'm used to the cold."

"Okay." It seemed to be her favorite word around him. Was there some kind of cosmic force at work? Even before they'd spoken a word to one another, she'd felt comfortable with him. As if she instinctively knew he was someone safe. But how was that possible? He was a stranger.

A stranger with a badge, but a stranger nonetheless.

Once she got some sleep and some distance from everything that had happened, she was probably going to come to a different conclusion or admit that her irrational reactions and actions were nothing more than spur-of-the-moment coping mechanisms. That said, there was nothing wrong with enjoying the moment, was there? Chances were that after tomorrow, she'd probably never see him again.

She wasn't the least bit surprised that, after climbing out of the car, he hurried around to open her door. Vivian couldn't shake the feeling of intimacy that struck her when he slipped his hand into hers and tugged her toward his front porch.

In the dim light of the porch lamp, she couldn't get a good look at or feel for the interior of his home. It seemed the second he opened the door the sky opened up and dropped a full blanket of continuous snowfall.

Once inside, a blast of warmth set her frozen cheeks to stinging as he drew the jacket off her and hung it on a hook by the door.

"Hang on. Let me get the lights." He left her in the entryway as he moved down the hall. A moment later, light blazed to life. Nate leaned out and waved her back. "I'll get the coffee going. Unless it's too late for you?"

"I have stratospheric caffeine tolerance," she said. It might make her jittery at times, but it rarely kept her awake. Especially when an adrenaline crash was coming. She strode down the short hallway to the kitchen, which she found surprisingly comfortable and practical. "Nice place."

"Yeah?" He shot her a surprised smile as he set his coffee machine to gurgling. "It serves a purpose. I'm fixing things up as I go along. Only been here a couple of years."

"Handy around the house, are you?"

"Well, I wield a mean paintbrush. The little touches are more my sister's doing. She's much more attuned to things than I am."

"Sister, huh?" She hugged her arms around herself as she wandered across the marble tile, nodding approvingly at the shiny black appliances and gold-flecked black marble countertops. "Younger or older?"

"Younger." He retrieved one mug from the dish rack by the sink and another from a cabinet. "We had a kind of complicated upbringing, but one thing we always had was each other. How about you? Brothers and sisters?"

Regret and that all-too-familiar pang of loneliness chimed inside her. She pulled out one of the two barstools at the counter and sat while he rummaged around in the refrigerator. "I was an only child. And not the best at socializing."

"Doesn't seem that way to me." He set a sealed container on the counter before going back in. "Let's see. I've got some leftover pizza in here. And some salad that..." He popped off the lid, then grimaced. "Okay, yeah, that might send you back to the hospital."

Vivian laughed. "Pizza sounds great, actually. And what's this?" She pointed to the first container.

"A neighbor across the street uses me as a guinea pig for his baking experiments. I thought you might appreciate them since you didn't get your promised dessert. Go ahead." He gestured for her to open it.

She did and felt some of the tension she'd been struggling with ease. "Chocolate chip cookies?"

"Double chocolate chip cookies," Nate corrected. "He has a secret ingredient."

"Espresso powder?" Vivian guessed and earned an arched brow. "I might not be the best baker, but I read a lot of books about food. The espresso's supposed to enhance the chocolate. I'll know for sure when I eat one. Later." She left the lid off and slid it out of reach. "Chocolate's best at room temp."

"Funny." The cardboard pizza box replaced the cookies as he went to get plates. "I've never been patient enough to prove that theory. Anything for your coffee?"

"Straight's fine." She could feel her energy beginning to drain. That adrenaline crash was barreling straight for her, no doubt coming on faster because of how comfortable she felt, both with Nate and in his house. "Can I ask you why you were following Wexler tonight?"

"You can ask me anything." He bit into an ice-cold piece of pizza, the corners of his eyes crinkling as he chewed and swallowed. "Doesn't mean I'll tell you."

"Why not?"

"Because you've had enough to deal with, and—honestly? I don't want you any more involved in this situation than you already are."

"So you're protecting me." Should that idea both appeal to and annoy her?

"Yes."

"I'd argue that I can take care of myself, but considering I couldn't find the courage to drive myself home tonight, I guess that argument's moot." She didn't think she could convey how relieved she'd been not to have to get behind the wheel of her car in the dead of night.

"You must have had high hopes for your date if you made the drive into Boise."

"Not high hopes." Surrendering to the rumbling in her stomach and wanting to give her pain pills somewhere to land when she took them, she reached for a slice. "But I did have a friend who wouldn't let me back out. Can't wait to tell Lizzy how wrong she was." That, at least, would be one silver lining to the night. She nearly had the pizza to her lips when the thought struck. The pizza clattered on her plate with a disturbing stale thunk. "Colton. Your last name is Colton."

"Yes." Nate frowned, concern rising in his eyes. "Are we starting over?" He reached out, touched a finger to her bandage and looked into her eyes. "Your head okay?"

"My head's fine." But her heart was racing so fast it nearly jumped out of her chest. "Nate Colton. Boise PD. Are you..." She swallowed hard as certain pieces fell into place. "Your sister's name? Is it Lizzy?"

His face went blank for an instant, as if her question had flipped a kind of switch. He gave a halfhearted nod and ducked his head. "One of them is."

"Oh, wow." She leaned back on the barstool, relief and shock tumbling through her. She laughed, pressed her hands against her cheeks before she jumped off the stool and raced around the counter. "This explains it." She grabbed hold of his arms and turned him to her. "Oh, my gosh. This… I don't know, this thing I feel with you. This ease. This…"

"Spark?" Nate said in a way that had her wondering if he'd heard that part of her conversation with Dean Wexler.

"How many Lizzy Coltons could there be?" Vivian challenged.

"Hopefully, only one," Nate said. "She's a bit of a firecracker, for want of a better term."

"You're her brother." She grabbed his face between her hands and looked more deeply into those blue eyes of his. "The brother she only just found out about. I don't know if I can see it, but I can feel it."

"Can you?" He looked a bit flummoxed at her comment. "What do I feel like?"

"Lizzy's the best friend I've ever had. Ever since grade school, she's just… She's always been there for me. No matter what. She's solid, you know?"

"Can't really agree or disagree." The humor in his eyes had been replaced by what she could only describe as pain. "I don't know her well enough to say."

"Oh." It was only then she remembered what Lizzy had said. "You and your sister." Her mind searched for the right name. "Your other sister, Sarah. You and she share the same mother with Lizzy and her brothers."

"Yep. Good old Jessie Colton. Fracturing families and setting the whole root system on fire." He extricated himself from her hold and ducked down into a lower cabinet. "Suddenly, I'm feeling the need for something stronger than coffee." He added a big splash of bourbon to his mug.

"I'm sorry." She didn't like the expression on his face, the way his entire body had tightened up, as if her realization had somehow unlocked a secret part of him he wasn't interested in sharing. "I should have realized the media coverage and fallout must have been horrible for you. Lizzy said things were complicated. *You* said they were. I'm prying. I'm sorry." She stepped away from him.

"No reason for you to be." Was his response more obligatory than polite? "Didn't think I'd be traversing that particular minefield of family history tonight is all. I'm glad Lizzy's your friend. I can call her if you want? I bet she'd be happy to—"

"No, please." Vivian held up both hands. "With everything that happened to her recently, I don't want to be another thing for her to have to worry about. Besides, last I heard, Ajay was taking her away for a little while to help her...decompress." Was that the right word when it came to being kidnapped?

"Good." Nate nodded and looked relieved. "That's good to hear."

"This is so strange." She returned to the chair. "From the second I saw you at the bar, I couldn't shake this feeling like I knew you. Even though I don't. Didn't. Does that make sense?"

"I'm going to say yes and leave it at that."

"Right. You don't want to talk about it."

"It's not that." Confusion filled his voice. "It's more... I don't know how to talk about all that, actually. I'm assuming Lizzy told you about me and Sarah and our... place in the family."

She nodded. "Yes. A few weeks ago, I think? She was trying to process finding out she had two siblings she knew nothing about."

"Yeah, well, Sarah and I always knew," Nate said, and it was then she was able to decipher what it was she was seeing on his face. In his eyes. It was definitely pain. But also sadness. "That whole Coltons of Owl Creek, the branches of the family who built that town into something greater than anyone believed it could ever be? Sarah and I found out a long time ago that we're related. So we've had a bit more time to adjust to the idea than Lizzy and her brothers and cousins. There's still a bit of...tension among us."

"You said you've had time, but you haven't adjusted," Vivian observed. "Have you?"

"Don't get me wrong." He started to play with his pizza rather than continuing to eat. "I've met most of them now, and I like them all well enough. They're good people. They have every reason to distrust us, especially given who our mother is. Maybe I can see a time in the future when we're closer." He shrugged. "But not now. I spent a good portion of my life accepting the fact I was never going to be one of them. It's a hard shift to make when you're suddenly presented with an opportunity you didn't think you'd ever have."

"I'm sorry." She reached out, grabbed hold of his hand and squeezed. "And here I am going all cheerleader on the situation."

That smile of his returned, if not a bit less bright than

before. "I'm sorry, but there's no way you were ever a cheerleader."

She laughed and squeezed harder. "See? You know that about me already. I'm thinking we were most definitely destined to meet." She surprised herself by yawning. Her eyes went wide as her cheeks went hot with embarrassment. "Oh, geez. Sorry." She covered her mouth, shook her head and pulled her hand free. But not before he clung to her for a few seconds more.

"I'm going to take that as a hint to show you the guest room. Give me just a sec."

"Okay." She nibbled on her pizza after he disappeared, then quickly cleaned up and put things back in the fridge and finished her coffee. She wandered around a bit, cookie in hand, looking for the bits and bobs of character that turned a house into a home. He didn't seem to be a collector type of person. Everything she saw projected a lifestyle of practicality and purpose.

Photographs were sparse. There was no mistaking the people in the few she found—one of whom she'd bet good money was his sister Sarah. The affection between them was palpable and made her smile. The man she'd been dealing with tonight seemed no different than the one in the picture. Whatever niggling doubt she might have regarding her current situation vanished.

"Okay, bedroom's good to go," Nate said from where he lounged in the door frame, watching her examine the photographs on the TV stand in the living room. "I set out some towels for you, and there should be other things like a toothbrush and stuff in the cabinet drawers. Sarah left a load of laundry last time she stayed here. T-shirts and stuff. You're about the same size, so take your pick."

"Thanks." That urge to shower returned with an unexpected ferocity as she finished what she had to agree was a pretty great double chocolate chip cookie.

"Help yourself to anything in the kitchen. I'm a light sleeper, so if you need anything, just knock on the door." He pointed to the one on the other side of the living room. "I'm usually up around six."

"Me, too." Nerves she thought she'd banked surged afresh. "Ah, I really am sorry. Bringing up all that stuff about your family."

"It's fine, Vivian." There was no animosity in his eyes. "I should probably take it as a sign that it's time to start dealing with it all head-on. They're family after all."

"Yes, they are." Vivian felt a pang of envy so sharp she nearly lost her breath. "Grab hold of it, of them, Nate. Trust me. I've been alone most of my life. There's nothing more important than being a part of something that's bigger than you are."

"As much as I'd like to continue this conversation," Nate said, "I think you're questioned out by now. For tonight, at least."

"I really am." The last thing she wanted to do was unload her particular tales of woe. "Whatever else you're struggling with…" She walked over to him, rested a hand on his chest and curled her fingers under ever so slightly. She wasn't certain if it was she who shivered, or if it was him. "You're a good man. That's what I picked up on when I walked in the bar. You radiate it. You glow with it." She lifted her other hand to his cheek. "Believe me, that is a very rare trait indeed."

She resisted the urge to kiss him again. Afraid that if she did, it would lead to something neither of them was ready for. "I'll see you in the morning." She moved past him, forcing herself to look straight ahead and avoid looking at him again as she closed the door.

Chapter 4

Nate lied. He wasn't up at six.

He was up at five thirty. Getting through today on a whole three hours of sleep was going to be so much fun. It wouldn't have been so bad if those three hours had given him a degree of rest. Truth was, he tossed and turned, his mind racing first around his options surrounding Dean Wexler, and then around the fact that Vivian Maylor slept only a few steps down the hall from his bedroom.

He couldn't recall the last time he'd started his day with an icy cold shower, but since first seeing Vivian, he'd been doing—and thinking—a lot of things he wasn't used to.

What were the odds that this woman would consider Nate's half sister to be her best friend? He shook his head as he set a fresh pot of coffee to brew. The universe must be having a serious laugh at his expense. Clearly, he hadn't been paying enough attention to the shift in his family dynamic. His stomach tightened. What would Lizzy think when Vivian told her about their meeting?

It was obvious his siblings hadn't decided if he was guilty by association just yet—his mother's antics and actions, including her recent involvement with the Ever

After Church and its leader, Markus Acker, had been the cause of much of the distress the Colton family was going through.

If he were to look at things from his siblings' side, he'd definitely be suspicious, not to mention cautious. Whatever he might be feeling about the situation, their reserved behavior had hurt Sarah more than anyone. His sister had always longed to belong to a big family, and it had been difficult when they'd discovered they had one that they couldn't reach out to. Wanting Sarah to have that now meant Nate would do what he needed to make that happen.

"Morning."

The sound of Vivian's sleep-husky voice triggered a smile Nate couldn't have stopped even if he'd wanted to.

"Morning." He turned and his knees went weak at the sight of her standing in the doorway, clad only in a rainbow-centric T-shirt that skimmed the tops of her thighs. "You, um, sleep okay?" His voice sounded a bit choked. He cleared his throat, tried to reboot himself into thinking clearly.

He'd spent a big portion of the night not imagining what her legs looked like. Now that they were on full display—those long, toned legs—he was forced to admit his imagination hadn't come close. Never in the history of the female form had a woman filled a T-shirt to the absolute perfection of Vivian Maylor. Judging from the slightly dazed expression on her face, she didn't have the first clue as to the effect she had on him. And the effect was…for want of a better word, *stimulating.*

"I slept great, thanks." Sleepy-eyed, she walked toward him. "Coffee going already?"

"First thing." He shoved his hands into the back pockets of his jeans, rocked forward, his bare feet scrunching into the hardwood floor. "Wanted it ready for you when you got up."

"Sweet." She touched a hand to his arm but didn't, as expected, come over to watch the coffee appear. Instead, she popped open the container of cookies. "My first shot of the day." She bit in and closed her eyes, sighed in a way that left Nate feeling oddly jealous of a chocolate chip cookie. "That shower in your guest room worked wonders." She leaned back against the cabinets.

"Glad to hear it." He cleared his throat again and distracted himself by putting away the dishes from the drainer.

Those kisses they'd shared in his car last night had been a pressure release, a way of coping with an adrenaline-spiking event neither of them could have prepared for. At this point, it would be unprofessional of him to pursue any kind of relationship or push for a quick encounter that could, in the end, cause her more emotional harm. It wasn't the time.

Or the place.

"Everything okay?" Vivian asked.

"Everything's fine." He'd never felt so grateful to hear his cell phone go off. He all but dived to where it sat on the counter across the room, skimmed the text message. "It's Detective Sullivan. He said he texted you, but you haven't answered."

"Oh!" Her eyes went wide. "I totally forgot to charge it when I got here. Geez." Muttering to herself, she hurried out of the kitchen, the T-shirt skimming higher up the backs of her thighs with every step.

"Heaven help me," Nate muttered to himself even as his jeans became increasingly uncomfortable. "I'm not going to make it another hour with her around."

"Did you say something?" She was already back, cell phone in hand. That wide-eyed, innocent expression on her face was more alluring to him than a classic femme fatale's come-hither look.

"Nope. Not a thing."

"I've got the message." She squinted at the screen. "I really need my glasses." She sighed. "Can you read it?" She held out her phone.

"Sure." Their fingers brushed when he accepted her cell. A zing of energy shot through him, from his fingers, straight down to his toes, then back up to where it settled significantly south of his heart. "Ah, he says the sketch artist can come in this morning. Time's up to you. She's free until noon."

"That makes two of us," Vivian said. "How about… nine?"

"How about eight?" The sooner he got her out of his house, the better. The longer she was here, the more his thoughts circled things other than work. Inappropriate things. She was his witness. He needed to remember that. "We can stop for breakfast on the way. This early, we'll miss the main weekend crowd."

"Sick of leftover pizza?" she teased.

"Something like that." He answered the message, then texted Sullivan on his own phone confirming the time. The message he received back was a simple smirk emoji that told Nate he was in for some serious ribbing from his fellow detectives and officers. "Okay, eight's good. There's a twenty-four-hour diner on the way, one of my favorite places, actually." But that didn't stop him from pouring them each a cup of coffee. "You hungry?"

"Always." Accepting the mug, she smiled and tilted her head, which sent her hair cascading out of its loose knot down around her shoulders. "I'll be quick." She grinned over her shoulder at him as she walked away. "Promise."

She'd done something wrong. Sitting in the passenger seat of Nate's SUV quicker than promised, she nibbled on her thumbnail. What was it? He'd been acting nervous from the jump today, like every word she said grated on his nerves. The tension radiating off him had been alluring at first, tempting. Even seductive, but the way he'd all but danced and dived away from her to get to his phone had left her wondering if last night's interaction had been a fluke. She hadn't dreamed kissing him, had she? Or that he'd kissed her back?

Oh. She frowned, panic grabbing hold of her heart. Last night hadn't been some weird hallucination. Or had it?

"Hey." Nate's voice broke through her circling doubt. "You okay?"

"Yeah, sure." She rested her hand against her stomach. His sister Sarah had a fun, quirky sense of fashion, at least when it came to her casual clothes. The bright, colorful T-shirt collection had given her a surprising choice. The jeans she found in the dresser were on the snug side, but at least the zipper had gone up.

Vivian's favorite all-purpose black dress was wadded up in his bathroom trash can. The second she'd tried to wash out the blood, the red in the water had set her head to spinning and her chest to throbbing. She'd never be able to wear it again without remembering the shooting. Best to toss it and move on.

"Why?" she asked Nate impulsively. "Everything okay with you?"

"Yeah, sure."

She caught her lower lip in her teeth and might have gnawed straight through if she hadn't stopped herself. "I appreciate everything you've done for me." She hugged her purse against her chest. "I'll be out of your hair pretty soon."

"You're not in my hair, Vivian."

"Tell that to your face." She'd meant it to be a joke, but even to her own ears it didn't sound like one.

He pulled into the parking lot of a throwback diner. Vinnie's boasted twenty-four-hour breakfast and a selection of cakes and pies that were, supposedly, second to none. The fact he had to circle the lot to find a space spoke of a dedicated clientele. She considered that an acceptable endorsement. As if it had a mind of its own, her stomach growled.

Once parked, Vivian scrambled to grab hold of the handle. The sooner she had a fork in her hand and food in her face, the faster she'd put some distance between them. She didn't jump when he gently grabbed her arm. But she did sigh silently at the way her body wanted to melt toward him.

"Vivian." He tugged her back before she could open the door. "I'm sorry if I'm making you uncomfortable."

"I think I'm the one doing that," she argued, determined not to look at him. She promised herself to stare out the window or at the floor. Anywhere that wouldn't force her to admit to the embarrassment flooding through her. "I'm sorry I kissed you last night."

"I'm not." His response sent chills racing down the arm he still held in his strong fingers.

"I didn't mean to—"

"I spent most of the night wishing I didn't have a guest room."

Her lips twitched and hope flared.

"The thing is…"

"Right." She sank back against the seat, and this time her sigh couldn't be stopped. "Of course there's a thing."

"I don't do well mixing business with pleasure. You're part of a case, however indirectly, and honestly, I'm worried I won't be able to do my job if I'm distracted by… you. And if I don't do my job, people get hurt. I definitely don't want one of those people to be you."

She blinked. Then frowned. His words soaked in, but she didn't quite accept them. "I distract you?" She broke her promise to herself and looked at him, unable to hide her disbelief. No one, certainly no man, had ever said that to her before.

"From the second you walked into Madariaga's." Nate released her and rested his arms on his steering wheel. "This can't come as a surprise. I didn't stop staring at you all through your dinner."

Her face warmed. So she hadn't imagined it.

"Add to that you're friends with Lizzy and I'm not entirely sure how she'd feel about us…connecting."

"Considering she encouraged me to go out with a con artist," Vivian observed, "I think me liking you would be an upgrade."

"Yeah, one would hope."

It was the first time she heard disappointment in his voice. Whether it was about her or his newly formed relationship with his siblings, Vivian couldn't be sure.

"For now, we have to keep things professional," Nate insisted. "I can't taint my case, and I don't want you getting more involved in something that could hurt you."

"What about after? Your case," she added when he seemed confused. "Can we see each other after you close it?"

"I—" Another shrug. "Well, yeah. I don't see why not."

"Be still my heart," she muttered. "What every woman longs to hear." But still she smiled. If only because she'd struck a nerve with him—a raw one, it seemed. And that was something that left her feeling more than a little bit powerful. "Okay. I'll leave it up to you if and when we... reconnect. Later."

"What every man longs to hear," he echoed with that charming smile of his. "You still hungry?"

"If I can't have you, at least I can have..." She leaned over and scanned the writing on the bank of windows. "A bacon buttermilk waffle with real Vermont maple syrup. Shall we?" She pushed out of the door before he could stop her again.

Or before she attempted to seal their pseudo-friendship deal with another kiss.

"Eight on the dot." Detective Sullivan was waiting for them at the Sergeant's desk on the first floor of the Boise Police Department. The fluorescently lit lobby boasted uniformed officers pinballing their way from door to door to staircase to elevators, some offering Nate a wave of welcome. Shoes squeaked on the linoleum floor that had probably been installed decades before he was born. "Looks like you got some sleep, Vivian."

"I did, actually. Thanks."

Nate hadn't known Vivian for long, yet he couldn't help but think she'd offered the other detective one of the most forced smiles he'd ever seen on anyone's face.

They stepped out of the way of a pair of officers dragging in a barely responsive suspect. Weekends might slow things down for everyone else, but for law enforcement, they went into overdrive.

"Thought you'd want to know," Detective Sullivan said to Nate, "patrol found a car about three hours ago, few miles away from the shooting. Burned out, but the VIN comes back to a beige sedan reported stolen two days ago in Conners."

"You think it's the one used in the shooting?" Nate asked.

"Fits the description, and it was completely torched. Whoever did it knew how to do it effectively. And they didn't try to hide it. We've taken it into evidence, but we aren't holding out any hope for prints or DNA."

"Right." Nate shook his head. Professional or not, like Sullivan implied, they'd probably done it before. "Hopefully, there's something to be gleaned from Vivian's sketch."

"Sure hope so. You ready to do this?" Sullivan asked Vivian.

"More than ready," Vivian confirmed. "Let's get it over with. Thanks for breakfast, Nate. And the guest room."

"Ah. Sure." Nate started to follow, but Vivian turned, held up a hand and shook her head. "I'm good from here.

Thanks for everything." She looked down at her T-shirt. "I'll get Sarah's clothes back to you as soon as I can."

"No rush. Let me know when you're done. I'll drive you back to your car." It hadn't taken him long to realize he'd completely messed things up. True to form when it came to women he cared about, he'd stuck his foot in his mouth. Only in Vivian's instance it seemed as if he'd wedged both feet—along with half his shoes—into the mix.

"That's okay. I don't want to be a bother."

"I can have a patrol car drop you off," Detective Sullivan offered.

"Perfect," Vivian accepted immediately. "We're all set then."

"We can have a patrol car follow you, just to be on the safe side." Nate wasn't ready to say goodbye. "Are you sure you don't want me to—"

"I'm sure." Her too bright smile was back in place. She did surprise him by rising up on her toes and brushing her lips against his cheek. "I'll be fine. Thanks for everything."

He had no response. Instead, he stood there, in the middle of the lobby, and watched Detective Sullivan hold the elevator door open for her. Nate was still trying to ease his disappointment when he got up to the third-floor bullpen where the criminal investigation department was housed.

"Colton!"

Nate turned as Lieutenant Luke Haig stepped out of his office. His commanding officer held up two fingers and circled them in the air to indicate Nate's presence was requested.

Just as well. He could already smell the over-brewed coffee spiking its way out of the break room. Peak distribution time had passed him by, probably back when he'd been trying to salvage something positive out of his time with Vivian. The fact he was already regretting how he'd handled things did not bode well for the rest of his day. Or weekend.

"Close the door," his superior officer suggested and gestured to one of the two hard-backed chairs on one side of his desk. The shelves behind his desk were lined with photographs of his superior, most of which showcased his close-knit ties to the community at large.

His focus on the Armenian community, the community he'd grown up in, connected him to various neighborhoods in ways other officers couldn't replicate. His successful years working undercover in the criminal investigation unit had given him his choice of commands and he'd chosen to remain here, in Boise. His home.

That said, his detectives called him the Mob Whisperer, and not only behind his back. The fiftysomething immigrant considered the moniker a badge of honor. "The desk sergeant tells me you requested Officer Cooper for protective detail at Boise General."

"Yes, sir." Because it was expected, he sat, even though the last thing he felt like doing was staying still. "Dean Wexler's condition is unchanged. There were enough cell phones recording the scene last night that it wouldn't be difficult for someone to assume he may still be alive."

"You're convinced someone will come after him?"

"Whoever shot him was willing to make a very public

attempt to take him out," Nate said. "If they think there's a chance to finish the job, we should be ready for it."

Haig nodded. "Agreed. And any progress connecting him to DeBaccian?"

"I'm going to do some more digging," Nate said. "But everything I've found so far leads to a connection versus not. Wexler's been maneuvering his way up the criminal success ladder for years here in Boise. If what we're hearing about DeBaccian is true, DeBaccian would have his eye on him. Wexler can't get any further without going through him. Debaccian takes a percentage from most career criminals working the Boise area. Considering Wexler's less than subtle tendencies when it comes to his targets—"

"And this woman from last night, this…" Haig leaned forward, his chair squeaking beneath his six-foot-six-inch height and significant muscle mass and checked his notes. "…Vivian Maylor, was Wexler's latest target."

"She fits the victimology." Just saying that word made him cringe. He didn't like to think of Vivian as any kind of victim. "I know Sullivan and his team are taking a closer look at the women already on file. But Vivian matches up in a number of ways, not the least of which is she met him through a dating app. She's a successful businesswoman, owns her own home. Is financially secure." He couldn't attest to any belongings that might appeal to a burglar with more fences than a prison yard, but then neither could Wexler. "Their date was a bust. Wexler was trying to save it, but she saw through him. He slipped up a few times. She knew something was off." She'd have ditched him at the restaurant if it hadn't been for that promise of chocolate. *Something to keep in mind*, Nate thought, then mentally kicked himself.

Nate had burned that bridge. Best to stop trying to rebuild it.

"If only everyone had such radar," Lieutenant Haig said. "Sullivan's report stated she thinks she saw a driver and one passenger. He's setting her up with Stacy? Putting a sketch together?"

"As we speak, sir." If anyone could get Vivian to remember the micro-details of what she'd seen last night, it was Stacy Crum. The woman was a talented artist, but her degree in psychology often aided in guided exercises that enhanced victims' recall. Put the two things together, and she was one of the best weapons the Boise PD had at their disposal. "But that's Sullivan's case." Time to cut the cord.

Haig eyed him with unveiled skepticism. "Is there anything I need to be apprised of in regard to Ms. Maylor?"

"Only that she spent the night in my guest room. Alone," he added just to make certain his boss understood. "Her glasses broke during the shooting, and with the storm, she didn't feel safe driving home."

"Glad you were there to lend your…support." Haig gave a nod of dismissal. "Okay, then. Keep me apprised."

"Yes, sir." It always amazed him, Nate thought as he returned to his desk, how a simple conversation with his superior felt like an interrogation session. The man was as no-nonsense as they came, but he was also cognizant of the fact that every detective in his unit approached the job in varying ways. He gave a lot of rope to his people and rarely, if ever, did they hang themselves with it. "Give me time," Nate muttered as he surrendered to temptation and headed into the break room for coffee.

Considering the way Vivian Maylor had been seared into his brain, chances were he wasn't remotely done with the fallout of having met her.

"So, I'm going to have you close your eyes, Vivian." Stacy, the sketch artist Detective Sullivan had put her in an interview room with, had placed Vivian in a chair directly in front of her. No table between them. Almost to the point of their knees touching. Stacy's red hair was pulled back from her face, and tiny springy curls bounced free to frame her bright eyes.

The large sketch pad sat on the table beside them, a series of sharpened pencils in easy reach. Vivian wasn't surprised by the nerves that struck, or that her hands were twisting themselves together like a frenetic acrobat troupe. She'd had a lifetime of learning to manage the anxiety that descended with any new situation. Anxiety that hadn't come close to appearing whenever Nate Colton was around.

She locked her jaw, shoved that thought out of her mind before it took hold. His explanation for backing off made complete sense. As disappointed as she was, she couldn't blame him. She could only imagine the dedication and single-mindedness it took to be a detective in this day and age. Becoming a clinging vine definitely wouldn't earn her any points.

"Why do I think this is going to be like one of my therapy sessions?" Vivian caught a quick smile on the woman's face before she closed her eyes.

"It's specialized therapy." Stacy's voice was calm,

even and gentle. "I've found this technique works really well when there isn't too much trauma involved. You seem relatively well-recovered from last night."

"It feels like it happened to someone else, actually." She focused on keeping her hands still and evening out her breathing. Truth be told, she was a master compartmentalizer. She hadn't let herself really dwell on anything that had happened last night, except her interactions with Nate.

"That may very well work to our advantage," Stacy said. "Did Detective Sullivan give you the information for our victim assistance department?"

"Detective Colton did." The card was wedged into the front pocket of her purse.

"I'd heard he was on-site right after this happened." The affection in Stacy's voice caught Vivian off guard. "He's a good one to have around in a crisis. Level-headed, cautious and a straight shooter. You always know where you stand with Nate."

"So I'm learning." The comment slipped out before she thought to stop it. She cleared her throat, shifted in her chair. "Do you know him well?"

"Well enough to have him on speed dial in case of an emergency." She paused. "Nate makes a habit of looking after strays. He doesn't limit his big-brother behavior to Sarah."

Vivian didn't know how to respond to that.

"Okay, so let's take some deep breaths and try to clear your mind," Stacy told her. "I'm going to talk to you for a little while, just to help you relax, and then we'll take small steps in getting you back to last night, okay?"

"Mmm-hmm." Vivian resisted the urge to nod. All

she wanted was to get this over with, put the entire incident last night behind her and move on with her life.

"Great. You're doing great, Vivian. Just keep listening to my voice, all right? There're no wrong answers. Everything is fixable. Details are my specialty, so I'm one of the few humans who likes change. Deep breath in, and out. In…and out."

Vivian instinctively focused on Stacy's voice and let herself fall into that space between full alertness and the brink of sleep. Stacy's questions gently guided her back, putting the memories into a kind of slow motion, but also kept Vivian separate from the action.

She walked behind herself and Dean Wexler. Her boots struck at the same place as her other self, and Vivian followed her motions, moving the same way. When Stacy asked what she saw, she talked about the store windows, the holiday decorations. The thick pine garlands winding up and around the lampposts accented with alternating tinsel bells and angel wings.

Her heart rate kicked up when she heard the car behind them. She turned in unison with her other self, seeing the bare details of the car.

"Tell me what you see, Vivian."

In the distance, Vivian heard the scratch of a pencil on paper. The sound was oddly soothing, she found. As if evidence of progress. Vivian knew as much about cars as she did NASCAR, meaning next to nothing. So color, the number of doors and the odd shape of the headlights were the only things she could mention.

"Who is in the car?" Stacy asked.

"Two men. Dark hair. Round faces." She squeezed her eyes tighter. "I don't know what I should say."

"Anything and everything that comes to mind."

"Right. Okay."

"Can you see them both?"

Vivian nodded. She hadn't realized that before. It was only now that she could see she'd originally merged her description into one person. "There's an older one driving. The passenger looks darker somehow. Meaner. Cruel. Sorry." Her lips twitched in apology. "I work in PR. I tend to pick up on personalities and intentions, even silent ones."

"That's good," Stacy encouraged. "Like I said, there's no wrong way to go about this. I want you to do something for me, okay? I want you to pretend to take a snapshot with your mind. Just like you do with your cell phone. Just click and store it for later. Can you do that?"

"I think so?" *Odd*, Vivian thought as she did just that. She even tried to zoom in and find more details that could help. A medal of some kind hung from the rearview mirror. A parking lot stub was wedged on top of the dashboard. The bucket seats were dark, almost black, and in the back seat…

Vivian gasped. Her eyes shot open. It took a moment to focus again, but when her vision cleared, she went wide-eyed when she looked to Stacy.

"What did you see?" Stacy asked.

"A third man." Her voice nearly broke from the tension winding through her body. "There was a third man in the back seat. He was wearing this big gold ring. That's what was glinting." He'd looked at Vivian and

Dean when the gun fired. For an instant—a blink of one—she'd looked him directly in the eyes.

"Did you see his face, too?"

"Yes." She whispered now, tried to ignore the shiver racing down her spine. "Yes, I saw him." She swallowed hard. "I saw all of them."

Chapter 5

As glorious as Nate's updated waterfall shower had been in the early hours of the morning, the first thing Vivian planned to do when she got home was jump into hers and wash that man right out of her hair.

"That man. Last night. And everything in between." She cranked up the throwback '80s station on her satellite radio. It was obvious from the moment Detective Sullivan had joined her and Stacy in the interview room that Vivian's description of not one, not two, but the three men from the car in the drive-by had exceeded everyone's expectations.

Detective Sullivan had tried to hide his surprise, and there was a flash of anger that glinted before he covered it. But she'd seen it. It had sent chills down her spine.

He'd always been polite. But his more solicitous attitude when he'd escorted her back downstairs and handed her off to a pair of uniformed officers who'd driven her back to her car had definitely left her feeling both accomplished and unnerved.

Almost as unnerved as the trio of dark, dangerous eyes that all but glowed from inside that car. She shuddered, gave herself a hard mental shake and took a cleansing breath. Getting all those details out and into Stacy's talented hands had offloaded a lot of the anxiety that had been churning inside her. But not all of it.

A glance at her watch eased a bit of her anxiety. She had plenty of time to make the half-hour drive to Owl Creek, get cleaned up and jump on her call with Harlow Jones, a rather ebullient relationship-expert client who always managed to lift Vivian's spirits.

Taking the back roads always gave Vivian a bit of comfort. Getting behind the wheel was one of her least favorite activities, but a necessary one. Not that she'd be making her way into Boise again anytime soon. Detective Sullivan had insisted that should he have any follow-up questions, he was happy to come to her. Again, that solicitous attitude seemed a bit of a stretch from the no-nonsense detective she'd first met at the hospital in the middle of the night.

Weekend traffic was nothing like it was during the workweek. She was just happy for the daylight, however gray it might be. As her eco-friendly car hummed down the four-lane road, she breathed out and flexed her hands on the wheel, wincing a bit at the cars zooming past her on the other side.

She hummed along with the music, but within seconds was belting out, off-key and with wrong lyrics, her accompaniment as the cold air swirled outside.

Behind her, a dark SUV surged close, giving no indication of slowing down. She eased her foot off the gas, pumped her brake just to make certain to be seen. But the car kept its speed up.

Her stomach clenched. Her hands tightened on the

wheel. Tailgaters were the worst, and her already shaky relationship with driving didn't make things any better.

"Just go around," she said as the music grew louder in her ears. "Go around, go around..."

She took her eyes off the mirror for a moment, checking for other vehicles that might be preventing the driver from moving over. Vivian slowed, debated easing onto the gravel shoulder, but there wasn't one for at least another half mile. The long, iced-over drainage ditches stretched endlessly.

The SUV was so close now she could see the muddied license plate.

"Go around!" she yelled, swerving to the right side. The left lane was clear. It didn't make any sense...

She screamed when the car hit her from behind. That deafening sound of metal against metal, that heart-stopping *bang*. Her hands gripped the wheel. She tried to speed up, but her little car wasn't having it. It stuttered a bit, then shot forward, but not before the SUV hit her again.

Every muscle in her body tensed up. She could feel each one of them from her shoulders right down to her toes. Terror tightened her throat and had her swiveling her head back and forth looking for somewhere, anywhere, to go. She could hear horns blaring when he hit again, but the sound didn't quite register before the SUV swerved around her and kept pace with her.

She pulled her foot off the gas. As if anticipating her action, the SUV rammed her from the side, sending her careening off the road before it sped off.

Her tires caught the top of the ditch and pitched the car up and over. She covered her face and, for a moment, felt as if she were almost airborne. The back of the car slammed down with enough force to flip one more time. The front windshield cracked and spider-webbed, the horrific crackling echoing in her ears for what felt like hours.

It landed diagonally across the icy ditch. Water from beneath the frozen top layer seeped in below the door, freezing her boot-covered feet. Around her, brakes screeched and people shouted while a car door slammed and footsteps raced closer. She could only breathe in short, painful bursts. Her fingers seemed frozen around the wheel.

"Ma'am?"

She screamed again when someone pounded on her window. It was a bearded man wearing sunglasses. His red-and-black flannel shirt gleamed in the early morning, cloud-breaking sun.

"Are you okay?" He pointed down, indicating she should lower her window.

She did so. Her hands were shaking so hard she could barely see them.

"Call an ambulance!" the man called over his shoulder as more people raced over. She could hear people asking if anyone had caught a plate number, or if they'd seen the driver. Vivian released her seat belt and tried to stop sobbing. All she wanted was out of the car.

"Get me out." She pulled hard on the handle before realizing the door was locked. She unlocked it and, with the man's help, shoved it open. She grabbed her bag, held it against her chest as she shoved her legs out of the car.

A couple of people grabbed her and pulled her free,

immediately sitting her on the level ground above the ditch.

"Ma'am?"

"I'm okay." She touched a hand to her head, expecting to find blood, but she didn't. "I'm okay." Her memory fogged over as if protecting her from recalling the event.

"An ambulance is on the way," one person called as they raced over.

An older woman, silvery hair knotted on top of her head. "Hon, what's your name? Can you tell me your name?"

"Viv-Vivian," she managed. "Vivian Maylor." She shivered hard enough that someone noticed and draped something warm over her shoulders. In contrast to the malicious driver, she felt concern and gentleness from the growing crowd.

"I called the police," another woman yelled.

"De-Detective Nate Colton," Vivian managed as she drew in a shaky, lung-aching breath. "Boise PD. He's…a friend." Tears burned her throat. She'd gotten snippy. Petulant even. Rejection never brought out the best in anyone, especially herself. She'd wanted to pretend he didn't exist, so she hadn't bothered to say goodbye. Maybe if she had… "I have his card…" She blinked hard to clear her vision as she dug into her purse. When she found it, she held it up to whomever snatched it from her hand. "I'd be grateful if someone could call him for me."

Nate leaned back in his chair, chin resting in his hand, a finger poised over his lips as he stared at his phone. The cell had buzzed a few times in the past couple of hours, but nothing came through of importance. Nothing from Sullivan about Vivian's session with the sketch artist. Nothing from the hospital about any change in Wexler's condition.

Just…nothing.

Irritated, he snatched the phone up and called Sullivan himself, only to get blocked by voicemail.

He swore, hung up, tossed his phone back on the desk and tried to refocus his attention on the file containing a list of Marty DeBaccian's arrests and his one conviction for armed robbery. Funny that was the only one, given his file was more than an inch thick. Since his release, he'd become as slippery as the lawyers who represented him. More so even.

He'd gone from being a one-trick pony to having his hand in everything from illegal gaming to loan sharking to felonious assault and, in at least two instances, attempted murder. But arrest-worthy proof was a completely different story.

Nate and most of the Boise PD had little to no doubt DeBaccian had committed far more crimes than he'd been arrested for, but that was only supposition, and supposition was not evidence.

At least Nate wasn't alone in thinking DeBaccian was one seriously bad dude. There wasn't a cop within a couple hundred miles of Boise who didn't have this guy in their sights. DeBaccian needed to be locked up, but even that might not do much to crush his growing criminal enterprise.

Nate was a realist if nothing else. He was well aware of the failings of the penal system. Oftentimes, convicts only became better criminals during their sentences, even to the point of continuing to run whatever organizations or rackets they had in place. But Nate was still of the belief that chopping off the head of the snake was the best way to kill the business and rid Boise of a good portion of organized crime. DeBaccian had become notoriously solitary. He didn't have a right hand or a number one. He had his favorites, but didn't completely trust anyone, which made the promise of information Wexler might possess all the more important.

Nate's fingers itched to call the hospital, but he'd already spoken to Cooper when the officer had returned to the station after being relieved at the hospital. Nothing out of the ordinary had occurred, no visitors, no strange happenings. As far as Cooper had been able to glean, there had also been no change in Wexler's condition.

Which left Nate standing completely still while the rest of the world kept spinning.

"Screw it." He pocketed his phone, grabbed his blazer off the back of his chair and took the stairs down to the second floor. He scanned the semi-empty bullpen for Sullivan, looking for that shock of red hair that always made the other detective stand out in a crowd.

"Hey, Nate." Stacy Crum headed toward him, bundled up in a bright purple down jacket and matching scarf. "I was just on my way out. If you're looking for Vivian, she left maybe a half hour ago."

"Left? Already?" He glanced at his watch. It was almost noon. Then he remembered she'd mentioned having a meeting with a client. "Where's Sullivan?"

"No idea," Stacy said. "Haven't seen him since he escorted Vivian downstairs. Your girl did great, by the way. Scary accurate, according to Sullivan."

His girl. Hearing that should have annoyed him, if for

no other reason than it confirmed the department gossip mill was running smooth and steady. Instead, the very idea of Vivian being his girl left him feeling oddly... warm. And slightly dim-witted at how he'd left things. "I'm not surprised." Despite finding herself smack in the middle of chaos, near as Nate could tell, Vivian had weathered the shooting pretty well. "Anything come of her description?"

"Sullivan didn't call?" Stacy frowned. "Must have slipped his mind."

"I'm sure it did." Nate didn't believe that for a second. The detective had a rumored habit of putting ambition above all else and he definitely wasn't enthusiastic about Nate's involvement with his case. "Can I see what the two of you and Vivian came up with?" He indicated the large, long-strapped artist satchel Stacy had slung over one shoulder.

Stacy shrugged. "I guess it'd be okay." She looked behind her. "Let's go back in Interview."

He followed, impatience hitting as Stacy took her time extricating her sketch pad from her bag. It took her flipping through a good half dozen pages before she got to the first one.

He let out a low whistle, shook his head. "Now that's some detail." The man's eyes chilled him to his marrow.

"I've never had anyone describe malevolence before," Stacy observed. "He looks real, doesn't he?"

"Yes, he does," Nate murmured.

"Here's the second one."

"The second...?" He flipped the page. "She saw both of them?" The Cyrillic tattoo on this one's neck would make him easier to trace. Chances were that was prison ink. "This clearly?"

"She saw all three of them," Stacy corrected and turned one more page. "She didn't remember until I took her under. Meet bachelor number three." Her smirk was one of pride, but the man looking back at Nate stole the air from his lungs. "Nightmare fodder for sure."

Something icy and slippery slithered up his spine as he looked at the face. And the ring on his hand. "Sullivan saw these?"

"Of course. Why?" Stacy frowned. "Or are you going to go all secretive on me and keep me in the dark? Who is this guy?"

Nate's mind spun. His instinct about Wexler being connected to Boise's latest crime boss was dead-on right. Had to be, otherwise DeBaccian wouldn't have come out to make sure the job was done himself.

"Thanks, Stacy." He turned and ran back up the stairs, beelined for his boss's office. Lieutenant Haig was getting to his feet when Nate's cell phone rang.

He checked the screen. Unfamiliar number, but no spam warning.

"Yeah. Colton." He held up a finger when Haig stood up and came to the door.

"Detective Nate Colton?" An unfamiliar woman's voice echoed. Beyond, he could hear sirens and shouts and rapid conversation. "I'm calling for a Vivian Maylor."

"Vivian?" He turned fear-filled eyes to his boss. "Why? What's happened? Where is she?"

The person gave him a location on the back roads between Conners and Owl Creek. "There was an accident.

She's okay. Pretty shaken up, but a car ran her off the road. Straight into a ditch. The car did this flip thing—"

"Flip?" His lungs turned to ice. "But you said she's all right."

"Near as we can tell. Miracle if you ask me."

His cop brain kicked into gear at the last second. "What about the car that hit her? Did anyone get a good look?"

"Long gone. No question it was deliberate. Road rage, I guess you could say. Hang on." Silence for a moment. "The ambulance just got here. I'm pretty sure they're going to take her in."

"Ambulance?" Nate demanded in a loud enough voice to garner the attention of his fellow detectives.

"Precaution, I'm sure. The car's totaled."

Despite the fear clutching at his heart, he let out a sigh of relief. "Okay. All right. Tell her I'm on my way and that I'll meet her at the hospital." Hopefully, that alone would stave off any argument she might make against yet another ride in an ambulance. "I'm on my way now."

"I'll tell her." The caller disconnected.

"Report," Lieutenant Haig ordered in a way that jerked Nate back to reality.

"Vivian was run off the road on her way home. Sullivan…" Anger surged. "One of Vivian's sketches is of DeBaccian. Right down to that family crest ring he wears." She hadn't missed a single detail, and those details may well have almost gotten her killed. "He was in the car last night when they tried to take out Wexler."

"Ballsy," Haig said in that stern, detached way he had. "If that's true, that's a change in behavior for him."

"Indulgent," Nate said. "Arrogant." And proof DeBaccian had it in for Wexler. His gut had been right. "He's covering his tracks." Which put Vivian straight in the man's crosshairs. "Sullivan knew she'd seen him, and he still sent her home alone." His hand tightened around his cell phone. "I need to get to the hospital." He hurried to explain. "The person who called me said Vivian's car flipped into a ditch. She seems okay, but..." He hesitated. "We need her car in evidence." He was ping-ponging between cop and concerned...whatever he was to Vivian.

"There might be trace evidence we can link back to DeBaccian. Nice shortcut to an arrest, even if it is a Hail Mary pass." Haig nodded. "Okay. Paulson, Renard." He snapped his fingers over his head so loud nearly everyone in the bullpen shot to attention. The two detectives stepped out from behind their desks. "You two head out to the scene, control what you can and make sure every single witness is questioned. We want Ms. Maylor's car impounded, and I want Cassidy Barrett brought in to oversee the evidence collection."

Nate's fellow detectives quickly grabbed their jackets and, after giving Nate a reassuring pat on the shoulder, headed out.

"I need to—"

"Go," Haig said. "Let me know of any developments. And Colton?"

"Sir?" Nate skidded to a stop before reaching his desk.

"Consider Vivian Maylor in protective custody," Haig ordered. "Yours and yours alone. Don't let her out of your sight. She might be the best witness we've ever had against DeBaccian, and he clearly knows about her.

I'm going to order surveillance on DeBaccian's known hangouts while we wait for a warrant."

"What about Detective Sullivan?" Nate demanded.

"Leave Sullivan to me." The chill in Haig's voice left Nate almost feeling sorry for the other detective. "Go. And report in when you can."

"Thank you, sir." He retrieved his gun from his desk drawer, strapped it into his holster. "Will do."

"Are you sure you're all right?" The desperate plea on the other end of the line only added to Vivian's anxiety. She'd gone her entire life without having ridden in an ambulance. Now, within the space of twenty-four hours, she was on trip number two. This was not an item she'd had on her meager and pathetic bucket list. At this rate, she was going to have a reserved bed in the ER.

"Harlow, I'm fine." She grimaced as the aches began to settle in. She was back at Boise General. Back in one of their triage rooms, only this time instead of the midnight glow of the moon, she got full-on sunlight. "I'm just sorry I missed our meeting."

"It wasn't a meeting per se," Harlow said with the teensiest edge of guilt in her voice. "I mean, it wasn't like official business or anything. You've already gone leaps and bounds beyond what I expected from a publicist. You hooked me up with Sandy Flemming, the queen of morning talk! I'm happy where I am at the moment." She paused. "Mostly."

Vivian frowned. "I don't understand." Harlow had been a bit cryptic in their last email exchange, mentioning some impulsive plans she was considering implementing. Vivian had assumed it was in regard to

Harlow's ever-expanding audience for her online relationship advice. Whatever was beyond viral, Harlow had hit it in the perfect sweet spot. Hence her needing a PR person to help manage the cascade of offers and opportunities while trying to grab hold of even bigger ones. "So our call wasn't business related?" She sighed as the nurse tightened the blood-pressure cuff around her arm, forcing Vivian to switch her cell to her other hand.

She might have shot the nurse a look but found her own irritation mirrored in the older woman's face. Vivian glanced down, noted the woman's name was Helga and offered a strained, apologetic smile. "Cell phones really aren't allowed in here," the nurse said without bothering to try to keep her voice down.

"We're almost done." The familiar drab-blue curtains hung as limp as Vivian was beginning to feel. Talking to Harlow was at least helping her set aside the panic over losing her car and being run off the road by some reject from a bad *Mad Max* rip-off.

"You should go," Harlow said. "We can talk later."

"It's fine," Vivian lied. "What did you want to talk about?"

"Well." There was that pause again. "I think I'm going to come back to Owl Creek for a little while."

"Oh?" Harlow's career in Los Angeles was just beginning to take off into the stratosphere. Seemed an odd time to take a break. "You sure you want to do that?"

"I think it's time, you know? To finally put my folks' house on the market and get all that behind me. I was hoping we could get together in person once I hit town. I'll be there for a while, so I'm sure we can eke out some time?"

"Oh." The prospect might have brightened her mood if it hadn't been sitting at rock bottom. "That sounds great. Of course we can get together."

"Great. It'll be nice. Change of scenery, focusing on something other than…work."

There was that hesitancy again, a hesitancy that signaled something deeper was bothering her client-turned-friend. Given the *tsks* Vivian heard emanating from her nurse, now wasn't the time to question Harlow.

"I've got some things to tie up before I head to Idaho," Harlow continued. "But I wanted to touch base with you first."

"I'm glad you did. Seeing you gives me something to look forward to."

"You're sure you're okay?" Harlow asked again. "Car accidents aren't anything to laugh about, and it sounds like yours was a doozey."

"Could have been worse." Vivian blinked back the sudden rush of tears, but she refused to give in. She was alive. That was all that mattered. "But I'm really fine. I'll figure out everything that comes next. I just didn't want you to think I flaked out on our meeting."

"You're incapable of flaking. If you're sure, I'll let you get back to the nurses hassling you. Take care, okay? You need anything, you know where you can find me. Seriously, I'm just a call away."

"Thanks, Harlow." It felt odd, Vivian thought after she hung up and stared down at her cell: she'd spent so much of her life alone. Other than Lizzy Colton, she could count the number of friends she'd had on maybe three fingers. At the rate she was going, she might be all the way to five pretty soon.

"I'll take that." Helga plucked the phone out of Vivian's grasp and plunked it out of reach on the table beside the bed. The satisfied smirk on her face seemed like overkill, but Vivian supposed nurses needed to find a way to make the most of a bad situation. And right now, Vivian was definitely on the precipice of becoming a difficult patient.

She hadn't wanted to come back to the ER. She wanted to go home and bury herself under her covers and sleep away the last couple of days.

"We've got a CT scan scheduled for you within the hour," Helga advised her. "You should rest until then."

"Great." A CT scan was going to take ages. She'd be lucky to get back to her cozy little town house before sunset.

The nurse left, pulling the curtain closed to give Vivian the spare bit of privacy possible in a bustling ER room. One bed over, the patient was dealing with some serious stomach pain that, unfortunately for Vivian's batlike hearing, was indicative of either a seriously infected gall bladder or ruptured appendix.

"All the more reason to be grateful," Vivian mumbled to herself as she scooted down in bed and curled up on her side. "At least you've only got bumps and scrapes." And one seriously aching body. At least she had a different cubicle this time, one with a gorgeous view of the loading dock at the back of the hospital. Still, it felt as if an avalanche of the past had landed on her full force.

She should sleep. She wanted to. But every time she closed her eyes all she saw was that black SUV barreling up behind her in the rearview mirror. She'd spent most of her life hoping, praying, that history didn't repeat itself and yet...

She turned her head, this way and that, trying to push aside the haunting, nerve-wracking sound of metal scraping metal. Hugging her arms around her body, she curled tighter, hating the tears and fear threatening to explode if she gave them half a chance.

She covered her eyes, repressed the urge to growl when she heard the rattle of the curtain being pulled back. "Please, just leave me alone." She was already shaking so hard her teeth ached. If she was going to fall apart, she needed to do so without an audience.

"Vivian."

She dropped her hand and looked over her shoulder. "Nate."

The tears she'd been trying hard to bank flooded instantly. She wanted to ask why he was here. What he was doing here. She hadn't wanted to believe the kind woman who had called him when she'd assured Vivian that Nate would meet her at the hospital. And yet...

He closed the curtain and approached the bed. Her gaze shifted to the chair in the corner, but he walked right past it to sit beside her on the bed, up close to where she could grab hold of him. Instead of clinging to him, she pulled herself up and slipped her arms around his neck.

She wasn't alone.

A sob lodged in her chest.

That he immediately responded by wrapping his arms around her and pulling her in so close she could hear his heart beating over hers had her closing her eyes again, this time in relief. And comfort.

"I was so scared," she whispered, hating the helplessness she heard in her voice. She knew how to take care of herself, but the last day had definitely left her wondering if leaving the house was worth it. Taking chances clearly wasn't for her. Except...

Except that it had led to where she sat now. In the one place that felt perfect.

"I never should have left you," he murmured against the side of her throat. "When I got that call, I'd never been so scared in my life." He caught her face between his hands, set her away from him.

The fear she saw on his face, in those blue eyes of his, made her feel, at least in this moment, that she mattered to someone.

"You aren't going to ask me what happened?" Her question came out slightly broken, hitched, as if her words couldn't piece themselves together any easier than the rest of her could.

"Not yet." He drew her back against him, cradled her head under his chin, against his chest. "I will. But later. I just need a few minutes first."

"I'm fine." Her fingers felt bruised, as did her forearms. From gripping the steering wheel so tightly she supposed. "They want to put me through a CT scan just to make sure."

"Good." He pressed a kiss to the top of her head, and it was, quite possibly, the most caring gesture she'd ever experienced. "I'm here. I'm not going anywhere."

"That's nice."

"You don't believe me." She could almost hear the smile in his voice.

She shook her head, still unwilling to release her hold on him. "You have a job to do. An important one."

"You're my job now." He shifted before he slid off the edge of the bed. "Lieutenant's orders."

"Oh?" That piqued her curiosity, and she sat back, just enough to look up at him.

"Definitely *oh*." He flinched and doubt rose in his eyes. "The man you ID'd, from the back seat of the car. His name is Marty DeBaccian." He paused. "He's the man I was hoping Dean Wexler could give me information on."

She blinked, processed. She blinked faster. "But...you told me the man you were after was a really bad guy."

"He is." He stroked his thumbs down her cheeks, before sliding one across her lips. "He's a very bad guy. I think that's who came after you this morning. I can't prove it yet, but unless you really ticked someone off while you were driving, I think it's a safe bet."

"I might have." He clearly thought she was joking. "I'm a terrible driver. I go way too slow. It's why I'm always going to the right. It's... I hate it. Driving. I've lost track of the number of tickets I've gotten."

"I don't think—" He nodded as if humoring her.

"My parents died in a car accident when I was nine." She chewed on her bottom lip, considered. "I was with them, but I don't really remember. One minute they were there, and the next..." She wanted to shrug it off as if that event hadn't defined the rest of her life. "I woke up in the hospital alone. All of this, it's just so surreal." And familiar. Far too familiar.

The sympathy on his face was almost too much to bear. "I'm sorry."

"I didn't get my license until I was twenty-two. Every time I climb into a car, I can't help but think it might be the last thing I do. And if I drive past an accident?" Her laugh was harsh. "It sends me spiraling back. I can't explain it any better than that. Nine years old and I was left all alone."

"Alone?" His brow furrowed. "You didn't have any family?"

She shook her head. "My grandparents were all gone by the time I was born, and my parents were only children. We traveled a lot and were spending the summer on a road trip. The crash happened in Boise. I spent the next nine years in and out of foster homes in and around Owl Creek. That's when I met Lizzy. Your sister. When I started school that fall." Tears filled her eyes again. "She made me feel as if life might be okay again."

"Yeah, well." He rested his hands on her shoulders. "We Coltons have a bit of an unofficial code. Family finds family."

She sniffled and nodded. "I really lucked out in that department." She lifted a hand to his face. "Twice maybe, it seems."

He kissed her, gently. Carefully. As if afraid of breaking her. Instead, it brought all the fear and panic back to the surface and gave it someplace to go. When she broke away, she scooted closer and hugged him, hard. For however long he was around, she planned to make the most of their time together.

"What happens now?" she whispered.

"First we're going to make sure you're in the clear medically," Nate said. "That'll give me time to make some plans. But fair warning—" he spoke as if he expected her to protest "—I'm not taking you home. Not for any length of time. Don't worry," he added when she sat back and gaped at him. "We'll figure it out so your life isn't completely upended. Last night, you said you'd trust me. I need you to trust me again, Vivian. And know that this time I won't leave you behind."

"You promise?"

He nodded and pressed his lips to her forehead. "I promise."

It was, Vivian admitted silently when she closed her eyes in relief, the only thing she'd needed to hear.

Chapter 6

Guilt was a funny thing. Oftentimes, Nate thought as he waited in the registration area of the emergency room, guilt was also blinding. It descended with a familiar ferocity that shoved everything, including irrational thought, aside.

This was a roller coaster he'd been riding for as long as he could remember. Growing up with a less than stable influence of a mother—one who, while physically present, didn't come close to being emotionally invested in the children she'd brought into the world—meant growing up fast.

There was no defining the type of pain one carried upon realizing early in life that you aren't remotely close to being the center of anyone's universe.

He'd become an overachiever, a protector, especially where his sister Sarah was concerned. When Robert Colton, his father, had all but disappeared from their lives when Nate was around ten, Nate found himself instantly stepping into the caretaker role. It was a role that brought with it a particular resentment, one that grew with each calculated, cruel step Jessie Colton took away from her family. But with all of that came guilt.

No matter how many years passed or how successful or accomplished he became, Nate could always find a way to feel as if he could have done something, anything, everything, better.

It was too late to reconcile with his father, or even have any kind of confrontation or conversation with Robert Colton. A stroke had ended his life earlier this year before any kind of emotional peace could be sought, for either of them. It didn't quite seem real, that his father was gone. It should have been easy enough to accept. Robert hadn't been around for most of Nate's life. But with all the questions Nate had, not to mention the family dynamics that continued to swirl into the realm of complicated, it also felt as if Robert was still smack dab in the middle of everything.

Even Jessie had seemed—what was the word?—*contrite* about the situation as a whole. Contrite to the point of...

Nate squeezed his eyes shut as if attempting to clear out his brain. His suspicious nature surrounding his mother's actions had no place in his thoughts. As far as he was concerned, Jessie herself had no place in them, but blood was blood. No matter how much he distrusted and disliked his mother, she was still his family. Whether he liked it or not.

Seated in a worn vinyl chair, he rested his elbows on his knees and stared at the linoleum floor. The attempt at festive decor didn't feel quite complete. Some windows were outlined with dollar-store threadbare tinsel garlands, while a pair of one-armed frolicking elves looked more demented than celebratory. Clearly, they'd been dug out of a holiday bin probably stored in the basement. He definitely wasn't feeling the holiday cheer.

He was being too harsh, no doubt. Internalizing what he should have been trying to find a healthy outlet for. But he couldn't help it. Dwelling on the *should haves* and *wished he hads* was pretty much a pattern for him.

He shouldn't have walked away from Vivian the way he had. He shouldn't have pushed her away and into Sullivan's irresponsible, self-centered hands. He'd built up her trust then turned his back when he felt himself getting too close. It would be so easy, too easy, to take that slide he could sense hovering before him and fall. A fall that terrified him far more than any dangers of his job.

He'd felt it the second she'd walked into the restaurant the other night. That pull that had only gotten stronger. That…gravitational force that seemed to have been created just for the two of them. And yet…

He couldn't let himself surrender to it. That attraction that had struck and settled dead center in his heart from the start. It had no place here, between them. Inside him.

Especially now that her life may very well depend on him remaining attentive, on guard, and most of all, ready. He needed to put her safety first. End of story.

If only he didn't know what it felt like to hold her in his arms…

The swinging doors bounced open. Nate shot to his feet as a young female nurse pushed Vivian's wheelchair into the open space. He hadn't noticed the bruises before, or the cuts and scrapes she'd received, no doubt, from the shattered glass. She had her arms wrapped tight around herself, as if cocooning against everything around her. A couple of new bandages had joined the one near her eye where her glasses had cut her during the shooting.

She looked as if she'd gone a good three or four rounds in the ring with a less than sympathetic opponent.

"And here we are!"

Nate couldn't tell whether Vivian was embarrassed or annoyed, but the way she rolled her eyes at her escort's cartoony tone told Nate, more than any clear CT scan could have, that she was just fine.

"I can take her from here," he offered in an effort to spare the nurse any potential reaction. He could only imagine how frayed Vivian's nerves must be by now. She'd been shot at, questioned by the police, spent hours with a sketch artist and been run off the road. All that was beyond Nate's own capabilities of coping. "Really." He reached into his pocket and pulled out his badge. That action earned him another eye roll from Vivian, but he accepted her reaction as another good sign.

"Oh." The nurse straightened and looked a little disappointed. "Sure, of course, Detective. Just make sure you leave the chair in the depository just outside?"

"You've got it." He was well aware how effective a perfectly aimed smile could be for some people.

She settled her bag in her lap as Nate wheeled her outside into the sunny yet frosty day. She shivered.

"We need to get you another jacket."

"I just want to go home." Her grumble made Nate worry she didn't recall what he'd told her just a few hours ago in her cubicle.

"I'm taking you home to pack," Nate said in a way that he hoped left no room for argument. "Then we're headed back out."

"Is that really necessary?" She yelped a bit when he bounced over the metal threshold.

"Sorry. And yes," Nate told her as he steered her over to where he'd parked in the ER lot. "It is. I'm also going to need your phone."

"My...phone?" She made it sound as if he'd asked her to cut off her arm.

"Can't take any chances you're being tracked. Whoever ran you off the road—"

"It could have been an accident." She glanced over her shoulder at him, barely there hope swimming in her hazel eyes. "We shouldn't overreact."

Nate bit the inside of his cheek and remained silent until he had her in the car. Before he left to return the wheelchair, he pulled out his phone and tapped open the photos he'd been sent from Lieutenant Haig. "If you can look at these and still tell me you think it was pure coincidence this happened to you, we can discuss further. I'll be right back." He closed the door and grabbed the chair.

Showing her the photos wasn't something he'd planned to do. Personally, he'd have preferred not to show her the evidence of her own attempted murder, but they both needed to start looking reality in the face. If only to make some smart decisions.

By the time he returned to the car and slid in behind the wheel, he didn't have to ask if he'd made his point. She'd set her phone on the console between the seats. The tension swirling inside the SUV was more than enough evidence of that.

"You okay?" It was, perhaps, the dumbest question he'd ever uttered in his life. But it was the only thing he could think to ask. He quickly turned off her phone, popped out the SIM card and placed both in the glove box.

"Not really, no." She handed his phone over, and he

pocketed it so he could use it again in an emergency. "I guess I'd convinced myself it wasn't as bad as it was." She sighed, sank down in her seat. "My car's totaled."

"Yes, it is." The images had been sent from their evidence station, where Lieutenant Haig had ordered Detective Sullivan to meet him. Nate's superior had wanted Sullivan to see the results of his dismissing a witness without thinking things through. Nate could only hope the conversation made some kind of impact, but he doubted it. Sullivan was a decent cop, but not the best human being. "But you weren't, so let's count that as a win."

"Go me."

Her sense of humor was intact, at least. "We'll worry about your car another time. Right now, let's get you home."

"What about you?" She looked over at him. "If we're leaving town, don't you need your stuff?"

"I keep a go bag in the back." He jerked a thumb toward the rear window. He reorganized the duffel every couple of weeks, just to be safe. He'd only had call to use it a handful of times since becoming a detective, but at least he knew it was reliable. Anything he might have missed they could pick up down the road. "I can live out of that thing for weeks if necessary."

"I still haven't given a statement about the accident." She took hold of the grab bar over the door and the center console when he reversed out of the parking space. "Sorry." Her eyes squeezed shut for a moment. "Getting back on the horse isn't easy. Stupid." She gave her head a hard shake and had him wincing.

"It's natural, not stupid. It'll get better. And I'll try

to go slow." Truth be told, he'd considered having her drive his car to her place. Slapping fear in the face was usually his mode for getting past things. But she wasn't him. Vivian would have to be eased back into the driver's seat. Or at least be strongly motivated. Tiny steps, he told himself. "As far as your statement goes, we'll get that taken care of once we get to where we're going."

"And where is that exactly?" She hadn't released her grip on the grab bar. If anything, she'd tightened her fingers to the point her knuckles had gone white.

Because Nate wasn't entirely sure himself, he shrugged. "Does it matter?"

She went silent for a moment. "I suppose not."

"It's not going to be for long, Vivian. Just until we catch whoever is behind these attacks on you."

"Despite your best efforts to prove otherwise, you aren't a superhero," Vivian said. "You can protect me, or you can work the case. I doubt you can do both."

"Oh, ye of little faith." How she underestimated him. And it would be something akin to a pleasure to prove her wrong. "I'm capable of multitasking all sorts of things. Besides, I've got lots of friends in the Boise PD, and most of them owe me more than one favor. We'll get you home and back to your life soon enough."

She caught her lower lip in her teeth and turned her head to look out the window. The sun still shone, but a light dusting of snow fell from the gray clouds hovering overhead. Days like this felt like doom and gloom with the barest hint of light on the horizon.

"My lieutenant said there were more than a dozen people who stopped to help you." He was grasping at straws to help identify something positive out of all this.

"They all gave statements and a description of the car that hit you. Most of them asked about you."

He couldn't see her reaction. "Do you think…" She stopped, took a deep breath. "When this is all over, do you think I could get their names so I can send them thank-you notes?"

It seemed both a ludicrous idea and so incredibly Vivian. "I think we can make that happen."

She glanced at him. "That's weird, isn't it?"

"Incredibly," Nate said without hesitation. "But more that you thought of it now, when you're still reeling from what happened." Her grimace told him she was doubting her own sanity. "Feel and think what you need to in order to get through."

"I can compartmentalize better than most people." Her voice was low now and carried a familiar sadness Nate could relate to. "Sometimes you have to do that in order to survive."

Like she'd had to when her parents were killed. Like he did when his father had returned to his other family. His *real* family.

"Don't ever apologize for being who you are, Vivian." Because he couldn't resist the urge, he reached over and laid his hand over hers. His heart jumped when she folded her fingers around his and squeezed. "You're you. That's the only thing that matters."

"You missed your calling, Detective," Vivian said softly. "You really should give poetry a try."

He laughed, shook his head, and because she cast nervous eyes at his driving with only one hand on the wheel, he released his hold and put her mind at ease. "My expertise with poetry extends only so far as the naughty limericks one of my school friends used to recite."

"You underestimate yourself," she said in a tone that left no room for argument. "I think you have more talent in the word department than you realize. Can I ask a favor?"

"Sure."

"Before we hit the freeway, can we please, *please* stop for some coffee?"

It felt strange having a man drive her home. Strange in a good way, perhaps, but strange nonetheless. It was as if she'd left her home Friday evening one person and was coming home a different one. Maybe it was the fact that Nate was the man.

She didn't think it was the badge he wore or the job he did or even the last name he possessed, but perhaps it was the combination that made Vivian feel utterly and completely safe and content when he was around. Even while her entire world seemed to be falling off its axis.

For a woman who had spent the majority of her life alone, she wasn't completely pleased with the idea of feeling even the least bit reliant on another person for her emotional well-being but…there it was. Reality. And his name was Nate Colton.

Guided by his onboard GPS, he parked in front of her garden-gated town house and turned off the engine. There was an unexpected relief at seeing her house again. There had been moments before she'd crashed that she had honestly believed she wouldn't ever see it again.

"Can I have your keys, please?" Nate held out his hand.

She frowned, looked down at his empty palm. "Why?"

"Because I'm not taking a chance that they don't know where you live. They spent enough time looking at your license plate. Getting your address wouldn't take much more effort."

"Awesome." She hadn't even considered that. She dug into her purse, wincing at the slight dampness of the leather, to retrieve them. She hoped the bag wasn't ruined by its time in the icy water after the crash. "I suppose you want me to wait in the car while you check things out?"

"I'll only be a couple of minutes."

"More than five and I'm coming in." She was already mentally packing as he headed inside. She was also attempting to come up with some argument, any argument, to change his mind about letting her stay. She finished the last of her extra-large double-shot latte without the usual guilt at the caffeine level. Jittery was better than feeling helpless. At least, that was the idea she'd had when she'd placed her order.

Her home was her fortress, the one place she always felt untouchable and completely herself. What Nate was proposing was leaving all that security behind. As much as she trusted him, she wasn't completely on board with this idea.

Watching him approach her gate gave her an unobstructed rear view of the perfection of the male form. She let out a slow breath, appreciating the way he moved, even as he reached behind him and pulled a gun out of the back of his jeans.

"And there's the reality check." She was really getting sick of them, to be honest. She was not a fan of weapons. She didn't own a gun. Heck, she'd never even fired one!

Now she found herself getting tangled up with someone who carried one for a living. As if a handful of steamy kisses equaled entangled.

The metal fence clanked shut, and he made his way up the short walk to her front door. He took a moment before sliding the key into the lock and disappearing inside.

Vivian's heart pounded hard against her ribs. What if someone was inside? What if Nate found them in there? Could she ever feel safe again after her space had been invaded? Or if he was hurt protecting her?

No sooner had she begun the internal debate than Nate reappeared and returned to the car. He pulled open her door. "Everything looks fine to me." He held out his hand, and for an instant, she had an image of a particular glass-slippered princess being welcomed by her prince charming. She rolled her eyes, shook her head and wondered when her teenage self had been reawakened. Clearly the last couple of days had made a jumble of her thoughts and long-suppressed longings and dreams.

"It shouldn't take me too long to pack a bag." The sensation of his hand against the small of her back felt incredibly intimate. "How long should I plan to be gone for?"

"A week." His answer sounded as if he'd given it some thought. "We'll re-evaluate after that."

"Right." She left her purse on the floor in front of the small entryway table before heading up the stairs. "I'll be back down in a bit."

"Take your time," he called up after her. "I'm not going anywhere."

* * *

Nate closed the front door to Vivian's town house and, out of habit, snapped the lock. He'd only given a cursory glance to her home's contents on his initial entry. He'd been looking for disturbances, signs of someone else's presence. Not a reflection of Vivian's character and personality.

Since he'd found nothing disturbed, he relaxed and took in his surroundings. Not that there was much to take in. The ground floor mostly consisted of a spacious living area, where she had a small sofa, coffee table and rather large television set up in the corner beneath the stairs. There wasn't any art on the walls or knickknacks on the shelves.

Behind the sofa, taking up the entire back wall, was a bookcase crammed with titles of every sort, forced into precarious storage as she clearly read more than her system could contain.

A collection of blankets covered the sofa. One in particular, a black one over the back, near the window, had an indentation in it. He frowned, walked over, touched gentle fingers to the blanket, which was coated with cat hair.

He turned, looked around and spotted a pile of cat supplies in the corner by the front door. A cat perch with a cubby, a scratching post and a paper bag filled to overflowing with toys, food bowls and water dishes.

There were only a small number of framed photographs on display. One showed Vivian cuddling a beautiful, sleek white-and-gray cat with enormous yellow eyes. Another photo gave him a start as it was most definitely of his half-sister, Lizzy Colton. The two of them wore their caps and gowns at high school graduation. They'd been caught mid-laugh, and the sight stole his breath.

The other three were of Vivian as a little girl, being cuddled between two people he assumed were her parents. One during the summer, one at the holidays and a third at what appeared to be one of Vivian's birthdays. The light in her eyes was almost blinding with happiness as she blew out the candles on her cake. Those three pictures were more faded than the others, had folds and creases in them. Five pictures seemed a small and sobering number to represent thirty years of life.

In the corner by the window stood a round table on which a small, not even three-foot fake Christmas tree sat. Without the lights, it looked more than a little sad, with only a handful of ornaments on it, but there was one small, handcrafted paper angel sitting on the top with stringy blond hair. Other than that, there wasn't a hint of the holidays around her home.

"Hey, Nate?" Vivian came down two steps and leaned over. Her wet hair spilled over her shoulders. Heat and the fragrance of flowers wafted off her skin, a result of the shower she must have taken.

Gone were his sister's jeans and T-shirt. The sweater she wore now over faded jeans was a deep turquoise blue that accentuated her beautiful eyes. "We are staying in civilization, right? Electricity and everything? Internet?"

"We are if I have anything to say about it," he confirmed and earned a smile from her.

"Cool." She disappeared back upstairs.

He wandered through to the kitchen and small nook where a table and two chairs stood. Files and papers sat stacked in what he assumed was a system only she understood. Outside, a collection of empty bowls sat alongside the sliding glass door leading out to a small garden that contained nothing resembling plants. Instead, there were tumbles of rocks where grass or pots might have been.

He stepped outside, checked the back gate and noticed the garbage and recycling cans out along the back road where tenants parked. Deciding he might be of some help, he returned inside and rummaged through her refrigerator. He was shoulder deep into a collection of leftovers and takeout boxes when she came up behind him.

"Hungry?"

"Yes, actually." He grinned over his shoulder at her. The warmth of her hand on his shoulder had him once again needing to remind himself that he was actually working. Now wasn't the time for flirtations. "But I thought maybe we should empty this out just in case you're away longer than a week."

"Probably." She sighed. "Shame. There's some good food in there. I found this new Peruvian place that... Where are you going?"

"I've got a collapsible cooler in the back of the car." He shrugged. "Like you said, it's a shame to let it go to waste." Because her smile of gratitude was almost more than he could take, he made a quick exit, taking deep, refocusing breaths as he retrieved the cooler. He'd no sooner slammed the back shut than he found himself coming face-to-face with an elderly man with glasses so thick he looked like a goldfish. "Hello."

"You visiting Ms. Maylor?" The man was a bit stooped and barely reached Nate's chest. He held a small package in one hand, a four-footed cane in the other. His

T-shirt declared him to be a marine veteran, as did the steely, almost suspicious look in his bright blue eyes.

"I, well, yes, I am. Nate Colton." He held out his free hand, refrained from flashing his badge. "I thought I'd take Vivian on a bit of a vacation."

"A vacation?" His eyes went wide. "Well, land's sake. Never expected to hear that. Don't really see her unless she's coming out to get her mail. I'm Edgar Bartholomew. I live next door." He indicated the town house to the right. Potted poinsettia plants lined the walkway, interspersed with solar lights that no doubt cast a festive glow onto the red and white petals. His front window was filled with an enormous lighted tree twinkling bright enough to be seen from the space station. "Folks just call me Eddie though. Vacation. Huh." He frowned again, quirked his head in question. "Really?"

"Really." It shouldn't have surprised him that this news came across as unexpected. Vivian didn't strike him as the impulsive type. "Was there something you needed, Eddie?"

"Me? Oh, no." Eddie shook his head, then shoved the box at Nate. "Delivery came for Vivian yesterday afternoon. It needed to be signed for, and I was out tending to my roses. Even in winter, they need tending to."

"Of course," Nate agreed, noting the line of blankets draped over the pruned bushes.

"I came over and rang last night, but no answer." His smile was quick. "Guess I know why now. Anyway. This is for her."

Nate accepted the box. "I'll make sure she gets it."

"Appreciate it." Eddie started to hobble away, then turned around and nearly toppled over catching his balance. "Nice to see she's found someone to take care of her. She's a lonely one, I think," he observed with a sad shake of his head. "Hate to see it. Put a smile on her face, would you? No one should be all alone. Especially during the holidays."

"I'll do my best," Nate assured him before he headed inside. He returned to the kitchen where he found her sorting containers and setting aside produce that wouldn't last much longer. The bowls that had been outside the back door were in the sink now. "I just met your neighbor, Eddie."

"Oh?"

"He accepted a delivery for you yesterday." He held out the box.

She accepted it with more than a question on her face. "I wonder what…" She read the label, then hugged it to her chest. She sighed and closed her eyes. When she opened them again, they were filled with tears.

"What is it?" Nate asked.

She grabbed a knife and sliced through the packing tape. Once open, she pulled out a small cedar box with *Toby* engraved on the top. "My cat's ashes. I had to put him down last month. Kidney disease." She sighed and touched her fingers to the polished wood. "I had him for over eleven years." Vivian attempted a laugh, swiped at the tears on her cheek. "Boy, when it rains, it pours. I wasn't sure when to expect this, but it makes sense it would come now. The hits just keep coming."

"Vivian." Her name was the only thing he could think to say. The toys and cat things in the corner made sense now. She was giving it all away because her cat had died.

"Thanks." She sighed. "Boy, I'm a piece of work, aren't I? Can't begin to understand why I'm still single."

"I, for one, am glad you are." He took hold of her shoulders and turned her to face him. "I'm sorry about Toby."

"Thanks." Her smile was both sad and sentimental. "He was the best cat. My best friend. My shadow. Never left me alone. Because of him I didn't feel quite so..."

"Alone?" Nate supplied when it seemed she couldn't.

"Yeah." Her voice was thick. "Geez, you don't want me blubbering all over you." She stepped away, bent down and grabbed a bag of cat food out of a cabinet. "I didn't want all this going to waste." She quickly filled four of the bowls to the brim, set them aside then did the same with water in the others. "I've been feeding the neighborhood strays in his honor. He was an indoor kitty," she said as if that explained everything.

"A fitting tribute," Nate agreed. "I've never had a pet."

"No?" She looked shocked.

"My mother had little interest in taking care of us. I didn't dare try to add an animal into the mix." As always, he didn't let that thought carry him very far. "Let me take care of loading up the food. You take care of the cats."

Her eyes were clearer now, and the two of them traded positions. Once she slid the back door closed again, Nate spotted two cats hopping over the fence and diving straight at the food.

"You all ready to go?" he asked, once he added a couple of handfuls of ice and zipped up the soft-sided cooler. She had her still damp purse on the counter, along with a different bag to transfer her things into. He didn't comment when she slipped the box containing Toby's ashes into the bottom.

"Just need to get my laptop and some files together." She did so in record time, and pretty soon he was carrying the cooler, one small suitcase and another smaller bag out to the car. She had her laptop bag over her shoulder when she locked up the house. "I'm going to ask Eddie if he wouldn't mind getting my mail while I'm gone," she said.

"Good plan." Nate stayed near the car while she did just that. That Eddie thought of Vivian as lonely had done something to Nate's heart. It wasn't fair, what life did to some people. The last thing Vivian deserved was to be pitched headfirst into this mess with Dean Wexler and Marty DeBaccian. Then again, if she hadn't gone on that date, then Nate never would have met her, and that, he realized as he pulled out his cell phone and stashed SIM card, would have been a terrible shame.

"Did you get a call?" Vivian asked when she appeared at his side again. "Is there any word on Dean Wexler?"

"No. I was just thinking about a call I need to make." One he didn't want to make in front of her. Mainly because he had no way of knowing how this call was going to go. "Why don't you get on in? I'll be there in a sec."

"Okay." It was obvious she knew why he was asking her to, but she didn't argue.

The now familiar dread that wound its way inside him when his thoughts turned to his siblings did so at extraordinary speed. His time in Owl Creek last month had been cursory and brief, but necessary given the events surrounding his sister Lizzy's kidnapping. He hadn't hesitated when he'd heard about the family dinner, but he'd also had to face a lot of truth by doing so.

Things had ended well, but it wasn't as if they'd all gotten to know each other very well. They were still, for all intents and purposes, walking on eggshells around each other. At least, that was the way Nate and Sarah felt.

Neither Nate nor his sister had summoned up the courage to call any of them to see if that truly was the case.

"Well, you've got a chance now," Nate muttered as he dialed one of the numbers he'd been given. His pulse kicked into overdrive as the phone rang.

"Detective Colton. Speak."

"Fletcher, it's Nate. Colton." He paused. "Your brother." Nate winced. Brilliant. "Sorry. You know that." He pinched the bridge of his nose and squeezed his eyes shut. "I don't know if it's okay that I called—"

"Of course it's okay." Fletcher's no-nonsense tone was, as far as Nate knew, his default and not to be taken personally. "What's going on?"

"I don't think there's a way to summarize." The last twenty-four hours spun in on him, robbing him of words but solidifying the one thing he knew to be true. "But I also don't think there's anyone else I can trust. I need your help, Fletcher." He paused. "More specifically, I think I need Colton help."

Chapter 7

"Are you sure no one is following us?" Not for the first time, Vivian twisted around in the passenger seat to look out the back window. The snowcapped mountain vistas ahead really should have captured all her attention, but she was used to seeing them, having lived in the area most of her life.

How she envied the ease with which Nate—and just about everybody else on the planet—maneuvered the highways and roadways, especially in the wintertime. Snow drifted down and coated the car in a delicate dusting as she scanned the vehicles behind them.

"I'm sure."

"How do you know?"

"Because it's my job."

She gave him points for patience. She was on the verge of annoying herself; she could only imagine how her continued paranoia must be coming across.

"I'm watching for it, Vivian." He took hold of her hand and gave a gentle tug, one she took to mean she should turn back around. "You need to stop worrying."

"Apologies," she muttered. "It's my first time being targeted for death." She glanced over in time to see his jaw tense. "They say your sense of humor is the first thing to go when you're stressed."

"Mine just gets more obnoxious," he said, and when she tried to tug her hand free, he slipped his fingers between hers and squeezed. "You aren't alone in this, Vivian. I don't know what else I can say or do to convince you of that."

"I don't know, either." She stared straight ahead at the sign that said the turnoff for Owl Creek was only a few miles away. "Things like this don't happen to me, Nate."

"Things like this don't happen to most people," he assured her. "How about we get your mind off the possibility of being followed and play a round of twenty questions? Anything you want to know, ask me."

Bold move. Not one she would have made. Or would she? She looked at him for a long moment, pondering how he affected her emotional state. What was it about this man that had her thinking in completely different ways than she normally did? There was such ease with him, such comfort, that her life-long developed fears took an almost back seat to reality. "Anything I ask, you'll tell me the truth?"

"It wouldn't be much of a game if I didn't," he said. "Go ahead. Try me. Question one. Let's have it."

"How old are you?"

"Interesting way to start." His lips twitched. "Twenty-eight."

"Oh." She blinked, not sure whether to laugh or frown.

"For the record, I've always had a thing for older women."

She snort-laughed, covered her mouth in surprise when he chuckled. "I'm not that much older than you."

"Two whole years according to your driver's license."

"Yeah, well, that license also gives me permission to drive, and we both know how that tends to go."

"What did you do for your thirtieth birthday last month?"

She narrowed her eyes. "I didn't realize this game was reciprocal."

"How else am I going to find out more about you?" He tightened his hold on her hand. "Come on. Give. What did you do?"

"Ah." She sighed. "I met Lizzy at The Cellar in Owl Creek for some wine tasting."

"That's it?"

She shrugged. "I'm not big on birthdays." Birthdays always reminded her of her parents, and the fuzzy memories she did have of them faded with each passing year. "That's our happy place. I drove down, and we went there after...well, after she was back home."

"I hope Lizzy gave you a great birthday present, at least."

"She signed me up for multiple dating apps," she deadpanned and earned a gasp from him. "Kidding!" She laughed at getting one over on him. "Actually, she tracked down a rare edition of *Pride and Prejudice* for me. It's my favorite Jane Austen book."

"That explains why you have an entire shelf of copies in your living room."

She didn't know why, but the idea of him noticing things around her home actually warmed her.

"Okay, my turn again." She started to look back again, but he squeezed her hand hard.

"Every time you look back gives me an extra question."

She resisted temptation. This time. "Why aren't you married?"

"Wow. Going straight to it." He shook his head. A strand of hair fell across his forehead, giving him a bit of a rakish appearance with that smile of his. "I could go with the usual, just haven't found the right woman. Which is true. Being married to a cop isn't something most women aspire to." He shrugged as if it didn't much matter. "The truth is probably more in line with the fact that I have no frame of reference for the institution."

"Oh." She instantly regretted the impulsive decision to ask. "I'm sorry. I didn't mean to—"

"You ever notice how much you apologize?" he asked. "Honestly, Vivian. It's a perfectly fine question, and considering where we could have easily ended up last night, you should probably be brought up to speed on my familial situation. Not to mention we're headed right into the heart of Colton country." Nate gestured to the increasing signs identifying Owl Creek. "What all has Lizzy told you about the family?" His eyes were glossy and unreadable when he looked at her. "I'm not asking so I can decide what not to share. I just don't want to rehash what you already know."

"Okay." Vivian's mind raced. She'd always found the Colton family tree a bit...confusing. Overwhelming to be sure. Lizzy came from such a huge extended family while Vivian had well, Lizzy. "You, Sarah, Lizzy and her three brothers share the same mother, Jessie, and she walked away from that family when Lizzy was really young. Like three or four, I think. They were raised by their father, Buck Colton." She smiled. "I like Buck.

He's a nice guy. Loves his kids. You can always tell, you know?"

"I've only met him a few times, but you're right. He seems like a good guy," Nate agreed. "Far more gracious than he has any right to be. What Lizzy and her brothers and cousins recently found out was that Jessie walked away from them to take up with Buck's brother, Robert Colton."

"Robert was married to Jessie's twin sister, Jenny, correct?" She really didn't want to get any of this wrong. It felt…disrespectful somehow.

"Yes. Robert and Jenny have six kids. Chase, Fletcher, Wade, Ruby, Hannah and Frannie."

"Frannie owns a bookstore in Owl Creek." She felt rather proud at remembering that tidbit.

"She does. Book Mark It," Nate said. "Should have figured you'd know that. I'm betting that's how Lizzy got hold of that rare book for you."

"Lizzy mentioned that Robert Colton died earlier this year."

"Yes, he did," Nate confirmed. "Unfortunately, my mother used that opportunity to make a familial comeback." His mouth stretched into a tight smile. "One of my dumber moves, believing she extended an olive branch on our behalf." His jaw tensed as if gnashing his teeth together. "She took his dying as her opportunity to tell the entire family about me and Sarah." He winced. "And no, she didn't give us any warning. And they didn't exactly throw out the welcome mat."

"Eeesh." Vivian cringed.

"Definitely *eeesh*. Personally, I don't think my mother took two breaths before she tried to stake a claim on

Robert's money by presenting me and Sarah as two of his heirs. She literally used us as exhibits A and B."

"Oh." Vivian chewed on the inside of her cheek. "Wow. That's…" She tried to find the words. "I seem to remember Lizzy mentioning some additional unpleasantness about Robert's passing. So, Robert was your dad."

"Father," Nate corrected. "I don't recall him ever being a dad. He was gone a lot when I was younger, then pretty much vanished from our lives when I was ten. I saw him maybe a handful of times after that. The story goes he had a change of heart and went back full-time to Jenny and their kids." He winced. "Couldn't have sat very well with any of them knowing that Sarah and I were born at the same time Hannah and Frannie were."

"I suppose not."

"Sarah and I were teenagers when we found out our parents were never married. Then there was the fact that our father was *the* Robert Colton, who was primarily responsible for putting Owl Creek on the map."

Her heart went out to him. "That must have been a lot for a teenager to process."

"It's been a lot for everyone to process," Nate said with a hint of sadness in his voice. "Maybe more when you're an adult. One of the reasons Sarah and I drove out to Owl Creek a couple months ago, to break the ice and clear the air."

"Did it work?"

Nate shrugged. "Can't be sure. I'd say we're in a bit of a strained time of existence. Sarah wants so much to make a lasting connection with our half siblings. It's like a dream come true for her, the whole big-family thing. But given who our mother is, our newfound family isn't totally trusting. I don't blame them." He hit the turn signal and moved two lanes to the right. "I don't blame them one bit. Jessie is unpredictable at best, malicious and cruel at worst. My mother doesn't have the capacity to care about anyone other than herself, so whatever her motivations regarding exposing our existence, you can bet they're self-serving." He flashed her a look. "Which brings us back to your original question about marriage. My perception of the institution of marriage is all a bit… What's the word?"

"Skewed?" Vivian offered. "Tarnished? Tainted?"

"Those work well enough."

She couldn't quite reconcile why that sounded so sad. "So, between Robert and Jenny's kids and Jessie and Buck's kids, you went from having one sister to having…" She did the math. "Ten brothers and sisters?"

"Yep." He took the turnoff leading into downtown Owl Creek, circling around the off-ramp before veering off to the left. "You out of questions or did I shock you into silence?" He shifted his gaze to the rearview mirror as he'd been doing since they'd started driving.

"I guess I'm wondering what questions are appropriate. New ones have popped to mind since we started."

"Already told you, nothing's off-limits."

"Okay." Time to put that to the test. "So, Robert went back to Jenny. What happened with your mom?"

"Jessie? She spent a good few years playing the victim and the martyr. That takes real talent in case you're wondering. Despite none of us being willing to give her even the time of day."

"Lizzy's never talked about her," Vivian said. "She's only brought her up recently because of what happened after Robert died." Coming face-to-face with the mother who had walked away and never looked back must have been excruciating for her friend. She'd covered, of course, and played it off like it wasn't anything other than ridiculous family drama, but how could it not have hurt?

"Sometimes, I think Lizzy and her brothers got the better end of the deal." Nate made easy work of the traffic. "They had to deal with Jessie being gone. Sarah and I had to deal with her...well, *with* her. I readily admit which road I'd preferred to have walked."

Vivian frowned. There was a kind of detachment in his voice, a tone that belied more than a tinge of resentment where his mother was concerned. It was, Vivian thought sadly, something she had no reference for. The vague memories she had of her mother, of both her parents, were so fragmented she couldn't piece them together. She'd tried to. For years. But they were just... ghosts.

"Hearing all this explains a lot about Lizzy. How she was growing up," Vivian said. Lizzy had always had serious trust issues and more than a suspicious nature when it came to anyone looking to the Coltons for a payout. "You said you were a teenager when you found out about your siblings."

"I was fifteen," Nate said. "I played basketball that year in high school. The team traveled to Owl Creek for a game. It was around the time some new construction project was getting off the ground. We were staying in this fancy—well, fancy to me—hotel in town. I went downstairs to work out and stopped in the lobby. There he was, my father, on the front page of the local paper. Along with his family. Jenny and all the kids." He hesitated. "His real family. Funny." Nate shook his head. "As shocking as that was—and believe me, I read everything I could about Robert Colton after that—seeing that picture, being in Owl Creek, walking through the town he was responsible for, everything about my own life suddenly made a lot more sense. It also made me a lot more self-conscious. I spent years worried about what would happen if the truth got out."

Her heart broke for the boy he'd been. How alone he must have felt in those days following his discovery. "But you didn't say anything to anyone."

"There was no point. I told Sarah a few weeks later. Once I'd worked everything out so I could answer her questions." A flicker of bitterness crossed his face. "I quit the basketball team first, though. I didn't need or want any more surprise trips to Owl Creek. We decided together to keep it to ourselves. We figured if our father wanted anything to do with us, he'd be the one to reach out. He'd already messed with the two of us. We didn't want to be the cause of destroying his other family."

Sympathy swirled through her. No. His mother had taken care of that, hadn't she? "I don't know that I'd have been that generous."

"It wasn't generous," Nate said. "It was survival. We had enough to deal with where Jessie was concerned, and honestly, if we had done things differently, who knows what might have happened." He frowned, gaze pinned to the rearview mirror. "Huh." He pulled his hand free of hers.

"What?" Forgetting the potential cost of looking, she

turned around, scanned the steady stream of cars. "Do you see something?" Everything seemed to blur together.

"Maybe." He turned right at the next light without signaling. "Let's see what this might be about."

Vivian turned back around, gripped the seat in her hands and squeezed until her fingers went numb.

"Nothing bad's going to happen, Viv." He didn't look at her this time, just kept his eyes straight ahead or on the mirror as he drove. "We're in this together, remember? Do me a favor? Write down this plate number?" He read off the letters and numbers once she took her phone out of the glove box and began typing.

He took a left, bringing them through a residential area coated with a light dusting of snow and varying degrees of holiday cheer. One fence line in particular boasted oversize Santa hats perched atop dividing posts. When she let her gaze drift to the passenger-door mirror, an SUV similar to Nate's turned behind them a distance back.

"That car look familiar?"

"No." She shook her head. "It's not the one that ran me off the road."

"You sure?" He hit the gas, and they sped up. The car still followed, but maintained its same speed, and the distance between them grew.

"That one had a weird decal on the front window." She gasped. Stacy had been right. When her mind relaxed, it seemed to set things free. "I just remembered that. I'm—"

He shot her a look that included an arched and challenging brow.

"Not sorry I didn't tell you before," she corrected herself. He was right. She really did spend a lot of time apologizing for innocuous comments or thoughts.

"You remembered now. That's all that matters. We'll put a call in to my lieutenant when we stop. Bring him up to date. Get that information added to the case file."

"Are we going to stop?" She couldn't have stopped her voice from squeaking if she'd tried.

"Not yet." He took another couple of turns and got them back on the road they were previously on. He tapped on his dashboard screen, scrolled down a list of names. Vivian frowned when he hit Call for Fletcher Colton.

Nerves tangled around themselves in her stomach. As close as she was to Lizzy, she hadn't seen her friend's brothers in years. When it came to the extended members of her family, she must have been ten the last time she was around any of them. "I thought you said you don't talk to your brothers?"

"Not on a regular basis, I don't." Nate said. "Given the situation we're in, couldn't really think of anyone else to ask for help."

"Nate." The deep voice bounced around the car like an echo. "You here yet?"

"We just got into Owl Creek. I've got you on Speaker with me and Vivian," Nate told him. "I'm pretty sure we've picked up a tail."

"Oh?" The alertness that came through on that one word added to Vivian's anxiety. "You close enough for a description?"

Nate rattled off the bare minimum. "And we've got a plate. Viv?"

"Hi, Fletcher." She swallowed the lump of anxiety lodged in her throat. "I'm sure you don't remember me—"

"Lizzy's friend from school," Fletcher said. "Sure. You spent Christmas at the ranch with us one year. You were what, fourteen?"

"Thirteen, actually." A very awkward, silent thirteen. Not that she'd ever needed to say much with Lizzy around. That was one of the reasons they got along so well. Vivian was always happy to let her take the lead. "It's nice of you to remember."

"That was the year Lizzy stuck a fake rattlesnake in my underwear drawer," Fletcher said. "I broke two of dad's favorite lamps trying to kill it."

Vivian's lips twitched. She'd forgotten about that.

"Every Christmas since," Fletcher went on, "someone buys me a lamp. The ugliest lamp they could possibly find. I hope no one shares that story with Kiki."

"Kiki?" Vivian asked before she thought better of it.

"She's a DJ here in Owl Creek. We're…dating."

Vivian shot Nate a look at the same time he gave her his own. They grinned at each other but didn't say anything more until Fletcher asked for the plate number.

Vivian read it back and was answered by silence.

"Well." Fletcher coughed. "Okay, then. How about you come on by the station for a bit? I'll meet you outside, and we'll see what the driver does when he realizes where you've led him."

"Okay." Nate frowned. "Is something going on?" He looked back into the mirror. The car was backing off but still visible.

"Nope. See you in a few." Fletcher disconnected before Nate could push harder.

"Didn't take long to get strange," Nate muttered. "Okay, then. Owl Creek police station it is." He accelerated through a yellow light and sped up again. "And the sooner the better."

Chapter 8

Nate's constant assurances to Vivian that no one would be following them had been uttered in good, solid faith. The chances DeBaccian's men would take another risk by running Vivian off the road twice in one day were, at least to Nate's mind, a million to one. And that wasn't even taking into account Nate's being along for the ride. Going after a cop was something DeBaccian wouldn't be stupid enough to do. Doubt niggled. Or would he?

That idea did not sit well. Still, lying to Vivian, intentionally or otherwise, was not something he ever wanted to do. Faith and trust were difficult enough to establish and build, especially with someone with Vivian's relatively solitary past.

"You're worried," Vivian said. Her voice was as quiet as he expected, as if she was worried about startling or offending him.

"A little." The full day was heading into the evening. Hard to believe things had been almost normal this morning when she'd walked into his kitchen wearing nothing but a T-shirt. What he wouldn't give to go back and take the day in a different direction.

"But going to the station is a good thing, isn't it?" The uncertainty rang loudly in Nate's ears.

"It is." He couldn't shake the idea that Fletcher knew something he didn't. It wasn't brotherly instinct—they didn't know each other well enough for Nate to claim that prerogative. But cop instinct was a completely different story. "You're going to be safe here, Vivian. I promise."

Her smile was almost wide enough to convince him she believed him.

Downtown Owl Creek opened up ahead and welcomed them like an old, festive frenemy. Nate's hands tightened on the steering wheel. He'd spent years limiting his trips here to official business and necessary excursions. Being this close to the Coltons was a lesson in tempting fate, and that was one thing Nate went out of his way to avoid doing.

Driving in like this, with his own trust placed firmly in the hands of a brother who would no doubt be happier not knowing Nate existed felt like a dangerous game to play. Especially where Vivian's life was concerned. But it was Vivian's life he was worried about, and—honestly? He couldn't think of anyone he could trust more when it came to her safety.

It was a bit like driving through a time portal, he noticed, as they made their way through town.

The town had developed into a year-round resort with skiing and other winter-centric activities taking center stage, yet during the warmer summer months, people flocked to the lake and consistent sunshine as a getaway. In February, the winter carnival would kick into high gear and feature incredible bigger-than-life snow sculptures, dog-sled racing and countless other events that would bring in a good deal of cash to the local economy. From the Tap Out Brewery that served local ales and pub grub, to Frannie's Book Mark It, the town had developed into a significant destination both for travelers and those looking for a laid-back, more relaxed way of life. Varying decor highlighted storefronts, walkways and lampposts. With the snowcapped mountains the perfect backdrop, it was like a kind of Christmas village had been plopped into the middle of civilization.

While the drive from Boise to Owl Creek was a good two hours, travel time—at least how Nate drove—from Vivian's town house was just shy of forty-five. Which meant the police station came up fast once they started down the main, business-lined thoroughfare.

"There's a space right in front of the station." Vivian pointed ahead of them. "Doris Day parking."

"What?" Nate glanced at her.

"You know, classic movies? How Doris Day always found a parking space in the front of wherever she was going? Sorry. I think of weird facts when I'm nervous." And with the way she kept looking at the car following them, she was most definitely nervous.

Nate shook his head. He couldn't recall the last time he'd watched a movie that didn't include explosions and car chases.

He pulled into the spot she'd pointed out, his attention partially divided and focused on the man standing with his back against the wall beside the entrance to the Owl Creek PD.

It was entirely possible, Nate thought, that Detective Fletcher Colton had a natural tolerance to the cold. With his worn jeans, thick, snow-friendly work boots and a khaki button-down shirt displaying his police badge, he may as well have been sunning himself in the middle of July.

"You look alike." Vivian's comment startled Nate back to reality.

"Do we?" Of course they did. Most of the male Colton offspring in these parts shared the brown hair and lighter color eyes. None of them could particularly look down on one another; height was another shared family trait. As was a natural propensity for athletic, fit builds and a low tolerance for bull. Yeah. Looking at Fletcher now, he definitely saw the resemblance.

Nate shifted, looked behind them as the car that had been following them pulled to a sudden stop in the middle of the street a few spots back. "Okay, here we go. Stay here."

Nate jumped out of the car, hand going to his back waistband for his weapon. He heard Fletcher yell his name, but it got carried off by the wind as Nate pulled out his gun and lifted it, both hands locked around the hilt, finger pressed against the side of the trigger. He aimed straight at the driver.

"Police!" Nate yelled. "Out of the car, now! Slowly!" He gestured with the gun as the man behind the wheel held up both hands. The sun visor obscured most of his face, but not so much that Nate didn't see the flicker of humor quirk his lips. A quick glimpse to the passenger seat told Nate that at least this guy was alone. Unless there was someone in the back seat…

"Nate—" Fletcher's voice sounded directly behind him now, but Nate wasn't going to take any chances. Not with Vivian's life.

"I said out!" Nate yelled again as he advanced.

Out of the corner of his eye, he saw Vivian push open the door and drop to the ground. She was bundled into the jacket she'd pulled out of the closet on their way out of her town house. Even from a distance, he could see her shivering.

"Nate, put the gun away," Fletcher said calmly.

"Not until he's out of the car." Despite the cold, he didn't shiver. He didn't move. He simply stared.

"Okay." Fletcher stepped around and motioned to the driver. "You heard him!" Fletcher called. "You'd best get out."

Nate stood there, staring as the door opened as he wondered why Fletcher was acting so nonchalant. Until the man stepped out of the car. Nate balked, glared and lowered his gun to his side. "Son of a— Max?" Max Colton, Nate's half brother through Jessie, slid out of the car, arms raised, an unfamiliar smile stretching across his mouth. "Did you skip surveillance-duty training back at the FBI?"

Max's expression came across as it usually did where Nate was concerned: guarded, suspicious and bordering on dark. But also, for the first time, Nate thought he saw impressed. That was a boost he hadn't expected.

"When did you spot me?" Max asked after he exchanged a hearty handshake and quick bro hug with Nate.

"About two seconds after you pulled out of the gas station parking lot just off the freeway." Nate holstered his gun, adrenaline draining. Only then did he begin to feel the December cold seep into his bones.

"We wanted to make sure you two were covered as

soon as you hit town," Fletcher said on a laugh. "This is one for the books. Max Colton, serial-killer hunter, bested by his baby brother."

Nate froze. Baby brother? It took a moment to shake himself clear of all that thought encompassed. He was still a bit foggy when Vivian appeared and touched his arm.

"Everything okay?"

"Yeah." Her question had him nodding absently. "Fine. I might have overreacted." As Max and Fletcher closed the distance, cars crawled around Max's SUV. Out of instinct or protection or perhaps wanting to make a point he'd never anticipated making, Nate slipped his arm around Vivian's shoulders and drew her against his side. He immediately felt warmer. "Vivian Maylor, you probably already know my…" He stopped at the other two men's sharpened gazes. He swore, shook his head. "Well, hell. Fletcher already started it. Might as well start to get past it. Fletcher and Max Colton." He swallowed hard around unexpected emotion. "My brothers."

"Of course." Vivian held out her hand. "Fletcher of the rattlesnake Christmas."

Fletcher grunted and grinned when Max chuckled.

"And Max." She shook both their hands. "It's been a while. Lizzy said you only get back to Owl Creek between cases."

"True enough," Max said, and immediately shoved his hands into the front pockets of his jeans. "I've got some downtime at the moment. Fletcher said you two ran into some trouble back in Boise." He eyed Nate, then Fletcher. "Glad you thought to call. Looking forward to being read in."

It was on the tip of Nate's tongue to admit he was out of options, but there was no need to go burning down a just built bridge. He hadn't known what to expect coming to Owl Creek, but he was planning to make the most of it.

"I'm waiting on a call to make sure the house is ready for you." Fletcher motioned them to the station.

"House?" Vivian blinked. "What house?"

"Max, park that thing somewhere legal, will you? We'll wait on you." Fletcher slapped a hand on the back of his shoulder before he motioned for Nate and Vivian to follow him to the station house. "You two hungry?"

"Not really," Nate said.

"We have food in the car," Vivian explained as if she thought Nate's response bordered on rude. "I cook to relax, and I'm feeling ready for a distraction."

"Understood. And lucky Nate." Fletcher pulled open the door and waved them in ahead of him. "I have a bet with Wade that Nate lives on toaster pastries and root beer."

"Close," Nate said without missing a beat. "Brownies and Mountain Dew. You going to tell me why you thought the escort into town necessary?" Nate asked the second the door closed behind them.

"I am." Fletcher accepted a clipboard offered to him by a khaki-uniformed officer, scribbled his name at the bottom before handing it back. Another officer handed him a manila file folder, and he nodded his thanks. "Had a long talk with your Lieutenant Haig a little while ago. He gave me the rundown. Extra precautions seemed warranted. Our break room doubles as our conference room, so we can talk in there. Monroe?" Fletcher rapped his knuckles on the counter, and another officer, this one looking as if he'd just stepped out of high school, shot to attention. "Send Max back when he gets here, will you?"

"Sure thing, Detective." Monroe's baby face stretched into an eager smile.

Nate sighed. He remembered being that young, but had he ever been so…innocent?

The station house was nicer than Nate expected. Cozier, with its wood paneling and collection of framed photographs, it didn't have quite the harsh, sterile yet aged feel his own station house did. Images of Owl Creek officers over the years were displayed among other ones featuring town events both big and small. Funny—the place had an unexpectedly homier feel than most police stations he'd been in.

"I'm going to make a quick stop in the ladies' room." Vivian pointed to one of the doors they'd passed before disappearing behind it.

"Does Lizzy know what's going on?" Fletcher asked as he grabbed a couple of clean mugs out of an overhead cabinet. "Coffee?"

"Yeah, thanks." At the rate he was going, coffee would soon replace the blood running through his veins. "With Vivian, you mean? Not that I know of." He grimaced. "I suggested Vivian call her, but she refused. Mentioned that Lizzy had enough to cope with at the moment." He paused. "How is Lizzy doing?"

"Okay." Fletcher didn't seem of the mind to elaborate. "She's good at covering, though. She mentioned using Vivian as a sounding board on more than one occasion. That's good since the rest of us have kind of been hovering. Ajay's been good for her."

That bit of information didn't surprise Nate in the least. He'd been impressed with Ajay Wright, a K9 search and rescue agent. No doubt Ajay would view what happened to Lizzy from every angle and help her accordingly.

"How about you?" Fletcher eyed him with more caution than Nate felt comfortable with. "The last few months can't have been easy for you. How've you been doing?"

Nate couldn't tell if Fletcher was being polite, big brotherly or simply curious. "Okay, actually." He shrugged. "I'll be doing better once a psychopath criminal isn't chasing after Vivian."

"I hear that," Fletcher muttered. "We seem to be a magnet for psychopaths these days." He paused as Max strolled into the room. "Found your way back here okay, then?" he teased. "I thought about leaving some breadcrumbs…"

"Ha-ha." Max glowered, but in a way that had Nate laughing on the inside. An unexpected yet sadly familiar pang of envy struck him with pinpoint accuracy. He'd spent years wondering what it would be like to have a relationship with his brothers. The brothers who hadn't known Nate existed. Sure, it would have been easier on everyone if he'd remained an unknown Colton element, but even now he could feel those family ties knitting and forming. "This is where you fill me in."

"Just waiting on Vivian." Fletcher motioned for them to take a seat in one of the chairs around a large, circular table.

"Got anything to eat around here?" Max started yanking open cabinets that had more office supplies inside than munchies.

"Doesn't Della feed you?" Fletcher teased.

Max glowered again but gripped an open bag of nacho tortilla chips in one hand. "Our brother, the wannabe comedian," he said to Nate. "We don't starve," Max said in a way that made Nate wonder if Max ever gave a straight answer. "Fletcher mentioned a guy named Marty DeBaccian."

"Are you familiar with him?" Nate pulled out a chair as Vivian joined them, quietly sitting beside him. Without even asking, Fletcher poured her a mug of coffee and set it in front of her.

"No, not really...we've never crossed paths." Max shook his head, drank some coffee and winced. "Wow." His eyes almost watered. "Congratulations, Fletcher. Takes some major talent to make a brew worse than what I get at headquarters."

"Look at you with the compliments." Fletcher closed the door before joining them at the table. "Eat your chips. CliffsNotes version—" he said, looking to Max "—Nate and his fellow detectives in Boise have been building a case against Marty DeBaccian. Wannabe crime lord with his hands in all kinds of dirty dealings."

"Up until last year, he'd made a name for himself loan-sharking and getting in on the local betting action," Nate added. "He's got a taste for things now. You name it, he's made a play for it. Drugs, extortion, protection rackets, which goes hand in hand with money laundering through local businesses whose owners aren't in a position to say no."

"Garden variety scum bucket, got it," Max said.

Nate glanced at Vivian. She had wrapped both hands around the brown coffee mug, but she'd hunched her shoulders and scrunched down almost into a shell of herself. Nate rested a hand on her knee, gave her a comforting squeeze. He'd needed it, but feeling the tension ease a bit in her body told him she'd needed it as well. She sat up straighter, offered him a quick smile that eased his mind a bit.

"DeBaccian's been building himself up as a kind of overlord of whatever criminal activity is running rampant in the city," Nate said. "I've had my eye on Dean Wexler for a while, trying to link him to a number of burglaries of single women. He's got a record that makes that possible. I thought if I could make the connection, I could use that information to flip him on DeBaccian."

"Apparently DeBaccian doesn't like it when people work outside of his purview," Fletcher added. "He likes to take his cut of the action."

"Which is where I come in," Vivian admitted. "Not the action part." She frowned, as if reconsidering her words. "I met Dean on a dating app. Seems I was his next planned target."

Nate didn't miss the ice flashing in both his brothers' eyes.

"Needless to say, our first date didn't go as expected." Vivian summarized it far more precisely than Nate probably would have. "Now Dean is in an induced coma, and I've become a material witness."

"Against Wexler?" Max's brows shot up.

"Against DeBaccian," Nate said. "He was in the car when Wexler was shot."

"And you saw him." Whatever Max had been thinking, his eyes turned to steel.

"Yes," Vivian said firmly. "I saw him."

"And he knows she did. Someone trying to run her off the road this morning proves that."

"It proves something, and I'm fine," she said at Max's suddenly sharp gaze. "Lucky, but fine. But Nate didn't think it was safe for me to be anywhere familiar or predictable for a while."

"Nate's right," Fletcher said. "And he was right to call. Lizzy would never forgive us if we didn't do everything we could to help."

"I appreciate that." Vivian's mouth curved. "And the trouble you're going to."

"It's no trouble, Vivian," Fletcher said. "If anything, Nate calling gave us all a bit of a kick. We're family. We need to start acting like it. We appreciate the faith, however tenuous."

Nate wasn't entirely sure what to do with that statement. So he did what he always did when emotions started clouding his judgment. He shifted back to the job. "You said you spoke with my lieutenant?" Nate asked.

"Yeah." Fletcher took a deep breath. "No change in Wexler's condition. He's continuing the protective duty you ordered in the hospital. No joy on the burned-out car they've identified from the drive-by."

"Awesome." Not a surprise, but still disappointing. That meant Vivian's description of DeBaccian was the only evidence they had that he was involved.

"There's been a bit more luck with the SUV from this morning." Fletcher leaned back and retrieved the folder he'd been handed at the front desk. "He emailed this over so it was waiting for you." He set it on the table and flipped it open. "The car was found abandoned about ten miles from where they hit Vivian. Same MO as the first car."

"They didn't do such a great job, this time, did they?" So much of the car was still intact. A break for them for sure.

Vivian gasped, pointed at the half-worn decal in the bottom corner of the windshield. "That's what I saw. The sticker. That's what I remember seeing in the mirror."

Nate's hand curled into a fist. He'd known they'd gotten close enough to ram her off the road, but so close that she got a clear look at a sticker? He repressed a shudder.

"Your lieutenant recognized the logo from a strip club in downtown Boise," Fletcher said. "Place called Shake It Loose."

Nate's stomach tightened. "That's one of DeBaccian's properties." He'd spent an unholy number of hours parked across the street while Dean Wexler was inside. "He's either getting careless or desperate."

"Or arrogant," Max said. "Never underestimate the destructive power of ego. It takes a lot more of these criminals down than you think."

"True enough," Fletcher agreed. "Evidence is still working on the SUV, but they've got a couple of sets of prints so far. They're rushing it through the system." Fletcher looked to Max. "Anything you can do about that?"

"Sure." Max shrugged. "But I'd advise you to leave me in reserve." He pulled the file close and scanned the reports, flipping up the pages. "I'd want to do this on the up and up, and if I do that, you get federal interest, which could pull this case out of your control." He eyed

Nate. "Unless you're looking for someone with FBI contacts to take the lead?"

Nate took his time answering. He wanted to make a good case against DeBaccian. Federal or state, locked up was locked up. His ego required a win. He'd worked this case a long time and had DeBaccian in his sights for months. He didn't like the idea of handing it off, even unofficially, without getting at least some credit.

Beside him, he could feel Vivian shaking. She was holding it together, but the longer this went on, the more anxiety and fear she was going to develop, and he didn't like the idea of being responsible for that—it was even worse than losing credit.

"I want DeBaccian taken down and out. I want Vivian out of the line of fire." He couched his words carefully. "Would I like a hand in that? Absolutely. But I'm more interested in seeing his operations shut down. Boise needs him gone." And so did Vivian. "If that means bringing the FBI in officially, I'm fine with it. Not my call, though." He looked back to Fletcher. "My lieutenant would have to take that up the chain in Boise PD."

Fletcher glanced at Max. "We're in a holding pattern for now on that front. He's got surveillance up and running on a number of DeBaccian's businesses and hangouts and his main residence. When he pops his head up, Haig will let us know." Something akin to admiration flickered in his brothers' eyes when they looked back at him. "In the meantime, it sounds like we're all on the same page."

Max grimaced, leaned to the side and pulled out his wallet. When he slapped twenty bucks into Fletcher's hand, Nate frowned. "What's this about?"

"That's about Fletcher betting you'd put the end result and Vivian's safety before your arrest record," Max said. "I was less…confident."

"Let me guess." Nate didn't have to hear more than that to understand Max's meaning. "Given who our mother is, you were thinking the apple didn't fall too far?"

He started to pull his hand away from Vivian's knee, but she dropped her own hand under the table and covered his. When she curled her fingers under and squeezed, he felt a boost of confidence and understanding surge through his system.

"More like birds of a feather," Max said easily. "But that's neither here nor there at the moment." His gaze slipped over Vivian, as if he didn't want to discuss their family drama in her presence.

"I know about your mother," Vivian said quietly. "I know the generalities of what she did going back to when you all were kids. Lizzy brought me up to date the last time I saw her. And, just so you know, Nate's been perfectly up front about his and Sarah's situation where Jessie Colton is concerned."

"Vivian—" Nate began.

"You all are Texas two-stepping around this, and no offense, but I've got enough to worry about without having to learn to dance," she said in a tone Nate hadn't heard from her before. "Nate's not his mother, Max. No more than you are. From the time this whole nightmare started for me, Nate has been the only consistent thing I could hold on to. Whatever else you might think of him, he's an honorable man who only has the family's best interests at heart."

The doubt in Max's eyes faded, not completely, but

enough that Nate felt grateful to Vivian for knocking down at least one invisible wall between them.

"It's taking us some time to come to terms with a lot of what happened over the past thirty years," Fletcher said slowly. "We got blindsided when Dad died. It's obvious a lot of mistakes were made."

"Yes, they were," Vivian insisted. "But by Robert and Jessie. Not Nate or Sarah. Not that anyone asked me, but I think you're all lucky to have them as siblings. So either talk it all out or set it aside at least until I can go home and get back to my quiet, unassuming life."

Nate couldn't have stopped the wave of affection washing over him if he'd tried. "I was wrong." He squeezed her hand. "You would have made a fantastic cheerleader."

Her cheeks went bright pink, and her hand tightened around his.

"There's something else your lieutenant thought you should know," Fletcher said. "Regarding a Detective Jim Sullivan."

"Let me guess," Nate muttered. "He's complaining about my being involved with the case."

"No one knows what Detective Sullivan's doing," Fletcher said slowly. "He's disappeared."

"He's…what?" Nate frowned. "What does that mean?"

"Would you like the dictionary definition or—"

"Max." Fletcher glared at his cousin and shook his head. "All your lieutenant said was that they've been unable to make contact with Sullivan since he left the station after Vivian's session with the sketch artist. He'll get back to us when he knows more."

"Get back to *us*?" Nate hedged.

Fletcher didn't flinch when he met his confused gaze. "If DeBaccian and his men are looking for Vivian, then they're probably looking for you by now. The less communication you have with anyone back in Boise, the better. For the foreseeable future, what you're told, I'm told." He looked over to Max. "You have what you need?"

"Yeah." Max leaned forward again, reached into his back pocket and pulled out a flip phone. He slid it across the table to Nate. "This is untraceable," he said easily. "A few numbers programmed in. Your lieutenant's. Mine, Fletcher's. And Chase's." He paused. "I didn't include Sarah's. I didn't have it, and I wasn't sure how much she knows."

"Nothing," Nate said instantly. "She knows nothing, and I'd like to keep it that way."

Max nodded. "Understood."

Relief surged through him. His sister was a schoolteacher, for heaven's sake. The last thing he wanted to do was put her in the sights of a career criminal. The further away she was from all this, the better. He scrolled through the solitary page of numbers. "Chase." Chase Colton was CEO of Colton Properties. He didn't have anything to do with law enforcement. "Why Chase?"

"Because it's thanks to him you two have a place to hole up until this is all settled." As if on cue, Fletcher's cell phone vibrated. He looked at the screen, shook his head in mild disbelief. "Speak of the devil. Looks like we're all set." He got to his feet and motioned for them to follow. "Let's get you two settled in."

Chapter 9

"You look like you've been caught in a whirlwind."

Nate's comment had Vivian pulling her attention away from the scenic, winding drive through the outskirts of Owl Creek and back to the reality of her current situation. "I kind of feel like it," she said. "From the outside, the Colton family feels like a force of nature."

"Newsflash," Nate said as he followed Fletcher's marked police SUV. "Doesn't feel much different from that on the inside." Behind them, Max followed, this time keeping a fair distance.

She wanted to smile, wanted to believe he meant that in good humor, but she couldn't be sure. The tension among the three brothers had been palpable. So much needed to be talked about, but she doubted it was ever going to happen where those three men were concerned. Not without a bit of a nudge. Which is what she'd been attempting to do by sticking her nose into something that was most definitely not her business.

"It's a pretty drive." She'd been to Owl Creek plenty of times over the years, mostly to meet up with Lizzy, but during the holidays, not so much. This time of year was always hard for her. It wasn't necessarily the being alone that triggered it, but the reminder that she was. Maybe it was being here with Nate or maybe the anxiety from the past few days, but she found herself feeling far more lighthearted about the season.

She loved how the dusting of snow cast the passing homes into a kind of exhibit in an art gallery. December in Idaho definitely put on a beautiful show. Add to it the festive outdoor lighting, the occasional decorated trees and decked-out front porches, and it was almost like stepping into a painting. The backdrop of snowy mountains conjured a longing for simpler, nature-focused times rather than the technological roller coaster the world found itself on these days. She had to remind herself, frequently, that it wasn't chance that had brought her to Owl Creek, or even that had put her in the vicinity of Nate Colton, but violence and danger that, even now, stalked her.

Surreal didn't come close to describing her current state. But she found herself wanting to push through the fear and embrace what had come to pass. Since walking into that restaurant the other night, she felt as if she were on some kind of self-awareness journey. One that was most definitely aided by the man sitting beside her.

Never in her wildest dreams would she have imagined finding herself traversing snowy mountain roads with someone who, near as she could fathom, might be responsible for reminding her she had a pulse. And a heart.

"Any idea where we're headed?" she asked.

"Not a clue." Nate did not sound happy about that, but she wondered if he realized the trust he'd displayed in the past few hours. He had, for all intents and purposes, placed both their lives in his brothers' hands, and that, she thought as her heart cracked open wide enough for a fraction of the Colton men to spill in, might make this entire situation worth it. "At this point, I wouldn't be surprised if it's a two-room shack with a padlock on the door."

She laughed, happy to pile onto the ridiculous suspicion, only to have every thought tip out of her brain. Fletcher veered off to the right and soon stopped at a guard post situated outside a large, iron-gated community.

"What the—" Nate's mutter only echoed her own disbelief. Eyes wide, she took in the vast area around and in front of them. The intricate welding of the gates offered both protection and elegant decor that stretched in both directions as far as she could see. "Guess the family business is doing pretty well."

The young, uniformed woman leaning out of the security office was pointing beyond the gate that was currently sliding open. She nodded and waved Fletcher through. Nate pulled up and powered down his window.

"Detective Colton." The woman offered a solid, welcoming smile. "Ms. Maylor. I'm Maya Baxter. Welcome to Colton Crossing."

"Nice to meet you, Maya." Because Nate seemed a bit tongue-tied, Vivian leaned across the center console and rested her hand on Nate's arm.

"Chase will give you the rundown for how to contact us here at the security office," Maya told them. "Someone will be here twenty-four seven. We've been made aware of your situation and will be on alert for anything out of the ordinary. If you have any questions or concerns, call the office at any time."

"Appreciate that," Nate said finally before he followed Fletcher's vehicle through the gate. Vivian checked her passenger-side mirror, saw Max stop for his intro then nip through the gate. "Apparently, I missed notice of this place in the family newsletter."

Vivian grabbed hold of his hand and squeezed. "This isn't easy for you, is it?"

"Entering Shangri-la?" His attempt at humor sounded strained.

"I meant dealing with your brothers. Your family." But he had a point. The sprawling homes that madè up Colton Crossing ranged in size. Some were smaller, bungalow-type homes while others stood two stories with wide, wraparound porches. The complex was obviously in various stages of construction. She counted a few dozen homes that appeared completed, while other foundations were mapped out, and other cleared-out areas were no doubt going to begin construction once the snow stopped falling.

It was only when she looked past Nate and out beyond the security gate that she noticed all of them offered a stunning view of the mountains along with Owl Creek nestled into the valley below.

"I don't think they're taking us to a shack with a padlock."

"I think you're right." Nate waved at Fletcher, who after parking and climbing out of his car, indicated he should pull into the long driveway just beyond. When he stopped the car, they both leaned forward and gawked up at the house in front of them. "Am I the only one thinking both your place and mine would fit inside this place?"

"You are not." So much for cozy and close quarters.

Disappointment and relief crashed against each other inside her. Something told her she and Nate could go days inside without seeing each other.

"I'll come back for our things." Nate pushed open his door and came around to open hers. "Looks like we aren't in Boise anymore." As if completely normal, he took hold of her hand, and they walked down the driveway side by side.

Fletcher and Max stood at the end of the walkway with another, slightly older man wearing a suit beneath his long wool coat. Vivian couldn't help but think he'd stepped off the cover of a men's quarterly magazine. Slightly lankier than his brothers and cousins, he had a professionalism about him that screamed competence and success.

"Nate." The man pulled one hand out of his coat pocket and extended it. "Good to see you again."

"Chase."

"Welcome to Colton Crossing." Chase's smile came a bit easier than either Fletcher's or Max's had, and she could feel Nate relax a little. "Ms. Maylor."

"Vivian, please."

"Vivian." Chase nodded in approval. "Welcome. I'm afraid the house is a little sparse furnishings-wise. We've got the bare minimum set up since this is going to be our first market model, but it should be enough for the two of you. On the plus side, there's a furnished office, and Nate mentioned you needed a place to work."

She probably looked a bit doe-eyed when she glanced up at Nate.

"Shall we?" Chase turned on his heel and took the lead.

"Like we're going to say no?" Vivian muttered so only Nate could hear.

They followed Chase inside, their footfalls echoing on the large porch landing. Up two steps and through an enormous, heavy wooden door. Inside, the foyer opened up and branched off into multiple hallways and directions.

"You met Maya down at the guard house," Chase said and led them straight ahead and off to the left. "The security company we've hired has been thoroughly vetted by multiple security experts, including SecuritKey and Max here."

"I love running background checks," Max said from where he trailed behind them. "Not that Sloan needed double-checking. I'm curious, Chase. Did you visit Versailles before you came up with the plans to this house or did you just wing it?"

"We call this the Colton-size house," Chase said easily. "Lots of room for a large, ever-expanding family. We've still got some touch-ups to do on the other finished homes, but this one is move-in ready. Permission to enter?" he called.

"Ack! Two seconds!" a female voice called back before a blond head popped around the corner. "Seriously. Just..." She held up a couple of fingers and had them stopping in the hallway.

"Ruby takes this kind of thing rather seriously," Fletcher said as he leaned back against the light yellow wall. "Especially these days."

"What kind of thing, exactly?" Vivian asked.

"Three things, actually," Max said. "Homecomings, the holidays and surprises."

"I'm guessing that makes us the family trifecta," Nate said.

"Okay!" A curvy, dark-haired woman with deep auburn tips and brown eyes jumped into view and waved them in. "Hey, Detective." She waggled her eyebrows at Fletcher, who moved in to catch her around the waist and pull her in for a kiss. "Nice to see you, too," she murmured and looked into his eyes in a way that had Vivian thinking they should all be someplace else. "You must be Nate." She held out her hand. "And Vivian. I'm Kiki Shelton. Ruby and Sloan recruited me to lend a hand."

"A hand for… Oh." Vivian blinked at the sight in front of her.

Not only was there a gourmet kitchen fit for a houseful of kings and queens, but the attached great room boasted a deep, comfy sofa, large-screen television and an enormous seven-foot Christmas tree in the corner. Lights had been strung to the point of setting it aflame with glowing white bulbs and a beautiful gold star sitting atop.

Two large plastic bins sat beside the tree, crammed full with colorful boxes and shiny ornaments.

"Hi. I'm Sloan Presley. We thought you could do with some holiday cheer." The woman stepped under Chase's outstretched arm and gave Vivian and Nate a wave. "There's more in the boxes if you want to play yourselves." She had her thick, curly dark hair pulled back from her round, friendly face. "Seeing as you're going to be stuck here for a little while, might as well pretty the place up."

Vivian was agog. The place was already prettied up near as she could tell. "The tree's a lovely addition. Thank you." The only other time she'd ever seen such a grand tree had been that aforementioned holiday she'd spent at the Colton ranch. "It wasn't necessary to go to so much trouble."

"No trouble at all." Ruby Colton, a familiar face from Vivian's childhood, came over and nudged Nate with her shoulder. If memory served, Lizzy mentioned Ruby recently had a baby boy. Named... Vivian's mind raced. Sawyer. Yes, that was it. And the baby's arrival also explained the new mother glow about Ruby. "We wondered what it might take to get you back to Owl Creek, Nate. Guess we know now, huh?"

"How about I show you around." Sloan stepped away from Chase and set her attention on Vivian. "Don't worry. We'll leave you two alone soon enough so you can get acclimated. Let's start with the best thing about this house." She tugged Vivian by the hand through the kitchen and dining area to the glass double French doors. She pushed them open and flung them wide to give an unobstructed view of the mountain range. "How about that view, huh?"

"Yeah." Vivian looked back over her shoulder to where Nate remained standing amidst his newfound family. He looked both shocked and awed, but also, whether he wanted to admit it or not, exactly where he belonged. Vivian smiled and released at least some of the tension she'd brought with her in the car. "That is most definitely a great view."

Chapter 10

Fletcher gave Nate his own tour well after Vivian's concluded. He'd also waited until well after Ruby, Kiki, Chase and Max had taken off under the guise of giving Vivian and Nate some acclimating time. Nate didn't need acclimating. He could settle in easily wherever he went.

But he had not missed the knowing looks that passed among his brothers. Looks that made the back of his neck prickle to the point of pain.

With the car unloaded and Vivian occupied with storing the cooler contents as well as going through the well-stocked refrigerator, freezer and pantry, Fletcher showed Nate the lay of the land, ending, to Nate's surprise, on the second floor and the balcony outside the massive bedroom suite that could have doubled as a ballroom.

"You worried about Vivian hearing whatever it is you're going to tell me?" Nate challenged.

Fletcher didn't blink. "More like I'm leaving it to you how much you want to tell her. Consider it my gift to you, offering a return of control you're going to be lacking for the next little while."

Nate almost grunted a reply. Seemed his new siblings really had thought of everything.

Outside, as it was coming up on five o'clock, the sun had begun its nightly surrender, and the chill factor dropped. The cold air blasting into the house was blocked by the bedroom door Fletcher had closed behind them.

"I'm guessing you all like your space." Nate twisted off the top of a beer bottle he'd grabbed out of the fridge and pocketed the cap. The house was beyond anything he could have ever imagined vacationing in let alone living in. *Tasteful elegance* was a phrase that came to mind.

"Colton Properties is Chase's baby these days. He's a fan of giving prospective buyers a wealth of choices." Fletcher pushed open a pair of French doors identical to the ones just off the kitchen downstairs and stepped outside. "He's hoping it'll offset some recent business blowback."

It didn't sit well, Nate realized, having this much space between him and Vivian. But Fletcher seemed to have a plan in mind, even if said plan meant turning them both into Popsicles. Good thing he'd noticed a stash of firewood by each of the fireplaces. He couldn't wait to get a fire started.

"Small homes, large homes, long-time residents, vacationers," Fletcher went on. "Chase has developed Colton Crossing for a myriad of income levels."

"It's called hedging one's bets," Nate countered and earned a nod of approval as Fletcher took a pull of his beer. "So, I give. What's with the cone of silence?"

Fletcher leaned back, sat on the edge of the banister and stretched out his legs. "I've been elected to broach a subject that might be considered a bit tricky."

"Elected by whom?" Nate needn't have asked. As

much as he'd been hoping for an uneventful arrival, it was unrealistic to think it wouldn't come with a price.

Fletcher dismissed the question with a smile that didn't come close to reaching his wary eyes. "What do you know about our father's death?"

Whatever Nate had been expecting to hear, it certainly wasn't that. "I read it was a stroke." He braced his feet apart, folded his arms across his chest, beer bottle dangling from two fingers.

"Read?" Fletcher's brow furrowed.

"Yeah, online. In the paper. Saw it on the news ticker." An unease he thought he'd left in Boise re-knotted low in his belly. This didn't have anything to do with Vivian's current situation as a target.

"You didn't hear about his death from Jessie?" Fletcher asked.

Why did everything have to come back to his mother? "Until Robert died, I hadn't seen or spoken to my mother in years. She wasn't thrilled with me becoming a cop, and when I made detective, I became persona non grata, for want of a better term." He didn't add that earning that status had been such a relief he'd privately celebrated. "I'd heard about Robert dying before she came knocking on my door a few days after it hit the press." At the rate he was drinking his beer, he was going to run through his supply pretty darn quick. "I know now she stopped by on her way to Owl Creek. She thought she had me, talking about regrets and how we'd lost the chance to mend family fences." He rolled his eyes, shook his head. "I didn't believe it for a second."

"Why not?"

"Because the only regret my mother is capable of feeling has only to do with her own failures. She tried to offer sympathy to me and then to Sarah. She tried to talk about the good times and bring back memories that, to be honest, I have no recollection of." Sometimes, he was convinced he'd lived a completely different life than the one Jessie recalled. "I remember him being around the first ten years of my life, but not really present, if that makes sense. He traveled a lot. For business, we were told." Business. Hardly. Unless maintaining two completely separate families was a new kind of Colton enterprise. The entire conversation was enough to turn his stomach sour. "I told her I didn't think it was a good idea for her to come here, but that fell on deaf ears. Next thing I know, she's back from having met with all of you here in Owl Creek, as angry as I've ever seen her, ranting and raving over being pushed out of the inheritance." He shook his head again. "As predictable as she is spiteful."

"*Pushed out* meaning you and Sarah?" Fletcher asked.

Nate smirked. "Hardly."

"So you're of the belief Jessie came to us because she expected a payout."

"Expected?" Nate shrugged. "Couldn't say. Wanted? Definitely." He shivered. "Is there a reason we're having this talk outside?"

"Extreme temperatures make it easier to tell when someone's lying."

"Huh." Nate had to give Fletcher points. The reality of being interrogated by his older brother hit him with a bit more force than expected. So much for happy families. He toasted Fletcher with his beer. "Thanks for living up to my very low expectations." Maybe he had made a mistake coming here.

"You and Sarah came out of nowhere, Nate." Fletcher's voice was even and calm. "Of course we were going to be suspicious. You have no idea the pain Jessie's inflicted on the family over the years."

"Fair." He nodded, but it didn't dispel the disappointment he felt. "Just like you don't know what it was like to grow up in her house." Or to find out your father chose one portion of his family over another. "It might be easy for me to say, but don't paint me or Sarah with any brush connected to Jessie."

Fletcher glanced down. "You said it had been years since you saw Jessie. How long exactly?"

"I don't know." Nate frowned. "Three, maybe four years? Sarah sees her more than I do. My sister's a lighter touch when it comes to our mother's financial failings and machinations." Guilt he didn't like to ponder surged. "It hurt Sarah, more than me, to know Robert kept us secret from all of you. That we had this enormous family living only a few hours away. Sarah's always wanted to be part of something bigger than just us. When I found out about you all, I was terrified about what it all would mean. But Sarah? It was all I could do to stop her from jumping on a bus and coming out here to introduce herself as one of the family. Right now, I'm real thankful I won that fight."

If Fletcher took offense, he didn't show it. "Sarah didn't care that our father lied about everything?"

"Sure she did." Nate ducked his head, let out a soft laugh. "She just got over it faster than me. Sarah's far more forgiving. Which explains why she always lets Jessie back into her life. Despite knowing it won't end well."

"Hope's a dangerous thing," Fletcher said.

"Especially in the hands of someone who knows how to wield it," Nate agreed. "So." He took another drink. "What is it you want to ask me that requires a deep-freeze lie detector?"

"I guess I was curious if you thought Dad's death was…suspicious in any way."

"I hadn't seen the man in almost a decade," Nate said carefully. "I'm not in a position to suspect anything about him." He paused, looked his brother in the eye. "Do you think it was?"

The clouds opened up and sent a heavy cascade of snow down upon them. Fletcher motioned him back inside, closed the doors, then led him into an alcove off the main suite that contained two overstuffed cream-colored chairs with matching storage ottomans.

"It's been discussed," Fletcher said as he got comfortable. "That there might be more to Dad's death than originally believed."

Nate tried not to react to the use of the word *Dad* where Robert Colton was concerned. Instead, he focused on putting the pieces of this conversation together. "If you're going to kill someone, especially a man as powerful and well-known as our father, there are better ways than to trigger a stroke."

"Unless someone is already prone to them. Then it would be—"

"Understandable and not wholly unexpected," Nate finished. His cop brain clicked on. "I take it his medical history proves that out?"

"He had a minor stroke a few years ago," Fletcher said. "And, okay, to be completely honest—"

"*Now* we're being honest?"

Fletcher looked at him. Really looked at him this time, then gave a slow nod. "Okay. I had that coming. We all had that coming, I suppose. Look." He let out a sigh. "I don't want you thinking we considered Dad some kind of saint or perfect father. Or a perfect man. He wasn't any of those things."

"Do tell." Nate took his last drink of beer.

"Jessie wasn't his first or his only affair. He had a lot of them," Fletcher said. "After Jessie, he stopped trying so hard to hide them. Near as we can tell, he didn't have any other kids."

Nate smirked again. "Time will tell."

"He was a hard-drinking, heavy-smoking, live-life-to-excess kind of man. His first stroke was a warning he didn't heed." Fletcher sounded both resigned and regretful. "The second one didn't come as a big surprise. Still, he was bigger than life, and it was a shock when he died. But then Jessie turns up. Out of the blue. And tells us all about their life together. Tells us about you and your sister." He rubbed a tired hand across the back of his neck. "Suffice it to say, none of us handled it very well. When we didn't acquiesce to her demands for an equal share of the estate, she talked to anyone who would listen. Papers, reporters, bloggers. She didn't just air out the family closet, she fumigated it."

"Yeah," Nate said. "I am well aware." He and Sarah had both needed to change their phone numbers multiple times to avoid the press's attention. At least the camp-outs on their front lawns hadn't lasted more than a few days. Small blessings, he supposed. Thank heavens for the media's short attention span.

"Chase has had to work nearly 24/7 to keep the scandal from destroying the family company," Fletcher said. "It took a while to stop the financial hemorrhaging, reassure our investors and shareholders. The rest of us just did what we could to wait it all out."

"He seems to have done a pretty good job of things. You all have," Nate added with some reluctance. "None of this answers the question you asked of me, though. About Robert's death. You haven't mentioned anything that argues the ruling of natural causes."

"That's because there isn't an argument. It's more a gut feeling. On the surface, yes, everything points to a stroke. But then there are other things to take into consideration." Fletcher pursed his lips. "You ever hear of the Ever After Church? It's run by a man named Markus Acker."

"Of course," Nate said. "It's hard not to living around here. They have some kind of church compound, don't they? Near Conners? Although calling it a church seems a bit of a stretch."

"Mmm." Fletcher nodded. "You'd be right on that front. It's a cult, pure and simple to anyone on the outside looking in. Acker's a con man, plain and simple. This Ever After Church isn't the first time he's pulled this stunt, but so far it seems to be his most successful. He's got about a thousand followers living with him. Living under his rules, working his land, giving over their life savings in exchange for atonement, forgiveness, who knows what else."

"Free labor in exchange for the promise of redemption?" Nate supplied. "There's dozens of men like Acker working scams like this all over the country."

"True enough," Fletcher agreed. "Acker's especially

insidious, though. He doesn't hide his love of money, or the power he thinks it gives him. He sucks everyone he comes in contact with dry, and once they are, he puts them into situations where they can get him more. And then there's his seduction ratio. He goes after what he wants, especially if he thinks it'll add to his coffers. Or if they're female." He paused, eyes shifting as he decided on his next words. "Jessie's one of his followers, Nate."

Nate blinked. Frowned. Opened his mouth to respond, then closed it. Tried again. "You're sure?" was all that came out.

"We're sure," Fletcher said. "From what we've been able to find out, she has been for years. Maybe even from before Acker hit Idaho four years ago." Another pause. "One thing Acker's followers all do is confess to him. They tell him every detail of their life before they found him, and no doubt he keeps impeccable notes. Jessie wouldn't have been an exception."

Nate could only imagine how a man like Markus Acker would have reacted to hearing one of his devotees had her claws in Robert Colton. "You think she told Acker about Robert and their life together."

"She had to have. And if Acker's as dangerous as we think…"

It took Nate a moment to pull together the threads of their conversation. "You're thinking Acker might have somehow had Robert killed so Jessie could make a claim on his estate."

"That's part of what I'm thinking." Fletcher watched him carefully, as if poised for a fight once Nate caught on to whatever else lurked beneath the surface of accusation.

It was Nate the cop who needed to step up now. The

cop who needed to stop lurking in the shadows and see this situation from the outside, taking into consideration everyone involved in the story. It took a moment to step away and look objectively, but once he did, the answer became more than evident. It became probable. "You're thinking it's possible my mother had a hand in killing Robert." He waited for the doubt or disbelief to land and steal the air from his lungs. But it didn't.

"As much loathing as there is for Jessie, we're struggling with that idea," Fletcher admitted. "We haven't brought the entire family in on this yet. It isn't time, and honestly, this isn't something any of us want to think possible. Right now, it's just you and me talking. Cop to cop." He hesitated. "Brother to brother."

For the first time, hearing that word didn't make Nate flinch.

"I think the timing of Dad's death is beyond coincidental," Fletcher went on. "Acker's rise to prominence, Jessie running out of cash, the companies' success. Given the resulting chaos Jessie's bomb created, it all feels a bit calculated. And cruel."

"My mother's specialties. Okay." His mind was spinning in a dozen different directions, not one of them good. "Okay, I'm not saying you're wrong, but I'm also not ready to say you're right." It should have hurt, far more than it did, to even consider his mother might be capable of murdering Robert Colton. But the truth was his days of predicting Jessie Colton's behavior had long ago passed. Given what he'd seen being a cop for as long as he had been, one thing was true in this life: anyone is capable of anything at any time. "That said, I'll agree this is something we should dig deeper into." He took a deep breath. "I hate to say it, but that should probably fall on me." As Jessie's son, it would be far less suspicious for him to go investigating the last few years of her life and any connection she had to Markus Acker.

Fletcher dropped his head forward as if in relief. When he lifted his chin once more, he had an odd grin on his face. "Max owes me another twenty bucks."

"Does he?" Nate didn't know why it mattered, but it did. Clearly Max Colton was going to take more time to be convinced about where Nate's lack of loyalties lay. "He doesn't have much faith, does he?"

"It's been hard on him, and Greg and Malcolm and Lizzy, knowing that Jessie chose to raise you and Sarah when she walked away from them. He was what, eight when Jessie left? That's a hard age to witness a family breaking apart."

Any age was as far as Nate was concerned. "And like I said before—"

"Yeah, I know," Fletcher agreed. "Living with Jessie wasn't a picnic. And I get it. I really do. But you've known about us for a while, haven't you?"

Half a lifetime, Nate almost admitted. Instead he simply said, "Yes."

"We've had months. Give everyone a bit more time to adjust. We'll get there, Nate. And believe it or not, we might all actually be worth it."

Nate wanted to believe that was true, but Fletcher didn't seem to be taking one thing into consideration. That Nate's mother may very well be responsible for what happened to Robert Colton.

And if that was the case, would Nate and Sarah ever truly be accepted?

* * *

"Good night, Vivian."

Vivian glanced up from her laptop screen, sliding off the barstool at the kitchen counter when Fletcher poked his head in to wave goodbye.

"Oh. Good night, Fletcher." She flashed him her best "not a care in the world" smile and lifted her hand. "Everything okay?"

"I've given Nate a crash course on the security system." He pointed to the keypad by the back door. "He'll fill you in on everything you need to know."

"Okay." It didn't escape her notice he hadn't answered her question, but it wasn't her place to push. Clearly what the brothers had to discuss needed to be addressed in private. Didn't mean she wasn't curious about it, though. "Thank you, again, for everything. I hope..." She moved closer to him. "I hope we won't inconvenience you for long."

Fletcher's cool expression immediately shifted and, for want of a better term, opened. "You're the one being inconvenienced, Vivian. Your life shouldn't have to come to a screeching halt because you accepted a dinner invitation."

"No, it shouldn't, should it?" Easy enough to say, but at the same time, if she hadn't said yes, she might not ever have met Nate. And that, she knew without a doubt, would have been a terrible shame.

"Don't let all this family stuff get to you," Fletcher continued. "It's taking us some time to adjust to everything that's happened these past few months, but you were right back at the station. Nate's family. It's time we started acting like he is."

"I'm glad to hear it." Despite Nate's detached attitude about his place in the Colton family, she couldn't help but think that deep down, in places he didn't even know existed, he really did want to belong. But he also was preparing himself for disappointment. Something she could relate to all too well. "Nate will be glad, too. Especially for Sarah."

"Yeah." Fletcher nodded. "Yeah, I got the message on that. We'll get there. Eventually. I'll check in with you both tomorrow." He walked back down the hall, and a few moments later, the front door shut behind him.

The silence in the house was beyond deafening. Nate hadn't been wrong earlier about the size of this place. It was nearly cavernous and even echoed in places. Despite its beautiful decor and design, it didn't feel remotely homey to her. Or maybe she was just too comfortable with the way her life had been up until now. These last few days—despite the disastrous underpinnings of misadventure—had been a kind of awakening for her. Lizzy had been right all those times she'd worried that Vivian had locked herself away to stay protected from the world. Sure it was dangerous and scary, but it also contained wonders and excitement. Like a particular detective currently occupying the same house.

A detective who had her thinking about all kinds of activities the two of them might do together. Her face went hot, but instead of pushing the fantasies away, she embraced them. And settled them into the back of her mind to dwell on later.

"I smell something delicious." Nate's declaration as he walked into the kitchen startled her out of her reverie. He opened three bottom cabinets before finding the one housing the recycling bucket for his and Fletcher's empty beer bottles.

"Kiki suggested I break the kitchen in," Vivian admitted. It had been almost an hour since Nate had followed Fletcher upstairs, and she was dying to know what they had talked about. "I've got the leftovers sorted, and there's a whacky cake in the oven."

"A what cake?" He wandered around the large center island that housed a farmer's sink and extensive counter space, as if transfixed by the aroma emanating from inside the oven.

"Whacky cake." She flexed her fingers. "It's the first thing I learned to bake, actually. It's a kind of ritual for me. First night in a new house, I make it. My first foster mother gave me the recipe. It's from World War II, when rations limited store supplies. No eggs or butter, just pantry items, you know, like flour and sugar and... Sorry, babbling." She had to stop herself from twisting her hands into knots. "I'm nervous." She slid back onto the stool and tried to refocus on the emails waiting in her inbox. There wasn't anything urgent. Nothing that couldn't wait until tomorrow.

"Nervous about what?"

"Everything." Deflecting, she gave in to temptation. "What were you and Fletcher talking about upstairs?"

He pulled open the fridge, had his hand on a second bottle of beer, then changed his mind and shut the door without taking it out. "Trust me, you do not want to know."

"Oh." She scrunched her mouth. "Okay, sure. I understand." She closed her computer and stood back up, made a beeline for the remote. "How about we find something on TV to watch while we—"

He moved so quickly and quietly she almost yelped when his hand gently wrapped around her wrist. "Vivian."

She squeezed her eyes shut. She didn't want to admit how her name on his lips made everything inside her quiver. She didn't want to get any more attached to this man than she already was. She wasn't the kind of woman men noticed or gravitated toward, and she certainly didn't want to lean into the whole damsel-in-distress modus operandi. It took all her confidence to believe that the attraction she'd felt when she'd first kissed him, that *zing* of excitement that coursed through her whenever he touched her, wasn't one-sided.

"Do I make you nervous, Vivian?" He stepped closer, so close she could feel the heat of his body radiating through both their layers of clothing. He made her shiver, that baritone voice of his, that way he had of making her feel as if she were the only woman in his world.

"You know you do," she whispered. Her thoughts tumbled over one another as if caught in an avalanche of unchecked emotion. "I don't know how to do this, Nate."

"Don't know how to do what?" His thumb moved across the pulse in her wrist, tempting. Teasing. The slightest touch of his skin to hers, and she could feel herself melting.

"You know what. Interacting. I'm terrible at…this." Only now did she turn, if only because she had nowhere to hide. She lifted her chin, forced her gaze up to meet the eyes of the man who had stoked every fire inside her from the moment she'd first seen him at the bar.

"Well, Ms. Maylor." He released her wrist, threaded his fingers between hers and lifted her hand to his lips. "I think this deserves further investigation." He pressed his lips to the back of her knuckles, nudged her a bit closer as his mouth trailed across her hand. "You don't seem so terrible to me." His smile silenced her, emptied her mind of every thought except what it had felt like to be kissed by him. "Shall we see what else you aren't terrible at?" He let go of her hand, smoothed both of his down her sides, until they rested on her hips.

She whimpered behind pressed lips. Desire weakened her knees, and she clung to him, catching his upper arms in her trembling hands and willing herself to remain on her feet. When his lips brushed against hers, she sighed, opened her mouth and let him in.

Kissing him in the car yesterday had been pure impulse. A way to remind herself that she was still alive. But now, being here, in his arms, every cell in her being fired as his tongue swept in and engaged hers in a dance instinct led. He tilted his head, took the kiss deeper, and she rose up on her toes, stretched her body against his.

Her breasts tingled as he drew her in to him. She could feel every part of him pressing into her. He dipped down, wrapped those muscular arms around her waist and lifted her off her feet, his mouth creating a miracle of magic on hers. She could feel her arms move, as if on their own, up and around his neck. Her fingers tangled in the thickness of his hair at his neck. Silky, soft. Sensational. She sighed and sagged into him.

In the distance, she heard a buzzing, a ringing of sorts. Loud enough to break the spell, but not so intrusive that she unwound herself from around him.

"I think," Nate murmured against her throat when she dropped her head back, "your cake is done."

"Mmmmm." It took a moment for her head to clear,

for his words to seep in. "Oh." Her smile came slow this time. "Right. Cake." She'd baked out of habit, and craving, only to find herself not the least bit satiated by the man in her arms. "I should get it out before it burns."

He nodded and the quirky smile that curved his lips felt as if it had been created just for her.

"I'll…just…" She let her arms drop and stumbled back. Her knees hadn't quite got their strength back, but given the self-satisfied expression on Nate's face, she wasn't going to add to his ego boost by falling flat on her fanny. Whatever else she might think, he was here protecting her; he felt responsible for her. And that cold splash of reality was enough to have the self-doubt surging afresh.

"I've got frosting to make." It was, quite possibly, the dumbest thing she'd ever said in her life. Nonetheless, she pushed her way around him and retreated.

She smiled to herself as something unexpected and powerful bloomed inside her.

For now, at least.

Chapter 11

While Boise wasn't sensory overload when it came to noise, the utter midnight silence of Owl Creek pressed in on Nate to the point of insomnia. He could feel the exhaustion creeping through his system, but every time he closed his eyes and tried to sleep, there was a kind of electrical zap that had him staring back at the ceiling.

He groaned, snatched one of the pillows off the bed and shoved it over his face.

How was it possible for a mind to travel multiple roads at lightning speed? It clearly wasn't enough for him to be worried about Vivian being targeted by a narcissistic Godfather wannabe, or what might happen should Dean Wexler, his best and only lead in the case, succumb to his injuries. Nor was his ever-expanding and confusing family dynamic happy to play second fiddle to the first worry. It wasn't even the fact that he had to consider that Fletcher was right and that Jessie, his own mother, could very well be responsible for his wealthy and estranged father's death.

He smushed the pillow harder on his face. Who was he kidding?

None of that was responsible for his inability to sleep.

What was keeping him awake was one beautiful, curvy, slightly timid brunette who could kiss like a dream and made magic cake with a snap of her fingers. It would have been easy, so easy, he supposed, to nudge her gently up the stairs and into that spacious palace of a main suite she currently occupied by herself.

He'd always prided himself on following the rules. He had no doubt where it stemmed from—backlash against his parental examples who both excelled at making the world bend to their will. Rules were in place for a reason. It was inappropriate, unprofessional and irresponsible of him to even be considering getting involved with a witness, especially one connected to a case that could make his career. And yet...

And yet.

Nate tossed the pillow aside and grabbed the ridiculous toy-like flip phone Max had given him in place of his usual one. Two in the morning.

"Hour of the wolf," he muttered before he sat up, wishing, not for the first time, he'd surrendered to the idea of taking the bedroom next door to hers. Instead he'd sequestered himself downstairs. "This is ridiculous." If he wasn't going to sleep, he could work. Or at least stop circling the same mental track over and over.

Barefoot, and wearing only a pair of pajama bottoms, he grabbed the bag containing his laptop and whatever printed files he had on him and quietly padded down to and around the living room toward the kitchen.

He saw the glow of the Christmas tree well before he rounded the corner. Kiki, Ruby and Sloan had put enough lights on that thing for it to act as an airport landing strip. It had been sweet of them to add some holiday cheer, considering everything Vivian was being put through.

With only the tree lights on, the kitchen was cast in shadows. It wasn't until he set his bag on one of the barstools that he noticed Vivian sitting on the sofa, legs curled in under her, her hands cupped around a mug as she looked at the lights.

She turned her head, casting her profile in a shimmery glow that stole the air from his lungs.

"Did I wake you?" Her voice was as soft as the snow falling outside.

"No." All thoughts of work evaporated. "No, I couldn't sleep."

"Yeah." She sighed and returned her gaze to the tree. "Me, either. It's beautiful, isn't it?"

"Stunning." He wasn't certain he'd ever seen anything, anyone, more so.

"I made some hot chocolate. It's on the stove if—"

"I'm fine."

He sat down, purposely keeping some distance between them. He could smell the sweet cocoa steam drifting into the air. He'd been imagining what she might wear to bed. Somehow, the simple turquoise blue tank top and loose-fitting flowered pants hadn't come to mind. His thoughts had included…steamier selections. But with her hair tumbling free down and around her shoulders, her creamy skin gleaming in the dim light, reality won, hands down.

"That first holiday after my parents died," she said quietly, "I was living in a foster home with six other kids. The house was chaos, but in a good way, I suppose. It was…different. Shocking, actually." Memories clouded her eyes. "It was just me and Mom and Dad before that. To be suddenly in the middle of..." She sighed, shrugged. "Something strange is going on."

"Given the last few days, that statement is definitely a multiple-choice selection."

She laughed, just a little, but the sound took the clouds from her gaze. "For so long, I've felt like I'm sleepwalking through someone else's life. Like mine stopped all those years ago, and I'm just...adrift. Lost. Or, at least, I did feel that way." She looked up at the tree. "A tree like this seems like such a luxury. I used to dream about having one just like it. But as I grew older, it didn't seem... practical. As if I somehow wasn't worth the effort."

"Christmas shouldn't have anything to do with practical." Something his sister Sarah had said on occasion, usually when she was elbow deep in ornament boxes and trimmings.

"I didn't see a tree at your place when we were there." It wasn't an accusation, he thought. More of an observation.

"No." He shrugged. "No, I usually take extra shifts during Christmas so the detectives and officers with families can be home."

"Of course you do." She leaned forward, set her mug on the large, square coffee table. It was only then he noticed the small, wooden box sitting there. "It's funny. Before you came in, I was trying to convince myself you aren't as perfect as you seem to be."

He couldn't help it. He laughed. "Allow me to set your mind at ease," he teased. "I am not remotely perfect. There's a reason I cycle through partners the way I do. I'm difficult to deal with."

"Not from where I'm sitting." She uncurled her legs and scooted forward to the edge of the sofa. "I've never felt safer with anyone in my life, Nate. And I'm not referring to my physical safety." He looked for the uncertainty, the apology that had been hovering in her eyes since the moment he'd first seen her. As if she felt the need to apologize for existing. "I'm me with you. I don't have this…this need to put on a show or pretend to be something I'm not. I can't explain it."

"You don't have to explain it," Nate told her as his heart expanded to double its size. "I'll simply take it for the compliment that it is."

"You know what else I was thinking?"

Given that spark he saw in her eye, he had a pretty good idea. His fists clenched. She faced him, inclined her head.

"I was thinking," she went on when he didn't respond, "that I'm tired of living my life in the shadows. I don't want to live—or die—with any regrets." She stood up, smoothed her hands down her hips, took one, two, three steps toward him.

"You aren't going to die, Vivian." He leaned his head back to look up at her. Behind her, the tree's lights set her to glowing. "I'm not going to let you."

"Hmmm." She nodded, moved one foot then the other until she straddled his legs. "Then that means I'm going to live." She lowered herself, lifted her knees until she settled herself on his lap. He went as hard as stone in an instant, his breath hitching in his chest when she rested her hands on his shoulders, kneaded them gently with her fingers. "I don't think I've really lived much of a life, Nate." She leaned forward, placed a soft, nibbling kiss against the side of his throat. "Maybe it's taken almost dying twice in two days for me to see that. Maybe this is an awakening after all."

He squeezed his eyes shut, kept his hands at his sides as the scent of her washed over him, enveloped him. Her hair brushed against his face, his throat, as her lips moved ever so lightly, ever so gently, across his skin.

"Vivian, I don't think—"

"Don't." She sat up, caught his face between her hands and waited until he opened his eyes before continuing. "Don't think. Not now. This is what I want. You. Us. Together. Tonight. For however many nights we might have in this...place. Our place."

He felt himself standing on the edge of a precipice he'd tried so desperately to avoid. "I don't know that I have anything to offer you, Vivian." He couldn't stop himself. His hands finally shifted, skimmed feather-light up her thighs, over her hips, fingers slipping beneath the hem of her shirt to caress her back.

"I don't need anything but you," she told him. "I'm not special, Nate. I'm not made of glass. I'm not...innocent."

His brow arched. "Aren't you?"

"I've had sex before." She inclined her head as if contemplating something he wasn't privy to. "What I haven't had is lo—" she stopped herself but didn't look away. "Intimacy. Sex is one thing." She brushed the backs of her fingers down his cheeks. "Giving myself over, letting go, actually being with someone is another thing entirely."

Love. Despite everything else she said, that was what he'd almost heard. The word shuddered through him and stole what was left of his breath. Was that what this was? Was that what he felt? This all-encompassing desire, the absolute determination to keep her safe, not only from what existed in the outside world, but from himself?

"You don't have to say anything," Vivian whispered. "I don't expect you to. I'm still trying to figure all this out myself. But it's there. It's here." She caught one of his hands, drew it around to her stomach, under her shirt and up to her heart. Her breasts. "I need to know what it feels like to have your hands on me. To feel you inside me."

She kissed him, drawing him forward as she took what she wanted, her core pressing against the hardness of him.

"Don't turn me away, Nate." Her breath was hot against his face, his lips. Her words singeing his heart. She moved his hand over until it cupped her breast, which filled his hand to perfection. "I don't want reason or rational thought or anything other than you. And me. Upstairs. In that big bed I can't bear to be in alone."

He stared up at her, unblinking. Transfixed.

She moved against him, let out a soft moan as his palm slid over her hardening nipple.

Seduced.

"Never let it be said I ignore a lady's request." Reason and restraint fractured. He surged forward, caught her mouth with his and dived in. Her thighs tightened around him as she folded herself around him, matching his kiss with one of her own that left him shaken to his core.

He pulled his hand free, and as if reading his thoughts, she leaned back far enough for him to draw the tank over her head. She moaned when he used both hands this time, cupping, teasing. Nate dipped his head, replaced his palms with his lips and drew one hardened peak into his mouth.

She gasped. Her head fell back as he circled her nipple with his tongue, leaving only to pay the same attention to her other breast. She clasped the back of his head, her hips rocking against him as she held him to her. She rubbed against him, the hot core of her against that which ached to be buried inside her.

"Stop." He gasped, struggled for control, and pulled his mouth free of hers. "Just…" He tried to catch his breath. "We need…" The word. What was the word he… "Protection."

She kissed him again, slowly, tortuously, slid off of him. She stood, slipped her hands beneath the waistband of her pants and slowly lowered them down her legs.

He groaned at the sight of her naked, glistening body against the blinding glare of the tree lights. She held out her hand, took a step back. He followed, rising from the sofa as if caught in a spell. When their fingers entwined, the explosion threatening to undo him built again.

When they reached the stairs, she turned, taking his other hand in hers and drawing him with her.

"It wasn't only the pantry they stocked," she said, her lips curving into a beautiful smile. "I found a nice selection of condoms in the main bath." Her eyes glinted. "Made it very difficult to sleep after that. Thinking how they should be put to use."

Nate wanted to respond. He wanted to spout poetic words of perfection, but any capacity to utter a word had been stolen from him. The last steps to the main suite seemed to take both an eternity and a moment. No sooner had they crossed the threshold than he had her in his arms again.

Beside the bed, the table lamp glowed and the box she'd found sat open and waiting. With the mountains cradling them in their snowy wonder, he lifted her, kissed her. Devoured her. And lost himself.

She wound her bare legs around his hips, gasped into his mouth as he walked them to the bed. Kissing her, tasting her, should have been enough. It might have been enough if he hadn't already known what it was like to touch her. To have her touch him.

He lowered her, gently, until she was lying on the bed. He backed away, only enough to see her writhing on the mattress as she opened herself to him. "Nate, please." Her voice beckoned him with longing, but not yet, he told himself. Not until…

He knelt down, gently grasped her open thighs and drew her forward. Until he could feel the heat of her against his chin. His face. His lips. He licked her, one steady, firm swipe of his tongue before nibbling at that tiny nub of pleasure at the apex of her core.

She whimpered. Her hands grabbed his head, dived into his hair as she lifted her hips against him. Her back arched off the bed. Her breath turning into gasps that created a surge of power inside him. When she came, it was an explosion of unreserved passion that left her limp on the bed.

Even as her arms stretched out for him. For more.

He had never, in his entire life, seen a more beautiful sight than that of this woman laid bare before him, wanting him inside her.

Nate made quick work of discarding his pants. He

had the condom on in record time, doing his best not to meet the teasing gaze of Vivian's oh-so-easily read eyes. Her hands reached for him, eager fingers clutching for him as he placed a knee on the edge of the mattress. She shifted back.

He moved forward, loomed over her, lowered himself and pressed his length against her.

"More," she whispered, bringing one leg up and around his hips, nudging him forward. "More, Nate. All."

He surrendered and sank into her. Her moan echoed in his ears, in his soul, as he moved, slowly at first, wanting her to get the feel of him, even as he held back. When she curled around him, her arms, her legs, he increased his thrusts, determined to set her climbing back toward release. There was no rationalizing what he felt being inside her. There was no way to describe the absolute bliss of joining with her. Her hips pumped in time with his. Their breathing came in gasps, even as he stared into her eyes.

"Come with me," she whispered when he felt the urge overwhelm him. Unable to hold back, unable to deny her, he erupted inside her.

And set her to soaring as well.

"Well." Vivian had never felt so utterly relaxed and fulfilled in her life. "There's only one problem with us having done this."

"Only one?" Nate said on a sleepy laugh. He'd been efficient in the way he'd adjusted them in bed, had them snuggling beneath the comfy, warm down duvet once they could both move.

She lifted her head from the curve of his shoulder,

rested her chin on her hand that was placed over his still rapidly pounding heart. "Well, only one comes to mind at the moment." She cuddled against him and felt her heart zing when he tightened his arm around her as if trying to draw her even closer. "One time isn't going to be nearly enough."

Vivian smiled and laughed at his arched brow. She traced a finger down his nose and allowed it to be caught in his teeth when she reached his lips.

"Did I mention I've always had a thing for older women?"

"You did," Vivian said seriously and moved her leg between his. She felt him stir, anticipated the minutes until they could try to outdo round one. "You're quite... adept for such a young man."

Nate snorted and laughed. "What do you think young men spend most of their time thinking about?"

"I don't have to think." She rose up, kissed him, all but melted into him. "I have firsthand experience." She tucked her head under his chin, closed her eyes against the sensation of his hand smoothing her hair, cupping her cheek. "Can I tell you something?"

"You can tell me anything," he assured her.

"Seriously. I don't want you to laugh."

His hand stilled. He tucked a finger under her cheek and lifted her chin so he could look into her eyes. "I will never laugh at you, Vivian."

"You know the first time I thought about this happening between us?" She hesitated. Exposing her body to him had been one thing. Exposing her heart? Well. She'd been wanting to take more chances with her life, hadn't she? "When I first saw you sitting at the bar."

"Yeah?" He looked inordinately pleased with himself.

"Yeah. It made focusing on dinner quite impossible, I can tell you." She trailed a finger across his chest.

"Tell me about it." He caught her hand and brought it to his lips. *Talented lips*, she thought as she pushed aside any regret or doubt. She was not going to let anything ruin this time she had with him. "You know when I first thought about this happening between us?"

She smiled, entertained at his amusement. "Tell me."

"When you took off your jacket at the restaurant." He blinked, and she searched for the teasing, for the lie. And found none. "It was like being hit by a lightning bolt." His hand sunk into her hair. "And that was before I even saw your face. Or your glasses." He tapped her nose and earned a laugh. "We should get bonus points for resisting temptation for as long as we did."

"Yes, well, you did your best to push me off. Didn't work though." She'd meant what she'd said earlier. Sex was one thing. Making love with Nate Colton had been entirely another. "I do believe almost dying...twice," she added quickly, "might have finally taught me not to be quite so...timid."

He kissed her, long and deep. Until her head spun.

"There is nothing timid about you," he assured her when she reached down and grasped him in her hand. "Not one little bit."

"No," she said as she slithered down his body and lowered her mouth to him. "I don't think there is anymore."

When Vivian opened her eyes, it took her a long moment to remember where she was. She wasn't staring at dull white walls or a mirrored dresser she'd found at a yard sale shortly after moving into her town house. She didn't feel the chill of the straining heating unit doing its best to spit out warmth on a cold December morning.

Instead, she was buried beneath a comfy, cozy down-filled duvet, looking out to the stunning mountain range encircling the town of Owl Creek. An unfamiliar yet welcome weight had settled over her, behind her. Around her.

The smile that spread slowly across her lips had her reaching up and resting her hand on the top of Nate's head. Her fingers sank into the thickness of his hair as she drew her fingers down. He shifted, moved more snuggly against her in a way that both brought a tint of color to her cheeks and a slow boil to her blood.

"Don't start something you might not have the energy to finish." Nate's voice rumbled against the side of her neck. He tightened his hold around her waist, pressed his lips against the pulse at her throat.

"Believe me," she said on a half moan as his hand wandered down her bare stomach. "If we start, I'll make absolutely certain we finish."

Still, she found her gaze drawn back to the mountains as she clung to the memory of this perfect moment. A moment that only months before she couldn't have conceived of.

His stomach rumbled, and she laughed. "Hungry?"

"Starved." He nipped at her neck, and she gasped as he rolled her onto her back. He gazed down upon her as if he were an art aficionado looking upon a classic painting.

"I can cook," she offered, linking her hands behind his neck. "Unless you have someplace to be?"

"I do not." He kissed her. "Have any place." Kissed her again, longer this time. "To be." This kiss had her melting beneath him to the point of becoming utterly putty in his hands as the sun completed its ascent into the sky.

She hadn't lied to him last night, when she'd told him she'd had sex before. But she wouldn't necessarily qualify it as…rewarding. A quick tumble with a boy her first week of college had been the result of curiosity rather than passion. It certainly hadn't been anything that warranted a desire for a repeat performance either on the boy's part or hers. As a result, she'd added sex to the list of things she could live without.

She caught a giggle behind her still vibrating fingers.

She definitely couldn't say that anymore.

"Do I even want to know?" Nate lifted his head from where he'd been dozing against her breast.

"I don't think you do." This time, it was her stomach that rumbled. "Okay, that's embarrassing enough to warrant me heading down to the kitchen. After I take a shower."

"Mmmm." He nuzzled his cheek against her. "Couple more minutes."

She sighed. It was so easy to forget everything, including what had brought them to this place, this moment. And yet the threats hovered, as did the reality of needing to return to her actual life. They both needed to return. Once she was out of danger, he wouldn't be responsible for her safety any longer. His job would be done, and if there was one thing she'd learned about him the past few days, it was that his job always came first. "Nate?"

"Yeah."

"Are you going to tell me what you and Fletcher talked about up here last night?"

She knew asking would break the spell, but one of them had to be practical about things. Fairy tales were all well and good as a diversion, but she knew, better than most, that real life rarely brought a happily-ever-after.

"It doesn't have to do with you." He rolled onto his back but curved an arm around her when she leaned over him, catching the sheet between them. He pinched the bridge of his nose, squeezed his eyes shut.

"So it's none of my business?"

He dropped his hand, looked at her, and she wondered if it was possible to actually fall into the ocean blue of his eyes. "I didn't say that. It's...complicated."

"I'm a smart woman." Funny. It was something she'd always known, of course, but rarely was it anything she said. Out loud, at least. "Maybe I can help?"

"What makes you think I need help with it?"

"This." She traced a finger from his furrowed brow, down his nose, to his swollen lips. "It appears every time you start thinking."

"Then it must be permanently etched on my face." He stopped, sighed. "I don't know that I'd even know where to start."

"Anywhere." She hesitated, then plunged ahead. "If it doesn't have to do with me, does it have to do with your mother?"

"Okay, flag on the play." He sat up and scooted back against the headboard. "Let's not put you and my mother in the same sentence. Or mention her while we're in bed, okay?"

She knew he meant it as a tease, a joke, but there was definite pain behind the thought.

"Tell me." She sat up and crossed her legs, pushed her hair away from her face. "Talk to me, Nate. You've certainly listened to me enough."

He looked a bit lost for a moment, confused, and she caught a glimpse of a younger Nate, struggling with the truth about his complicated family life. When he spoke, it was with a resoluteness that made her heart ache for him.

"Fletcher thinks my mother might have had a hand in our father's death." His smile was quick and cursory. "Surprised you, didn't I?"

"Not...exactly." She frowned, frantically searching for the right words. But she didn't have a chance to say anything else before he went on.

"How about this, then? Apparently, for the past few years, she's been involved with this Ever After Church, and the guy who runs it. Markus Acker. You've probably heard of them."

"I definitely have." She nodded as her blood ran cold. "One of my clients, he runs a Fortune 500 company out of New York. He hired me to do some damage control when his son got caught up with Acker last year. Just press releases and statements to the media. He didn't want it to be full-blown news, but he didn't want his shareholders thinking he was being held hostage by the fact his boy was being used to essentially extort him."

"Did he get out? The kid?" Nate asked, a bit more alert.

Vivian ducked her head. "I don't know how much I'm legally allowed to say since I signed a nondisclosure agreement, but…" She nodded. "Without going into details, I can tell you my client hired a specialized team to get him out."

"Like an off-the-books mercenary kind of group?"

She shrugged, a non-answer. "The last I heard he'd had his son sent to a facility overseas that specializes in… I don't know if this is the right word…*deprogramming.*" While she'd been relieved the boy was safe and out of the cult's reach, she hadn't found working that kind of job to be anything other than stressful and gut-wrenching. She much preferred working with authors looking to sell their books and brand, or actors and actresses hoping to up their profile. That particular client had helped her learn to set boundaries and not jump at every professional opportunity just because it might up her profile. "Do you think… Is it possible Fletcher's right about your mom being involved with this group? Does he have any actual evidence?"

As horrific as the stories were about Jessie Colton—and she'd gotten an earful from Lizzy as well as Nate—the idea Jessie may have murdered Robert came across as a little too *Game of Thrones* for her liking.

"Do I think it's possible?" Nate's brows went up. "Yes. As far as evidence? He doesn't have anything concrete. It's a gut feeling on Fletcher's part. Others, too, if I was reading him right. I don't know if he's talked to Max about it or not."

"I would think yes," she said and rested a hand on his thigh. "They might be cousins by birth, but they're brothers by choice. Something like this, if Fletcher truly believes it, enough to talk to you about it, then Max knows." She caught her bottom lip in her teeth. "That could explain why Max has been a harder sell on you."

"I told Fletcher I'd look into it. Later," he added quickly. "Once we're on the other side of this DeBaccian mess, and you're safe."

Once they were back to their real lives. Where neither one of them particularly fit with the other. When his job with her was done. "Then we'd best get to that." She tugged the sheet with her as she scooted off the edge of the bed. "I'm going to jump in the shower, then fix breakfast while you take one."

"Or." He caught her around the waist before she took two steps from the bed. He spun her around and kissed her breathless. "We could conserve water and shower together." The grin he gave her contained none of the hopelessness she'd seen shining in his eyes moments before.

"I do like conservation," she agreed, but her attempt to remain completely serious failed, and she laughed as he scooped her into his arms and carried her into the bathroom.

Chapter 12

Nate quietly stepped into the front downstairs bedroom that had been set up as a home office. It had made sense for Vivian to set up shop in here, where she'd have privacy to conduct whatever work she needed to take care of. When he set the fresh mug of coffee onto the coaster, he earned a thankful smile as she pressed a finger to her ear and the headphones for her online call.

"No, Wanda, this should work out fine. I'll send you my compiled list of agencies I think we should send your press release to, and we'll go from there. Uh-huh. I'm hoping to be back up and running sometime next week."

Nate offered an encouraging nod.

"Great. I'll check in with you then. Okay, bye." She clicked off and sagged back in the leather chair. "I could get used to this. Gorgeous view." She pointed out the front bay window that overlooked the sloping view of Owl Creek below. "Despite the constant run of construction trucks and crews."

Nate grimaced. The banging and buzzing of construction equipment had started right at eight. The fact that winter meant everyone was working on home interiors only made the noise echo louder, near as he could tell.

"Could be worse." They could be dealing with cement trucks and paving equipment.

"I also have coffee at my beck and call."

"Not just coffee." He bent to kiss her, determined to keep it quick, but, as always seemed to happen, the moment he tasted her, he wanted more.

"Stop." She laughed and pushed him away. "I've got one more client to call and a ton of emails to answer." She gestured to her laptop. "Give me an hour, maybe ninety minutes tops, then I'll be all yours."

"Sounds like a plan." He walked backward out of the room. "I'll check in with Fletcher and my lieutenant. See if there have been any developments."

She nodded and spun around in her chair, but not before he saw a flash of sadness in her eyes. Before he could ask, she was clicking into her video system to make another call.

Later, he told himself. He'd ask her what was bothering her when she wasn't as focused on work.

He returned to the kitchen, where he'd set up his own makeshift workstation at the table near the door to the backyard. He was already getting antsy, being stuck in one place, but the view helped. As did the woman who would soon be joining him.

He'd spent the better part of the morning digging through police reports that contained any mention of Marty DeBaccian, going back the last few years. Even if Lieutenant Haig had someone doing this already, it was research that felt like they were making progress. More information was power moving forward. There was little that irritated him more than being bored and useless, so he'd take what he could get.

He was compiling lists of any businesses mentioned, any suspected co-conspirators and even the names of former detectives and officers who had come across him. Leaving no stone unturned was the only way they were going to catch this guy.

No stone... Nate pursed his lips, stared at the screen and the list of detectives he'd been making. "Sullivan." It didn't sit well with him at all that the detective assigned to Vivian's case had done a disappearing act. In his experience, that meant one of two things.

Either Sullivan had gotten too close to something and DeBaccian had reacted or...

"Definitely leaning toward *or.*" He hated voicing it, hated the very idea of it, but there was no getting around the fact that Detective Jim Sullivan could very well be on DeBaccian's payroll.

Someone had to be, Nate reasoned. DeBaccian had been staying a good few steps ahead of law enforcement for a while now. Having someone on the inside of the Boise PD could explain that. Accusations like this were never made lightly, however. Even a false accusation of corruption could follow a cop around for the rest of his life, and if Sullivan was clean...

That thought didn't develop beyond that. He couldn't shake the feeling there was more going on, given Sullivan's recent disappearance. The timing couldn't be a coincidence.

Like Fletcher had said yesterday about their father's death: too many coincidences.

"Down the rabbit hole we go, then." He hunched over his laptop and got to work.

When his phone rang a little while later, he had to

remind himself how to use a flip phone to answer. Distracted, he all but growled a greeting.

"Catch you at a bad time, Detective?" Lieutenant Haig's voice sounded surprisingly lighthearted.

"No, sir, sorry." Nate cringed, pushed his laptop back and blinked his eyes wide to clear the blur. "I've been doing some digging." Tapping his pen against one of the notepads on the table, he wondered how best to approach this.

"I just got a call from the hospital," Haig told him. "Wexler's stable enough for surgery. They're taking him in later today."

Finally, Nate thought. *Progress.* "What's his prognosis?"

"Fifty-fifty." Nate could all but hear his commanding officer's shrug. "If he comes through, we should be able to question him in a day or two."

A day or two. He gazed around the house that, because of Vivian, felt more like a home than his own ever had. It would be a shame to leave it. And her. "Sounds good, sir."

"Good to hear it. Now, tell me about your digging."

"Ah." Nate glanced over his shoulder as Vivian came in. Barefoot and with her hair loose and long around her shoulders, she wore silky, flowy pants that hung low on her hips, along with a short-sleeved shirt. The color reminded him of the syringa, Idaho's state flower. She looked like a summer oasis in the middle of a snowy, frigid winter. "I'm not entirely sure you'd approve of where I've been excavating, sir."

Vivian frowned at him, as if trying to decipher his

code. She walked over to sit across from him, pointed to some of his notes as if asking permission. He nodded.

"Then it's a good thing this isn't an official call," Lieutenant Haig said. "Out with it, Colton."

"I've been looking for a connection between DeBaccian and Sullivan." Before giving his boss a chance to push back, he plowed ahead. "It's just a thought, and a rough one, but unless Sullivan's popped back up—"

"He has not. I sent a couple of patrol officers to his place this morning under the guise of a wellness check. His car's gone. No sign of him. We're hoping to locate his wife—"

"Officially separated as of last year," Nate said. "Near as I can tell, neither has filed for divorce. Haven't been able to track where she's gone."

"So he's rudderless," Haig murmured. "Okay, I'll get someone to track her down. Did you find the connection you were hoping for?"

Hoping wasn't exactly the word. Nate couldn't think of any police officer who hoped to find evidence of a dirty cop. "Maybe." He shuffled through his notes as Vivian rested her bare feet on the bottom rung of her chair. "Seven years ago, DeBaccian was arrested as a suspect in a string of electronics store burglaries. Sullivan was one of the investigating detectives."

"Is that it?"

Like Fletcher, Nate trusted his gut. And his gut told him there was something more. "The case was dismissed when one of the key pieces of evidence went missing. Security tape footage." He scrolled through the online evidence-storage database. "The assistant DA prosecuting the case had the evidence brought to her office. A day later, she had it sent back. According to her statement, she placed everything back in the box before it was picked up. When they retrieved it for court, the recordings were gone."

"Whatever it is you don't want to say—"

"Detective Sullivan was responsible for the transport, sir. According to the sign-in sheet, he was the last person to have access to the evidence box."

"All right, then." Haig lowered his voice. "Keep following this where you can. Put it together for me but keep it with you. Right now, there's no place safer for any evidence against DeBaccian than with you in Owl Creek."

"Yes, sir. Anything else, sir?"

"Not at the moment, no. I'll check in once I get word on Wexler's condition."

Nate slapped his phone closed. "You get all that?"

"I did." Vivian nodded as she flipped through his scribbled notes. "Looks like we're both making progress where our jobs are concerned. I've officially moved into the world of new client referrals."

"Yeah?" He wasn't entirely sure what that meant, but she seemed happy about it.

"Oh, yeah. Someone recommended me to this digital content company out of Texas. Their website certainly makes them sound promising." She frowned. "I had to email them and let them know I wasn't available for a consult for a while yet. But if they're really interested, they'll wait."

"Because you're the best at what you do," Nate said.

"Yes." She straightened in her chair, a hint of surprise in her eyes. "Yes, I am."

"Hopefully, we'll have you back to your life sooner

than later. My lieutenant called to let me know Wexler is going in for surgery sometime today. If he wakes up and talks, I'm hoping we won't need your testimony against DeBaccian."

"A girl can dream." She flipped more of the pages of his notepads. "You really think Detective Sullivan is a bad cop?"

"The more I look into him, the more it looks that way." Despite needing to, this wasn't something he felt any pleasure in undertaking. "Personally, I just want him found so we at least know where he is." DeBaccian coming after Vivian was one thing. Like Max said at the station, criminals often let their egos get the better of them.

But having a trained cop hunting her? A person who knew the ins and outs of protecting witnesses, who understood how the police went about their jobs in the most detailed of ways? The very thought made the bitter coffee churn in his stomach. Her face tightened. The tension he'd been hoping would melt away for them surged. "You know what I saw out on the back patio?" He stood up, carried his coffee to the sink and set it to soak. "A hot tub."

Vivian looked out the window, into the graying, threatening sky, then back to him. "In December?"

"You've never been in a hot tub when it's snowing?"

"Ah, no." She laughed, shook her head. "Is that really a thing?"

"Let's find out." He returned to the table, held out his hand.

She didn't look convinced as she grabbed hold and allowed him to pull her up. "Funnily enough, I didn't think to pack a swimsuit."

He grinned and tugged her close, kissed her hard. "Neither did I."

Her brow arched, and she pulled her hands free, slipped them beneath the hem of his dark T-shirt. "Well, in that case…"

When Vivian was little, before her parents died and before discovering the unpredictability of life, one of her favorite games to play had been "house."

She'd recruited her dolls and stuffed animals, lining them up on the bed while she cooked pretend food on the pretend cardboard stove her father had made for her out of an old shipping box. On occasion, she'd snuck into the kitchen, opened the cabinets she could reach and pilfered whatever items her mother had stashed away. A bag of rice. A potato. A dented can of tomatoes. She'd spent hours "feeding" her companions as she talked to them, telling them about all the fun things they were going to do together.

Funny. Vivian sliced through an onion and set to chopping. She'd never imagined playing house again since becoming an adult. But being here, now, with Nate, it felt exactly like that. She wouldn't outgrow it this time, but she would have to leave it behind when everything was resolved and life returned to normal.

Her eyes filled with tears, but she had the perfect excuse. She turned and slid the chopped onions off the cutting board and into the pan that had been heating on the stove.

Post—hot tub—and they'd definitely given it a workout in more ways than one—he'd returned to his computer, losing himself in chasing down the people who meant to do her harm. To prevent her from returning to that normal she'd existed in.

Normal.

The word didn't seem quite so defined any longer.

It hadn't taken her more than waking up in Nate's arms to realize that aching void of loneliness she'd lived with for so long was gone. She pressed her lips together hard, wiped the back of her hand under her eyes as she sorted through the meager selection of dried herbs.

She'd run on a handful of emotions her entire life, and never to extremes. Anxiety had tamped all that down and back to where, most of the time, she didn't have to acknowledge or deal with it. But being with Nate, loving Nate, she couldn't help but feel as if every emotion possible had jumped on board the spinning carousel that was her heart.

Loving Nate. She squeezed her eyes shut. She'd almost said it last night. Before she'd let herself think about it. Before she'd come to terms with it. It was one thing to fall in love with a man. It was quite another to admit it out loud and have him with no way to escape.

"So, what's for dinner?" Nate's domestic-tinged question had her thinking of her long-lost stuffed animals and dolls and how they'd remained silent. And forever perfect in her memory.

"Pasta." She had to assume it was Sloan, Ruby and Kiki who had stocked the kitchen, and they'd done so with an overabundance of attention to carbs. "I'm making my homemade meat sauce."

"Sounds great." He flashed her a smile. The way he looked at her—even as he plowed through the potential criminal activity of a fellow cop—had those unbelievable fairy tales surging to the surface of her thoughts once more.

"I'd have made bread, but I didn't have time." Time to get back to the teasing and playing of the relationship. "Someone distracted me in the hot tub."

"Totally worth it," he said. The humor in his voice sounded forced. His cell phone vibrated to the point of dancing across the table. He flipped it open. "It's my lieutenant."

Vivian turned the flame down on the stove, grabbed a towel and circled the island.

"Sir? Any word on Wexler?"

She stood beside him, tempted to touch him, but also worried it was too familiar a gesture. How was it she could share a bed with this man, make love with this man, and still be afraid? Not of him. But of what he made her feel. Even now, she could see the concern on his face, and she knew it was because of her.

He was a man dedicated to his job, so by extension she was his concern. And maybe, for a little while, a distraction.

"Okay. Great. Thanks for letting me know. Yeah." His gaze met hers, and in those blue depths, she saw a glimmer of hope. "I'm just about done with my report. I'll check in with you tomorrow. Yes, sir. Thank you."

He clicked the phone closed and sagged back in his seat. "Wexler's surgery went well."

"Yeah?"

"They got the bullet, but most importantly, he's stable. Lieutenant Haig thinks we'll be able to talk to him as early as tomorrow."

"That's great news." She let out a sigh she hoped

would be heard as relieved. "That should make your job a little easier."

"We'll see. You know what's even better?" He collected his papers, stacked them up and, after hitting Save, closed his laptop. "I'm calling it a day. Just in time, too, since it's after five."

"Keeping bankers' hours now, are you?" She returned to the kitchen and searched for a cheese grater. She found one, on a shelf under the center island. When she popped back up, he was standing across from her, hands planted on the gold-specked black marble countertop.

"Can I help?"

"I don't know." She eyed him. "How good are you in the kitchen?"

That grin of his reappeared.

She was onto him this time. Even as she laughed, she held up both hands. "Oh, no. Not again. Not now."

"Why not now?" He challenged, stalking around the counter in a very precise and familiar way.

"Because nothing interferes with me making my meat sauce." She turned, tried to dive away, but he caught her around the waist, spun her around and straight into his arms. "Nate—"

Whatever else she was going to say was caught by his mouth. His wonderful, talented, undeniably tempting mouth. Bittersweet tears burned the back of her eyes. She felt so lucky, to be wanted by him. And he wanted her. There was no denying that.

When he lifted his mouth, and she blinked dazedly up at him, he reached out and turned off the stove. "What room would you like to try next?"

* * *

Nate's eyes snapped open.

What was that?

He sat up, dislodging the blanket he'd dragged over them from the back of the sofa. Mind racing, he jumped to his feet, shoved both hands into his hair. "Vivian?" Her name all but echoed through the kitchen and great room.

The tree lights burned yet again. The remnants of the pasta dinner she'd finally found time to make for them still sat on the stove. Food didn't come close to satiating him, not since he'd gotten his first taste of her. But something felt...

Wearing only his jeans, he retrieved his gun from where he'd left it and his holster on the back of a kitchen chair. Something... He turned, scanned the room. Something was different.

He froze, listened. An empty house had an entirely different feel to it. The energy was lower but nonetheless heavier. As if the silence were pressing in on him.

"Vivian?" he called again as he searched the first floor. No sign of her.

He raced to the stairs, skidding to a halt with one hand on the banister. His keys. He'd kept them on the small marble table by the front door. They were gone.

He walked to the door, heart pounding.

It had been left ajar.

He swore, pulled the gun free and tossed the holster to the floor. He carefully placed his bare foot in the opening and pulled open the door.

The cold blast of air hit him like an avalanche. Locking his jaw, he stepped onto the porch, weapon poised at his side, ready to react.

"Vivian?"

He heard it again. A *click*. A *beep*. He swung toward the SUV he'd parked in the driveway. Gun raised, he made quick work of the path, circling down and around to the car, which, only now could he see, had its passenger door open.

Nate almost forgot to breathe until he saw two feet dangling from a pair of white pants. He grabbed the door and yanked it all the way open. "Vivian!"

She yelped, sat up and nearly slipped right off the seat. "Geez, Nate." She glared at him, pressed a hand to her chest. "Who needs a hitman chasing them when I've got you?"

"What. Are you. Doing?" It took every ounce of patience he had to quell his anger. "You aren't supposed to leave the house. Especially not without telling me."

"You wouldn't have heard me, anyway. You were snoring." She snapped the glove box shut and got out of the car.

"I do not snore."

She rolled her eyes. "I wanted to get my phone." She waggled it in front of him. "Okay?"

"Not okay." He snatched it from her hand. "Who were you going to call?"

"I wasn't—" She scrunched her mouth like a petulant toddler. "None of your business. Give it to me."

"No." He held it up over his head, well out of her reach.

"Give me my phone, Nate." She jumped once, twice, then growled and stepped back, slammed the car door so hard his teeth rattled. "I'm well aware of your sensitive areas, *Detective*, so unless you want them to meet my knee—"

"You don't have anyone to call," he reminded her. "Lizzy's out of town, and everyone else is a client. So I ask again." His patience wore thin. "Who were you going to call?"

She straightened, an odd, dim light flashing in her eyes that had him lowering his arm. "I wasn't going to *call* anyone."

With unnerving speed, she snatched the phone out of his grasp and spun on her bare heels. Head down, she turned on her phone. The glare of the screen cut through the darkness of the night.

Feeling ridiculous, he trailed after her. "Vivian, what is this all—"

"Here, okay?" She shoved the screen in his face. The screen that displayed a picture of Toby. Her cat. "I was missing him. I woke up and saw that stupid box with his ashes, and I was missing my cat, and I didn't have…" She stopped, tears glistening in her eyes. "I didn't want to wake you up and ask permission to see his pictures."

"Vivian." He heard it, the sympathy, the pity that had anger erasing the grief he saw on her face.

"There!" She stabbed a finger into his face. "Right there. I didn't want that. Just…forget it." She made it only a few steps before a car, headlights blazing, turned the corner.

His hand tightened around his gun. "Get inside."

"Nate?" He heard the fear, the uncertainty, but she didn't move toward the house. She moved toward him. The car stopped.

Nate shoved her behind him, feet braced apart; he

watched, then gaped and rolled his eyes as he glared at the familiar face beyond the window as it slid down.

"Just checking the neighborhood to make sure all is calm." Max Colton leaned over, his expression, as always, unreadable. "'Tis the season, you know."

"Seriously, Max?"

"Della's working late, so I told Fletcher I'd just drive past." He shrugged. "I'd ask what the two of you are doing out here this late at night, but I'm not entirely sure I want to know."

Nate could feel Vivian shiver behind him. "Go on back inside, Vivian. Please." He could only hope his more solicitous tone would work better than his irritated one had. He didn't like to admit it, but scared was not a mode he operated well in. And finding her gone from the house had definitely scared him. "You want to come in?"

Max's eyes went wide with surprise. "You sure?" He watched Vivian make it up the path. "I've got time before picking Della up, but I don't want to intrude."

"Just park already." Funny how easily they'd fallen into the big-brother/little-brother routine. Nate wasn't entirely sure he was comfortable with that. Nate headed inside before his feet turned to blocks of ice.

"I put the coffee on." Vivian was already headed up the stairs. "I'm going to bed."

"Don't put the card back in your phone. We don't want anyone tra—" The second the words were out of his mouth he wanted to take them back.

"Thank you, yes." She gave him a look that had previously active parts of him withering. "As I have the IQ of a turnip, I was in need of the reminder."

"Wow." Max closed the door behind him as Vivian

went upstairs. "Chilly in here." He detoured straight past him into the kitchen.

"It's December," Nate called as he retrieved his holster and keys and followed. "It's chilly everywhere." But his brother had a point.

Something told him he was about to experience his first-ever deep freeze where Vivian was concerned.

Chapter 13

Vivian prided herself on not dwelling on the dumber things she'd done in her life. Picking a fight with Nate over her phone—and Toby's pictures—would no doubt remain at the top of that list for the foreseeable future. At least that was the thought she woke up to late the next morning.

That she found herself staring at the box containing her cat's ashes rather than debating how to extricate herself from her lover's arms didn't seem an ideal way to start the day. Like most people, she didn't do well with being embarrassed or being caught. Of course, she'd overreacted last night, but honestly, she hadn't expected to take more than a few minutes to retrieve her phone.

Still feeling cranky, she slugged out of bed and took a shower, got dressed and headed downstairs. She found Nate eyes-deep in his laptop, and while it didn't improve her mood, she was grateful for the distraction. And the delay in needing to apologize.

"Sleep okay?" Nate asked as she poured herself some coffee.

"Well enough." She'd slept like crap, but criminals weren't the only ones susceptible to ego. Hers had definitely been dented, but mostly by her own behavior. "I'm sorry I worried you last night."

"I'm sorry I overreacted. When I woke up to an empty house, I got scared. The things that went through my head—"

"Blame your car." She pulled open the fridge despite having no appetite for breakfast. "If the stupid alarm thing would have disconnected on the first try, you never would have known I was gone."

"I'll make a note to share that with the manufacturer."

She squeezed her eyes shut. She did not want to fall further under his charm. They couldn't afford for her to. "Nate—"

He was standing behind the fridge door when she closed it.

"Yes?"

She had so many questions for him. What happens after she isn't in danger any longer? What happens if they don't catch DeBaccian? What happens if Wexler dies and she ends up having to testify in the murder trial?

What was going to happen to them when there wasn't a case pulling them together? Or ripping them apart?

None of those questions made their way out of her mouth. Instead, she retrieved her coffee and moved away. "How long did Max stay last night?"

"Long enough to clean up the kitchen."

"Oh." She frowned, hoisted herself up onto one of the barstools and sipped. "Dishes. Totally slipped my mind."

"Worked out okay," Nate assured her. "I told him he could eat whatever he wanted in exchange. You earned his seal of approval as far as meat sauce goes. And he might have taken a container of it home to share with Della."

"That's fine." There was always more sauce to be made. "I think we need to talk."

"I'm glad you're the one to say it." He leaned his arms on the counter and pinned her with those blue eyes of his. "Or *am* I?"

She frowned, confusion finally taking hold despite her best efforts to avoid it. "What's going to happen when this case is over?"

He hesitated, but didn't pull his gaze from hers. "I'm going to assume you don't mean with DeBaccian and the justice system."

She inclined her head. "I don't... I don't know how to do this, Nate. Getting caught up in all this excitement and danger, it's been a bit of a mind-spinner for me. You have been. And I'm afraid we're becoming blind to the reality of our situations."

"Right." He nodded, then shook his head. "Nope, sorry. Not getting it at all."

"Do we just stop everything now, before it gets too messy?" she asked. "Or do we take it as far as we can go and then worry about it? If I have to testify, the DA probably won't like the fact we slept together—"

"It's none of the DA's business—"

"Nate." She dropped her voice and the shield of protection she'd been unwittingly wielding. "Of course it's his business. You don't want the case corrupted because you were sleeping with your main witness. But that's neither here nor—"

"I don't want to stop." He blurted it out so fast he seemed to have surprised himself. "Seeing you. Sleeping with you. Being with you." He shoved his hand into his hair and sighed. "I had a feeling I was going to botch this up. Okay." Nate took a long, deep breath. "Okay, let me come at this a different way. Once this is all over, however it ends, I would like to continue to see you. Socially." He frowned. "Why does it sound like I just stepped out of a Jane Austen book?"

She tried to catch the laugh behind her lips but didn't quite manage.

"Look." He leaned on the counter again, only this time he reached across to capture her hands in his. "I don't know how to do this, either. You're a new experience for me, Vivian. This...thing between us. It feels special. Like a gift. And I don't want to walk away from it before we find out if it's something serious, we can make a go of."

She wanted to believe him. All her life, she'd wanted to belong to someone, anyone, who was willing to put their heart on the line for her. But thirty years of life can tarnish even the most hopeful of dreams. "You're no Jane Austen hero," she said finally. "Mainly because none of them ever say so much at one time. I..." She'd told him the other night she'd felt as if she'd been awakened, thrown into a life she'd only been a passive participant in up until now. He was giving her a chance to embrace that fully.

What a fool she'd be to walk away from everything being offered to her. Even if it was for a fraction of time.

"I would like to continue to see you, socially, as well. Maybe even carnally," she added in a moment of inspiration. She earned a smile and his raised brows. "And maybe we'll both be more clearheaded about the future once we don't have this whole DeBaccian thing looming over us. Speaking of..." She looked over her shoulder to the kitchen table, which was once again a mess. "Did you finish your report for your lieutenant?"

"I did." He released her and turned back to the fridge. "I worked some things out with Max. He suggested I run it past Fletcher, too."

She wasn't going to discourage him from spending more time with his brother.

"You hungry?" He bent down and pulled a box of frozen waffles out of the freezer.

"Seriously?" She narrowed her eyes.

"Yeah, why?" Nate looked at the bright yellow box. "What's wrong with—"

"You want waffles, I'll fix waffles." She joined him on the other side of the counter, dropped the box back into the freezer, then grabbed his shirt and pulled him toward her for a kiss. It was, to her mind at least, a new start. A reboot, so to speak. Something she planned to use to keep the hope she was determined to cling to alive. "Go clean up the table while I try to remember where I saw a waffle iron."

"Remind me to talk to Chase about the noise level around here," Nate grumbled as he tossed the remote onto the coffee table and gave up on whatever the plot might be of the movie Vivian had chosen. "Those trucks are driving me nuts."

"Just block them out." She sat beside him on the sofa, her bare toes tucked under his thighs as she typed away on her laptop. "I've got a pair of headphones in my bag if you think they might help."

"No. It's fine." He sighed and dropped his head back on the sofa. "Sorry. I'm just…"

"Antsy?"

"Frustrated."

"And bored?"

He rolled his head to the side, expecting to find her looking at him, but instead all her interest was on her screen.

"Go get your cell phone," she said. "You must have some kind of game or something on there you like."

"I don't want to play any games. With my phone," he added and earned a roll of her eyes.

"What time are you supposed to meet with Fletcher in town?"

"I'm not going."

"What?" She had something akin to panic in her eyes when she looked at him. "Why not?"

"Because you're here and I'm charged with protecting you. I'm not leaving you here alone."

"Are you suggesting I come with you?"

"No." They needed to keep her locked up tight until they had DeBaccian in custody, and last he heard, that wasn't remotely close to happening. "No, you need to stay here."

She sighed and closed her laptop. "Nate, go."

"Nope."

"If you don't—" her voice had an almost too sweet quality to it "—Fletcher's going to have another crime scene to worry about. One that involves your murder." Her smile promised much pain. "I've got plenty to work on getting ready to pitch to this next client. Plus, Harlow's got some new interest from a production company.

I know how to operate the security system and the panic button. Plus, there's security down at the guard gate. If anything happens, I'll hit that first and call you second."

"On what?" he countered. "You won't have a cell phone."

"I have one." She opened her computer again. "I'm just not allowed to use it as anything other than a photo album."

He didn't move. But he was thinking.

"The faster you close this case, the sooner we can get started on a real relationship." How she could make perfect sense to him and keep typing away like that was a multitasking miracle. "Go meet with your brother. I'll be fine. I won't leave the house. I won't even use the hot tub if it makes you feel better."

A car door slammed outside, followed by the quick staccato sound of heels against the concrete. He was up and moving even before the doorbell rang. When he pulled it open, he felt both relief and uncertainty.

"Lizzy."

"Hi, Nate." His half sister, with her long, strawberry blond hair draped over her slim shoulders, flashed familiar, worried blue eyes at him. "Ajay and I just got home this morning. I ran into Sloan in town, and she told me..." She peered around him, her gaze frantic. "She told me Vivian's here? Where is she?"

"Lizzy?" Vivian stepped clear of the hall, a surprised smile on her face. "Yes, I'm here. It's okay. I'm right here."

"Oh, my gosh, Vivian!" Lizzy pushed past him and enveloped Vivian in a hug so tight Nate could feel it himself. "You're okay! When Sloan told me... I imagined all sorts of horrible things."

Vivian looked over Lizzy's shoulder at him, and he immediately regretted not pushing Vivian harder to call her friend. His sister.

"What on earth is happening?" Lizzy demanded. "What are you doing here in Owl Creek? In this house? Sloan said you were shot at? That you're some kind of witness to an attempted murder?" She swung on Nate. "Tell me what's going on, please? Why didn't you call me? You should have called me."

"Okay, Lizzy, stop." Vivian surprised Nate by grabbing Lizzy's arms and spinning her back around to face her. "Everything's fine. I will tell you everything, I promise. But all you need to know right now is that Nate's been watching over me, and I'm here and safe because of him. Okay?" She touched a hand to his sister's cheek. "No need to spiral. Everything's fine. It's going to be fine." She looked to Nate again. "I promise."

He understood. She wanted him to know that he was an integral part of making certain her promise was kept.

"Okay." Lizzy sighed and sagged a bit. Nate closed the door and followed them back to the kitchen. "Okay, I'm sorry. I kind of freaked out after talking to Sloan. Sometimes, I swear it's like this switch gets flipped, and I—"

"You've been through a lot lately," Vivian assured her. "Which is why I didn't want to call you just yet. Sit down." Vivian pointed to the kitchen table.

"Should I make coffee?" Nate offered.

"Don't think she needs any caffeine," Vivian muttered under her breath. "How about some tea? We've got plenty of that, so hot water will do. Tell you what, Nate. Since you were worried about leaving me alone, why don't you take off and go see Fletcher, and Lizzy can stay here? Get this whole ball in motion, yeah?"

"You sure?" Nate eyed Lizzy.

"I'm sure," Vivian said as he gathered up his things. "I can handle this. And you need to get out of here before you go stir-crazy."

He both liked and didn't like the fact she recognized that about him. "Lizzy, can you stay with her until I get back?" Nate asked.

"Sure." Lizzy nodded and shrugged. "Sure. I'm not meeting Ajay at The Tides until five."

"Five, okay. Got it." Nate checked his watch. That gave him a few hours. "I'll be back by then for sure. Vivian?" He inclined his head to draw her over. "I've never seen her like this."

"You haven't been kidnapped before," Vivian said quietly. "It comes in waves. Most of the time, I've been around for her to confide in. You Coltons are pretty good at keeping your feelings to yourself." She arched a brow at him. "Never show any weakness, right?"

"Tell me she's getting professional help."

"We've talked about it." Vivian looked back as Lizzy wandered over to look out the back glass doors. "We'll be talking about it again. And hey, we have a few more things in common now. Me with the flying bullets and killer SUVs. Her with… Yeah." She steered him to the door. "It'll all be fine. Just give us some time."

"Some." He was already counting the minutes until he could get back. "But not a lot."

It took two full mugs of tea before Vivian felt as if Lizzy was back on even keel. She'd bet just about every penny in her bank account that Lizzy Colton had kept things together for everyone else. There was an unexpected burst of pride in knowing that Lizzy felt comfortable enough to break down in front of her. But it also waved a red flag. Trauma was tricky and insidious and often snuck up to slap its victims when they least expected it.

A lesson for Lizzy, Vivian wondered. Or herself?

"I'm so embarrassed." Lizzy curled up in the corner of the sofa, a half-full mug clutched between her hands as Vivian dug out one of the many packages of cookies that had been left hidden around the kitchen. "I can only imagine what Nate might think."

"I can tell you exactly what he was thinking." Vivian pulled out four crunchy chocolate chip cookies, set them on a plate, then left those on the counter and brought the entire package over. "He's worried about you. Here." She handed Lizzy the package and plopped down beside her. "Which means congratulations, you're now on his list of people to take care of." She snatched a cookie and bit in. "Welcome to the club."

Lizzy's eyes had stopped spinning more than an hour ago, once Vivian had gone through everything that had transpired since she'd first walked into Madariaga's. She'd felt odd rehashing everything, as if it were some kind of story she'd committed to memory.

"Is that a club I'm happy to belong to?" Lizzy's knowing look had Vivian squirming in her seat. "You and Nate? You're…together, right?"

"We are." Vivian had wondered how her best friend would feel about her getting involved with Nate. Given the strained family dynamic at the moment, there was no way to predict what was coming next. "Do you remember telling me the first time that you met Ajay?"

Lizzy ducked her chin, but not before Vivian saw the healthy pink tint to her cheeks. "I have a vague recollection of that conversation."

Considering the amount of wine that had been poured that evening, Vivian was impressed. "When I was sitting there, listening to you, all I could think at the time was that you were still caught up in the excitement of everything that had happened. That you were, I don't know, too susceptible to his charm. That you'd fallen as much for the romance of the situation as you had for him."

"You think being kidnapped was romantic?"

"No, of course not," Vivian said. She wasn't explaining this very well. "I think the end result has proven itself out though. You seem to have this, I don't know, calmness about you." Despite the anxiety that had sprung up. "As if you've stopped looking for something you were unaware you needed." Vivian sipped her tea, considered her words carefully. "The first time I saw Nate, sitting at that bar, that kind of warning in his eyes, like he was already protecting me, I don't know if I can explain it."

"Like finding your other half?" Lizzy suggested.

"No." She didn't need someone to complete her. "It was like being around him unlocked my other half." Her silent, intimidated half. Even now, the doubt remained. But since her conversation with Nate, her faith was stronger. "I'm not…afraid around him."

"Afraid? Oh, Vivian." Lizzy tilted her head.

"I mean I'm not afraid to be myself. There's no expectations. No show to put on. I don't have to impress him or pretend to be something or someone I'm not. He sees me." The admission lifted her heart. "Who I really am. And he has from the start. Everything I never thought I would have has clicked into place. Which brings me to a question I have for you."

"For me?" Lizzy frowned. "What about?"

"About Nate. And me. Lizzy, you're the best friend I've ever had. The only friend, really." She was already slipping into excuse mode, something she knew Nate would call her on. "But given everything that's going on with your mom and finding out about Nate and Sarah…" She screwed up her courage and just put it out there. "You're okay with me dating him, aren't you? I don't want to complicate things further."

"I could approach this question in a couple of ways." Lizzy ate another cookie, sipped her tea, looked at Vivian over the top of her mug. "But I'm not going to draw this out any longer than necessary. What's going on where Nate and Sarah and the rest of the family is concerned has nothing to do with you. There's only one thing I've ever wanted for you, Vivian. To be happy. And to be honest, until I saw you with him before he left, I don't think I ever have seen that side of him. You care about him, don't you?"

"I love him." The simple statement rocked the foundation of her life. "I haven't told him, of course." She laughed a little. Cried a little. "I haven't lost all my senses." But the time was coming when she would. She had to. If for no other reason than to put her heart out there one more time.

Lizzy's eyes filled. "Then take that ride with him, Vivian. Don't let go. Even when things get difficult or complicated or… I think he's probably worth it. You're right. About the family. Things are weird and frustrating, but everything I know about him—that he stands up for his family, even when he doesn't really know us? That's about as good a guy as you can find." She grinned. "That said, you might want to give him fair warning that he and I are about to become a lot closer because where you go, I go. End of story."

"Okay, then." Another weight she hadn't realized she was carrying lifted off her shoulders. "I'll do just that. And I'll go on that ride." For however long it may last.

Chapter 14

Sitting across from Fletcher in his office at the Owl Creek Police Department, Nate watched his brother read through the report he'd put together on Detective Jim Sullivan and his plausible connection to Marty DeBaccian. The situation reminded Nate of his trips to the principal's office once upon a time.

Either his brother read at the speed of a comatose turtle, or Fletcher was committing every word Nate had written to memory. The only thing that made the waiting tolerable was Max, who, seated on the side cabinet by the door, kept rustling an open bag of chips that he'd found in the break room.

Nate checked his watch. The afternoon was ticking away, but he had plenty of time to get back to Vivian before Lizzy left. Storm clouds had accompanied them on the drive, which meant the snow would be coming in hard and fast. All the more reason to get all of this behind them.

"So, Lizzy," Max said between crunches. "How'd she seem when you saw her?"

Fletcher's gaze didn't flicker from the printed file Nate had run off as soon as he got to the station.

"Stressed." It was, Nate thought, the best word he could think of to describe their sister. "Worried. I think she might need some assistance dealing with what happened to her last month."

Max nodded, dug deeper into the bag. "I thought the same thing before Ajay took her away for some downtime. Good to know we're all on the same page."

"We'll make sure Lizzy gets whatever help she needs." Fletcher sat forward in his squeaky chair. "Vivian's always been a solid support person for her. It's good Lizzy showed up at the house. Means she's getting back on track. I appreciate you running this past me before sending it to your lieutenant."

"Figured it would be safer to send it from here on one of your more secure computers than from the house." Nate pointed to the pages Fletcher had insisted on printing out. "Took some finagling to track down all of Sullivan's logins for the past few years. Seeing the cases he was keeping an eye on tells me that when we get him into custody, we should look beyond DeBaccian. He's worked in a number of departments over the years, which means he's had access to more information than I feel comfortable with at the moment."

"No, I think you're exactly right," Fletcher agreed. "And I think the sooner we shoot this over to Boise PD, the better." He glanced at Max. "You've read this?"

"I have." Max chomped a chip. "Last night. Early this morning," he corrected.

"Thoughts?"

Max wrapped up the bag and set it aside. "I think, once Sullivan's been questioned, he might prove quite beneficial to a number of federal investigations currently on the books. Half the names DeBaccian has been in contact with are being actively investigated. More to the point, if you can flip Sullivan, you get him a deal to turn on DeBaccian and you remove Vivian from the equation altogether, which, let's face it, would be a major win for everyone involved."

"Not going to argue with that." Nate nodded. "I'm anxious to head back to Boise and try to put this whole thing to bed."

"Yeah, well, that isn't happening just yet," Fletcher said in a warning voice. "You're about to bust open what is tantamount to a nationwide organized crime ring. The longer you keep your head down, the better."

"Actually…" Max slapped his hands together before wiping them on his jeans. "I was going to recommend the opposite. Make some noise. Get down there and pull the attention off Vivian."

"Give DeBaccian a bigger target, you mean," Fletcher clarified.

"The second this report of Nate's hits the Boise PD system, all hell is going to break loose," Max went on. "Unless either of you can convince me that the server and anyone with access are locked down one-hundred-percent."

Nate considered it, and he didn't like the implied suggestion. "You're thinking Sullivan isn't the only one we should be worried about."

"Where there's one bad apple…" Max trailed off. "There's something to be said for scaring the crap out of people, even cops. Makes them do stupid things. Careless things."

"It also might push someone into coming forward

with information you can actually use as evidence against Sullivan." Fletcher nodded. "It isn't a horrible idea."

"You do have a way with compliments, Fletch," Max said.

"I don't know." Nate's reluctance had more to do with the idea of leaving Vivian alone even longer than planned.

"I can have one of my deputies sit on the house, if that's what's stopping you," Fletcher said. "Unless Max wants to take on protection detail?"

"Can't." Max slapped his hands together. "I'm going to Boise with our baby brother. Just to make sure he stays out of trouble."

Nate waited for the irritation. Or the embarrassment at his newly acquired nickname. Neither descended. But a smile lurked. A smile that came far more easily since Vivian had entered his life. One thing he'd learned in the past few days was that there was definitely a lot more to life than just work.

Fletcher laughed as his phone rang. He answered with a brusque "Detective Colton."

"Do people get confused, do you think?" Nate asked Max. "With all the Coltons in law enforcement."

"Nah," Max said easily. "We all sound different."

"Hang on, Lieutenant." Fletcher eyed Nate. "Let me put you on Speaker." He tapped a button on his phone, hung up the receiver. "You're on with me, Nate and our brother, Max Colton, who's a special consultant. You want to go through that one more time?"

"What's going on?" Nate asked his boss.

"We found a set of partials in the SUV that ran

Ms. Maylor off the road," Lieutenant Haig reported. "I went with your gut, Nate. I ran them against Sullivan's. They're a match."

Nate swore. So Sullivan had tried to kill Vivian. "He must have followed her from the station house."

"Probably," Haig said. "I've got Renard and Paulson running the security footage from the station to confirm. I've got an arrest warrant in the works."

"What about DeBaccian?" Max asked. "Any sighting of him yet?"

"None." And Lieutenant Haig didn't sound pleased about it. "But I'm not giving up hope. He's out there. We'll find him. In the meantime, Nate, I'm afraid your presence is required."

"In Boise?" He shook his head when Max opened his mouth, no doubt to tell Nate's CO they were already planning to head south. "Why?"

"You have a confidential informant on record who goes by the name Ferret Face?"

"Yeah." Nate frowned. "Real name's Colin Michaels He's a hacker. Specializes in virus creation. Nasty ones that take down entire computer systems, but usually only for his own amusement. Did he call in with some intel?" Odd. He hadn't heard from Ferret in months.

"Not exactly," Haig said. "Someone tried to kill him a few hours ago."

"Tried?" Nate couldn't quite process. "And failed?"

"He's still alive. A bit crispy around the edges, though," Haig told them. "Said he did a job for someone, only instead of paying, they tried to shoot him. Bullet grazed his head, and he played dead. Then tried to put out the fire they set to take out his network with his bare hands."

"Ouch." Max winced.

"First I've heard of Ferret going commercial," Nate said. "Makes sense, I suppose. He's been putting his younger sister through college, and his mother's had medical expenses."

"Is that information in your CI file?" Fletcher asked.

Nate nodded. "Sure." He liked being able to use specific motivations when approaching one of his sources for information. Ferret might be one of the smartest computer hackers he'd come across, but compared to other criminals Nate had dealt with, the guy was a kitty cat.

"Did he say who hired him, Lieutenant?" Fletcher asked.

"That's the problem," Haig said. "He's not saying anything. He'll only talk to Nate. Either him, or he'll lawyer up. We've got him in an interview room, but he's going to start asking for additional medical attention pretty soon. I'd rather not take him out of the station until we have to."

"Ferret's always been wiggy," Nate told his brothers. "Makes sense he'd get more squirrely after something like this." If someone had tried to kill a rather insignificant hacker like Ferret, he must have taken on a really big job.

"Yeah, well, Mr. Wiggy underestimated our lab techs," Haig said. "They tapped into the security feed at his warehouse hideout." Haig paused. "Did Ferret ever mention Sullivan to you, Nate?"

"No." Nate couldn't make sense of this. "Cops don't poach other cops' CIs." What would Sullivan want with Ferret Face?

"Sullivan's not other cops," Fletcher said. "Lieutenant, I'm sending you the report Nate's put together on

Sullivan. Right…" He turned his attention back to his desktop and clicked a few buttons. "Now. You should have it soon. In the meantime—"

"I'm on my way," Nate told his boss. "I can be there in—"

"*We'll* be there in a little under an hour." Fletcher hung up on Haig and headed for the door, grabbed his jacket off the hook. "Work out who's riding shotgun," he told Nate and Max. "Because we aren't stopping once we hit the siren."

"I should not have drunk so much tea." Lizzy straightened her pale yellow shirt as she came out of the bathroom. "I'm going to be lucky to make the drive before I have to pee again."

Vivian smiled, closed the door to the refrigerator, where she'd been taking mental inventory so she could figure out what to fix Nate for dinner. "Yes, well, I'm sure you'll have a great night with Ajay, nonetheless."

"Oh, I know I will." Lizzy's cheery smile was back in place, a welcome sight compared to how she'd looked when she first arrived. "I'd say we'll have to compare notes in the morning, but seeing as it's my brother you're seeing…" She gave a little shudder. "Yeah, best not to have those images running around my head." Her cell phone rang from deep in her purse. "I bet that's Ajay now, checking in." She dug around, pulled out her phone, looked at the screen. "Huh. Totally wrong on that." She tapped Answer. "Fletcher? What's going on? Oh." Lizzy headed straight over to Vivian. "Sure, Nate. She's right here." She handed her phone over. "Nate needs to talk to you."

"Hey." She tried not to let the butterflies that had fluttered to life in her belly multiply. "Everything okay?"

"Honestly?" He sounded on edge, and the background noise surging through the phone included a siren. "I don't know what's going on. I'm with Fletcher and Max. We're headed into Boise right now. Something about one of my informants being in contact with Detective Sullivan. He's refusing to speak to anyone other than me."

"Oh." She glanced at her watch. Outside, the construction crew's trucks began heading out as a bright white van carrying custom glass drove in. "So you'll be later than you thought. That's okay." If anything, it was brilliant. She could get a jump start on her to-do list for tomorrow.

"You want me to stay?" Lizzy whispered.

Vivian shook her head, waved her off.

"Fletcher sent a patrol car to sit on the house until I get home," Nate said. "It's a Deputy Jeff Bricks. You probably saw him at the station the other day."

She'd seen a lot of people at the station.

"He left when we did," Nate continued. "So he should be there any time now. Even with the storm that's coming in, I should be back soon."

"Okay." As she approached the window, she saw the patrol car pull up and park right in front. "I'll check in with him. I'll be fine, Nate. Do what you need to do. Be careful."

"You sure? Maybe Lizzy—"

"Lizzy is already on her way to meet Ajay for dinner." She wasn't about to ask her friend to change her plans. "We had this conversation before. I know how the security system works, and now there's a cop right outside. Focus on your job, then come home, Nate." She paused. "To me."

"Yeah." She could almost hear the smile in his voice. "Yeah, that sounds like a perfect plan. I've got the deputy's number. If I need to call, I'll reach you that way."

"Got it. Oh, and Nate?" Those butterflies swarmed to life, but this time she embraced it. "I've got something to tell you when you get here. Something...important."

Lizzy tilted her head, pressed a hand to her heart.

"Even better. Stay safe." He clicked off.

"You two are just so cute," Lizzy said. "Are you sure you don't want me to—"

"I'm sure." Vivian handed her back her phone and walked her to the door. "He won't be gone that long, and it's starting to snow. Go. Have a good evening with Ajay."

"Always do," Lizzy confirmed.

Vivian followed her outside, waved her off in her car before she headed to the patrol car. "Hi." She smiled as the young deputy powered down his window. "Nate called and said you were coming. Vivian Maylor." She held out her hand.

"Jeff Bricks." With his dark hair and boyish smile, he reminded her a little of what she imagined Nate had looked like shortly after becoming a cop. "I checked with the guard at the gate. Updated them on what's going on."

"I'm sure we're in for a quiet evening. I'll be working. You want anything? Coffee? Snacks?"

"I'm good." He patted the green thermos sitting in one of the oversize cup holders. "Hopefully, you won't have any need to see me again."

"Okay, then." She stood up, gave him another smile.

"Thanks for doing this. You change your mind about wanting something to eat, just ring the bell."

"Lord love a duck, Ferret looks like he spent this morning in an air fryer." On the other side of the two-way mirror, Nate stood bookended between his brothers and his lieutenant.

"We had him sign a waiver stating he'd postponed medical attention," Lieutenant Haig said, hands shoved into the front pockets of his slacks, gray-haired head shifting against the fluorescent recessed lighting. "EMTs did the best they could."

"He's got to be in pain." Even Max flinched.

"Which means whatever it is he has to tell me is worth postponing treatment." Nate shook his head. "Guess I'd best get in there and find out what it is."

A knock sounded on the observation room door. The four of them turned as it popped open. Detective Julia Renard poked her head in. "Sorry. Lieutenant, patrol just radioed in. They've got movement at Shake It Loose."

"Is it DeBaccian?" Nate demanded. There were only two things he wanted right now: DeBaccian and Sullivan in custody, and to be back home with Vivian.

"Unconfirmed," Detective Renard said. "Our guys are too far away for a positive ID."

"I'm going to send two more cars out there for backup," Lieutenant Haig said. "Detective, get in there, and let's get to the bottom of this."

"Yes, sir." He looked to his brothers.

"You've got this," Fletcher told him. "But we're here if you need us."

"Thanks." Nate nodded. "Appreciate that." He didn't

give himself much time to think. Thinking might lead to mistakes. He needed to be impulsive, even as he reminded himself how to deal with Ferret Face. He tended to be cagey, hyper and, more often than not, smarter than he looked.

He didn't knock, just walked right into the interview room. "Colin." Using his hacker name wasn't something he tended to do. He needed to talk to the man behind the moniker. "What's going on, man? I hear you need to talk to me." He couldn't stop his wince of sympathy at the sight of the burns on Ferret's face, neck and arms. A stark white bandage had been taped to his right temple, and his hands, both of them, were thickly bandaged and wrapped up. "Just looking at you, I can see you're in over your head."

Beady brown eyes, usually magnified behind thick glasses, widened as Nate took a seat across from him. "You're here. Nate, dude, I need your help."

"That's why I'm here." Hands folded on the table, he did his best to keep calm and maintain his patience. "You been working with Detective Sullivan behind my back, Colin? I thought you and I had a deal."

"We did, man, we did." Ferret leaned forward. "I didn't want anything to do with this guy, right? I told him, I only work for you. Detective Nate Colton. Because you have my back. You always have."

"You'd best come out with it, then, just to make sure our relationship stays intact."

"But that's just it. I can talk now. Because you're here." The relief shining in Ferret's eyes seemed out of place. "This was part of the deal I made with him."

"Deal you made with who?" Something slimy and uncertain slithered in Nate's gut. "Detective Jim Sullivan?"

"So you know already?" Ferret squeaked. "Ah, man, does that mean Laura's okay? You've got her?"

"Your sister?" Nate glanced at the mirror, hoped Fletcher and Max got the message. "Sure, yeah, we've got her, Colin." Now wasn't the time to tell the truth.

Colin sobbed and lowered his head, banged his red, raw skin against the table. "Okay. Okay, I knew you'd get her. I knew you wouldn't let me down. He said he knew where she lived, that he could get to her anytime if I didn't do what he wanted."

"Detective Sullivan?" Nate had to be careful how he asked. It could just as easily be one of DeBaccian's henchmen, or even DeBaccian himself. "Colin? Look at me. Stop banging your head and come clean, okay? I can't keep helping you if you don't. Was it Detective Jim Sullivan? Describe him for me."

"Yeah, yeah, that's the name he gave me. Red hair, mean eyes. He shows up at my place a couple of nights ago, says he's heard about this new program I've created. Might have gotten too chatty at the Down and Dirty a few weeks ago in that poker game—"

"Colin," Nate warned. "Focus. What's this new program?"

"It's a virus that doubles as a tracker. Send an email with a virus, not as an attachment, but embedded in a link. Like in a sig line. It's mad brilliant, man. They click on it and *bam!* We can trace whatever device they use."

Nate nodded as if he understood completely. "So you did what he wanted, yeah?"

"Yeah, I sent the email that night. Told him I wasn't

sure it would work. I'm still, like, beta testing it and everything, but he promised me ten K if I took the job. That's like a semester and a half for Laura's school. And sure, yeah, he threatened her if I didn't take the job, but ten thou!"

"I get it, Colin." Nate resisted flinching. "She's family. You do what you have to do for family. That's all he had you do? Send the email?"

"Yes. Well, no." His eyes shifted, and he sank back in his chair. "He came back last night. Man, I'm sorry. I didn't want to do it, but it was the only way he said he wouldn't kill me. The only way he wouldn't go after Laura. And my mom. He threatened my family!"

"You told the officers who brought you in that this guy tried to kill you." Nate pointed to the bandage on his head.

"I had to tell them something!" Ferret cried. "It was the only way they'd call you, and I needed to get you back here, to Boise!"

"Get me back..." The pieces fell into place as if in slow motion. "He didn't really try to kill you, did he, Colin? Colin? Ferret!" Nate slammed his hand hard on the table. Ferret jumped. Guilt swam in his watery eyes. "Was all this a setup? Did you set fire to your own place?"

"It was the only way, man! I'm sorry! I didn't want... You've always been—"

Nate looked up when the door swung open. Fletcher and his lieutenant stood in the doorway, looming. Brooding.

"What?" Nate demanded.

"DeBaccian's club, Shake It Loose?" Fletcher said.

"What about it?" Nate asked.

"We just got a 911 call," Lieutenant Haig said. "It's on fire."

"Unbelievable," Max muttered from where he stood beside Nate, across the street from the now smoldering building that housed Shake It Loose. The parking lot contained a handful of cars, two fire engines and one ambulance. The fact the strip club had been closed for the past two weeks had probably saved lives. DeBaccian knew how to run a successful—if sleazy—business. "They should rename this city Coincidence Central."

Lieutenant Haig had accepted Fletcher's offer to be a second pair of eyes and ears when speaking with the fire chief leading the charge to douse the remaining embers of the fire. The fire had been out for a good half hour, but the smoke continued to billow as water dripped into frozen rivers and streamed into the street.

"Patrol units at each corner around this place, and none of them saw who was inside?" Max said. "How does that even happen?"

"Nate!" Detective Kevin Paulson, Renard's partner, hurried over from where he'd been speaking with two of the uniformed officers. "Patrol officer in the third car on scene hit Record on her body cam. Not sure if she caught anything, but it's worth a shot. We've got the footage coming through anytime."

It was something, at least. He'd feel a heck of a lot better if he could speak to Vivian, but between spotty cell service and the frenetic activity, there hadn't been a chance. "Any updates on who was inside?" Nate had never prayed so hard for a dead body in his life. If De-

Baccian was dead, that would kill any case the feds might be able to build against his associates, but it would put Vivian in the clear.

"Firefighters found three bodies in the back office." Fletcher joined them, his voice low and intense. "Just finished talking with the chief. Fire was started near the front, so it didn't get to them."

"Cause of death?"

"They were shot," Fletcher confirmed. "Close range."

Nate held his breath. "Tell me one is—"

"Chief's got a picture." Fletcher signaled the chief over, and she approached, still loaded down with equipment. She flipped up her face shield. "Chief Gibbs?"

"Detective Fletcher and Lieutenant Haig filled me in." The shorter, stockier woman handed over her cell phone. "Goes against protocol, but I took this. Hope it helps."

"There, bottom left corner." Fletcher pointed to the image. "Zoom in."

Nate took the phone and did just that. The familiar family crest glinted. "That's DeBaccian's ring."

"Looks like he didn't make it out of town after all," Max muttered before he swore and turned away.

"So he's dead." Nate couldn't quite let himself believe it.

"We've got the medical examiner's office sending out a team now," Lieutenant Haig said. "You should get back and finish with Ferret Face, Nate."

"Evidence tech is working with him at the moment," Nate said. "Ferret said he could access his cloud storage to retrieve the virus information."

"Probably go a lot faster if the guy could type quicker with those bandages," Max said.

Lieutenant Haig's cell rang. "Yeah." He turned away as he answered.

"So, that's it?" Nate looked at Max. "After all this, it's just over?"

"Sometimes that's the way a case breaks." Max shrugged.

"And all these coincidences?" Nate challenged. "They don't bother you?"

"Didn't say that." Max waited a beat. "They bother you?"

Yes, but his gut wasn't capable of overriding actual evidence.

Lieutenant Haig rejoined them. "Security at Boise Airport just stopped someone using Jim Sullivan's ID to board a flight to Mexico."

Fletcher, Max and Nate simply stared at him.

"Yeah." Lieutenant Haig smirked and ducked his head. "I'm not buying it, either. He'd know we'd have locked down the airports, train stations and bus terminals in the city. No way he's that careless. I asked the officers to send me a photo..." His phone chimed. "And there it is." He turned the phone around. "Definitely not Jim Sullivan."

"Misdirect," Fletcher said. "A stupid one."

"None of this explains Sullivan going to Ferret Face," Nate said, more to himself than anyone else. "What good would a tracking virus be...?"

"Was Sullivan tracking someone for himself or for DeBaccian?" Fletcher asked.

"Only person that we know of that DeBaccian would want found is Vivian," Max said. "Do we have a copy of the email he sent yet?"

"Still working on it," Lieutenant Haig said. "Apparently there are seven levels of security that need to be traversed in order to gain access to Ferret Face's cloud storage."

"No one's more paranoid than a hacker," Nate growled. Smoke continued to plume into the air from inside Shake It Loose. "Only three bodies inside. No one else?"

"As far as surveillance reported," Lieutenant Haig said. "No one else went in or came out the front or back in the past eight hours."

"What about the alley?" Nate asked.

Lieutenant Haig blinked. "What alley?"

"There's a narrow one between the club and the abandoned building next door. I read about it in one of the initial surveillance reports from a few months ago. It's not wide enough for a vehicle, but DeBaccian used it as a private entrance. And he had at least two security cameras working twenty-four seven."

Lieutenant Haig shook his head. "I just reread all those reports this morning. No mention of the alley or the cameras."

"That list of databases Sullivan accessed that you came up with," Fletcher said to Nate. "One of them was the official records files, right?"

"He could have deleted the mention from the report," Nate said. "I couldn't go deeper than a cursory examination without raising an alarm." He looked back to the club. "We need to get in there. There might be security footage. Proof of Sullivan getting away." Maybe even proof he was guilty of murdering DeBaccian.

"Chief!" Lieutenant Haig called to Chief Gibbs.

"We're going to need your help. And a couple of helmets. We need to get inside."

With the television on for background noise—she preferred old Hollywood musicals to keep her mood elevated—Vivian made slow and steady progress on her always growing to-do list. Cyber-handholding had become her specialty. Selfishly, she preferred clients who liked communicating via email rather than spending countless hours on video or phone calls.

With the Christmas tree providing ambient lighting and the dim glow from over the stove, the house felt even cozier than before. Instead of tea—she'd definitely had her fill for a while—she had opened one of the bottles of wine she found in the dedicated wine refrigerator. Nothing rounded out the day quite like a bold Bordeaux. Sipping, she sighed and resisted the urge to check her watch for the hundredth time.

As the sun set and the night crept in, she couldn't help but feel anxious for Nate to return. Not just because she didn't relish being alone in this big house. Because she missed him.

Needing to stretch, she set her laptop on the coffee table and stood up, twisting and reaching her arms over her head to work out the kinks. She took a short walk down the hall to the front of the house. The patrol car hadn't moved. The now familiar shadow of Deputy Jeff Bricks shifted in the darkness. She waved, whether he could see her or not, and headed back into the kitchen.

She caught the oven timer before it started beeping and retrieved a pair of potholders to pull out the pork roast she'd set to cooking earlier. She tented it with foil, telling herself she could reheat it should Nate be much later.

With Bing Crosby and Danny Kaye singing on the television, she settled back onto the sofa and picked up her laptop again.

The second she started typing, the power cut out. The house went dark.

"Good thing the fire inspector won't be here until tomorrow morning," Chief Gibbs grumbled at their backs as Nate and Lieutenant Haig made their way through the burned-out strip club. It had taken some convincing, letting any of them inside, but she'd eventually given in, probably just to get the lieutenant off her overburdened back.

They'd donned evidence booties—those lovely blue cloth shoe coverings that would prevent them from dragging any trace evidence of their own onto the scene. Nate was relieved she hadn't put them in hazmat suits.

The alley door had been left ajar. Ash and soot had spread outside the club. Fletcher and Max remained outside, acting as a point of communication should they need it.

It wasn't Nate's first fire scene. The charred, wet wood gave off its own particular aroma, and the smoke settled into his lungs like an unwanted resident. He'd be smelling this place for weeks, no doubt. Maybe the hazmat suit would have been okay. He could hear the *drip, drip, drip* of the hose water used to knock back the flames.

"At first glance, I'd say whoever started it hedged their bets. I've got traces in the front and back entrances," Chief Gibbs called over her shoulder, a hand keeping her bright yellow helmet steady on her head. "Be careful where you step, please. I really don't want to fill out a report about you two being in here."

"Consider yourself having earned multiple favors from the police department," Lieutenant Haig told her.

She stopped outside a barely holding together door frame. "I'll remember that." She stepped back. "Your bodies are back there, near the desk. What's left of the desk," she corrected. "I'm going to take another walk-through, make sure we didn't miss anyone. Ten minutes," she told them. "That's it."

"That's all we'll need," Nate assured her. Unable to choke down any more smoke, he pulled the collar of his T-shirt up over his nose, stepped carefully through the debris and burned carpet and flooring. "Well, I see three." He didn't know what he expected other than what had already been reported.

He crouched down, carefully lifted one of the three bright yellow tarps covering the bodies. The flames hadn't done enough damage to obscure the markings on both men's skin.

"These two match the description Vivian gave of the shooters." He flipped the tarps back up, stood up, turned and took four steps the right. The exposed hand, stretched out as if for help, displayed the now familiar ring that had, for years, represented DeBaccian's growing power. He'd wielded it like a weapon, frequently shifting it to his right hand in order to leave a lasting mark.

"Nothing surprising." Lieutenant Haig nodded to the large safe across the room. "That's been emptied out."

"Guns, no doubt. And cash," Nate said, shaking his head. "Chief Gibbs was right. This was a waste of time."

"I heard that!" Chief Gibbs called from outside the room.

Nate almost laughed. He pushed to his feet, slipped his foot free of the corner of the tarp that caught against his shoe. The tarp fluttered and settled, exposing part of the victim's face.

Shock cut through him like a knife. Nate dropped back down, ripped the tarp back and stared at the body, with its dead wide eyes. "Lieutenant? You seeing what I'm seeing?" He pointed to the red hair gleaming in the dim light of their helmet lights.

"It's Jim Sullivan," his lieutenant confirmed.

"Nate!"

Nate pivoted as Fletcher dived into sight.

"Hey!" Chief Gibbs stalked toward him, hands up. "I told you to wait—"

"Nate, we've got the email Ferret sent." Fletcher plowed right past her. "It was an inquiry addressed to PR Perfection."

"PR…" Nate's heart skipped a beat. "That's Vivian's company. Ferret was hired to track Vivian's laptop." He stared blankly at his boss, then turned to look down at the body. "Sullivan's dead," he murmured. "Which means DeBaccian isn't." Fear wrapped its talons around his heart and squeezed. "He's going after her."

"We have to get back to Owl Creek," Fletcher commanded. "Now!"

Chapter 15

Vivian groaned and dropped her head back. The marvels of living in snow country. At home, she had a generator that would kick in when the power went out. But up here? She used her laptop as a light and untangled herself yet again from the sofa.

She heard a car door slam and quickly hurried to the window. The handful of street lamps that had been installed had gone dark as well. The only things casting any light were the moon and the interior of the deputy's car.

Deputy Bricks headed up the walkway, zipping up his jacket.

She set her laptop on the floor, hurried to the door and pulled it open. "What's going on?" she asked.

"No idea," the deputy said. "I'm going to take a walk around. There might be some crews working late... Maybe they tripped something." He offered a smile. "You okay in there?"

"Everything's fine." She shrugged.

"Let me take a quick look, just to be safe."

She shrugged and stepped back. "Okay. I think I saw some candles in the pantry."

"Great." He closed the door behind him and headed down one hall while Vivian retrieved her laptop.

"Oh!" She snapped her fingers, remembering her cell. It might be useless for calls, but it made a better flashlight than her computer. She headed upstairs to the bedroom, grabbed it from where she'd set it last night when she'd spent almost a half hour looking at pictures of Toby. She left her laptop on the bed, turned on the flashlight.

A soft thud echoed from downstairs.

She froze. "Deputy Bricks?" Taking slow steps, she moved into the hall, walked to the landing of the stairs. "Deputy?" The light wavered as her hand shook. "Hello?"

She cast the light around, eyes adjusting to the harsh light against the shadows.

"Deputy?" She yelled this time and winced against the echo that shot back at her.

Footsteps sounded. Dull, heavy.

Growing closer.

She shivered against a sudden chill and only now realized she could hear the wind blowing. Her mind raced. Everything she'd been told about the house seemed to tumble in her head. Alarm. Guard house. Panels.

She raced back into the bedroom, forced herself to be quiet when closing the door.

The keypad on the wall seemed to mock her as she flipped open the panel and hit the emergency button.

Nothing happened.

She pounded a fist against the console.

Frustrated tears burned the back of her throat. Blurred her eyes.

The footsteps were coming up the stairs. Slowly. Closer.

Her bare toes scrunched into the hardwood flooring.

She spun around, looking for something, anything, with which to defend herself. Moonlight shimmered against the glass door.

Swallowing her panic, she ran forward, threw open the doors, raced to the balcony railing, then forced herself to slow down, turn and return to the bedroom, placing her feet in the same prints she'd made in the snow.

She left the doors open, ran quietly tos the closet and ducked inside, pulling the door closed behind her as the bedroom doorknob rattled.

She killed the flashlight, hugged her phone against her chest. Moonlight streamed across the slats of the closet door.

She stepped back into the corner, into the darkness, as a large, shadowy figure stepped into the room.

"I'm not getting any response from Bricks," Fletcher said from the back seat. Max had reached the driver's side first and had them speeding out of Boise, siren blaring. "I'm calling the station now."

"We'll get there," Max said. "I promise, Nate, we'll get there in time."

"You know as well as I do that's an impossible promise to make." He was a cop. He'd been a cop for almost a decade. He was well aware of the realities of the job. "I shouldn't have left her."

"Don't go down that road," Fletcher ordered. "It doesn't lead anywhere good. If we can't get to her, I'll get someone who can. Yeah," he yelled into the phone. "Monroe, I want all hands on deck and up at Colton Crossing. We've got a wanted suspect on-site." He recited the address of the house. "Be on the lookout for

Vivian Maylor…" He rattled off Vivian's description. "I'm about— Max! Watch it!"

Nate gripped the passenger seat with both hands as Max weaved his way in and around slowing traffic.

"We need to get there alive to help her," Nate ground out between gritted teeth.

"Doing my best," Max said as he pressed his foot even harder on the gas. "Don't worry. I'm motivated. Lizzy will never forgive us if anything happens to Vivian."

"*I'll* never forgive us." Nate stared into the snowy night and did something he hadn't done in a very, very long time.

He prayed.

Terror, Vivian thought as she watched the figure pass, worked as a surprisingly effective mental reboot.

She knew what she didn't have at her disposal—the alarm and warning system she'd been told about time and again. No communication because her cell phone was little more than a door weight. She was currently a sitting duck. But hopefully a silent one.

Vivian stepped forward, angling her head to peer through the closet slats.

The man was following her footprints, stepping outside the bedroom. Onto the balcony. One step from the door. Two…three…

She pushed open the closet door and squeezed out. She couldn't risk closing it again for fear he'd hear. Moving as quietly as she could, she hurried out of the bedroom door toward the stairs.

She was three steps down when she heard him. No. She *felt* him. An energy of rage that pulsed through the house and nearly knocked her off her feet. She lost her grip on her phone, heard it skid away after it hit the floor.

Panic had her scrambling, tripping, nearly tumbling to the landing, but she stayed on her feet, using the banister to propel herself to the front door.

He'd locked it. Bolted it. She tugged on the handle, tried to flip the lock, but he was coming down the stairs. Too close.

Too, too close.

Her feet slipped and slid as she scrambled toward the kitchen. There had to be something—anything— she could use...

"There's nowhere to run." His voice didn't echo through the house. It settled inside her mind like a dark mantra of warning. "No one to help. I'll make it quick. And painless."

She sobbed, feeling her way down the wall and imagining the path she'd taken countless times in the past few days. Vivian cried out when she ran straight into the corner of the kitchen island. She could already feel a bruise forming as she grappled her way around the stove, knocked over the salt and pepper shakers. Biting back a sob, her hands flailed almost desperately until she finally felt the curved neck of the oil bottle.

His presence pressed in on her. Moonlight shone through the doors, and her eyes adjusted enough for her to grab the bottle and douse the top of the stove.

He stood only a few feet away now, his height making her tilt her head back to see the top of him. He flexed his hands, the leather of his gloves creaking in the silence.

Braced with her back against the stove, she reached behind her and twisted the knob. *Click, click, click, hisssss...*

Vivian dropped to the ground as the gas burner flamed to life.

The flames exploded up, straight into his face. The man screamed, held up both hands to protect himself, stumbled back and crashed down onto the coffee table.

The fire alarm blared, the horrific screech cutting through her head like a hot knife.

Vivian didn't stop to evaluate her actions. Or the damage she may have done to the kitchen.

She raced around the island, down the hall, wrenched open the locks. She flung open the door and ran out into the stormy, snowy night.

"What on earth did they teach you at the FBI academy?" Nate demanded as Max took the off-ramp that would lead to Colton Crossing at nearly twice the legal speed limit. "Holy... Is that black ice?"

"Maybe." Max plowed over it anyway, leading Nate to believe, without a doubt, the tires of Fletcher's SUV weren't even touching the ground.

"My officers are four minutes out," Fletcher yelled over the noise of the engine, the storm and Nate's frayed nerves. "We had a multicar accident in town. They couldn't get away until that was settled."

Nate clenched his jaw tighter. Four minutes. A lot could happen in four minutes.

Max rounded the first corner on two wheels. The siren continued to blare. Nate had no doubt he'd be hearing it in his head for years to come. He should have let her have the stupid cell phone. He needed to talk to her again. Needed to hear her voice again. Needed to tell her...

"Almost there." Max raced down the road as the snow

continued to fall. Another left turn and he zoomed up the final hill.

"There! I can see the guard house!" Fletcher pointed between their seats.

Behind them, more sirens screeched through the night. Nate looked back. Down, in the distance, he could see three patrol cars making their way up the mountain.

Max screeched the SUV to a stop in front of the guard gate.

"Where's the officer?" Nate yelled as he jumped out of the car. He all but leaped at the door that swung open by the hand of a middle-aged man with a full, dark beard. "Open the gate!"

"Power's out!" the guard, whose badge identified him as Angelo, yelled back. "I've been trying to reset the generator, but it's not connecting. Must be the storm!"

"It's not the storm." Nate shoved his way inside, Fletcher right at his heels. "How do I..." He started flipping switches, anything that might trigger the eight-foot wrought iron gate to open.

A red light started blinking, and an alarm sounded.

"What's that? What did I do?" Nate demanded.

"That's a fire alarm," Angelo said. "There's only one house that's occupied."

"Vivian." Nate slammed out of the guard house and went for the fence, looking for a way to squeeze through the slats or pull open the lock.

"Get back!" Max yelled before he ducked back behind the wheel. He screeched the car back, set the tires to spinning and hit the gas full throttle. Nate dived out of the way seconds before Max ran the car straight into the gate.

It didn't open. But the crash jarred it enough to break

the connection on the lock. Nate wedged his hands into the fractured opening, pushed with everything he had. His forearms burned with the exertion, but all he could think was that Vivian was on the other side of this gate. He had to get through. There wasn't any other option.

"Let me help!" Fletcher appeared, and sliding in behind Nate, he got his own hold on the frame. Together they shoved, crying out as the gate finally began to shift down the track.

Nate didn't wait to be sure he'd fit before he shoved his head through, then squeezed through the rest of his body. He tripped on the way out to the other side.

"Go!" Fletcher yelled when Nate looked over his shoulder. "We'll be right behind you! Max!"

Nate didn't have to be told twice. He turned and ran.

Vivian stopped out in the street, the house she'd escaped well behind her. She spun in a dazed circle. The thin fabric of her clothing gave even less protection than she would have imagined. Her feet had gone numb. The rest of her body was quickly following.

Above the gentle roar of the snow, she swore she heard sirens. But it could also be the alarm still blaring from the house. Which way to go? One way would take her to the guard house. The other...to the partially completed construction site. But which was which? She could barely see the sidewalks. But there...in the distance, whether her imagination or not, she saw lights.

She saw hope.

She only had one choice. Trust herself.

Ducking her head, she tightened her arms and, moving as fast as she could, headed into the snow.

* * *

The distance from the guarded gate to the house was a lot longer on foot than it was by car. Nate didn't have the luxury to stop and reevaluate his route. He went by memory, hoping, praying he was headed in the right direction. He ran full out, lungs expanding to the point of catching fire. His legs had long ago gone numb, his feet hurting with each strike on the ground. He was having trouble seeing as the snow flurries whipped around.

He skidded to a stop. There. He squinted, tried to peer closer. He saw something. A flash of shimmering white amidst the white. Like a sharp slice through the night.

"Vivian." He knew it was her even before he saw the whip of dark hair. She was moving slowly, but in the right direction. "Vivian!"

He heard his name on the wind, a sob of relief, of desperation. He couldn't be certain which. Nate raced forward, only to feel his heart leap into his throat at the sound of her scream.

"Nate!"

He kept moving, his line of sight clearing just in time to see the dark shadow of Marty DeBaccian. He had one arm locked around Vivian's throat. And with his free hand, he held a gun to her head.

Nate reached back, pulled out his gun and held it up. He shook his head, tried to see through the falling snow. He couldn't get a lock. He aimed up, then down, to the side, shook his head. He couldn't get a lock.

"There's nowhere to go, DeBaccian!" Nate yelled as he did the only thing he could. He stepped closer. "You've got the Owl Creek cops and an FBI agent coming behind me. You're not getting away."

"There's more than one way out of here!" DeBaccian yelled back.

Nate was close enough now. Close enough to see the abject terror in Vivian's eyes as she struggled to breathe. As she clawed her hands at his arm to dislodge his hold.

"She comes with me!"

Vivian gasped as he lifted her higher, to where her bare feet dangled inches above the snow.

He felt rather than heard his brothers behind him. That charge in the atmosphere could only be one thing: backup. The sound of car engines, the reflection of spinning lights exploding against the falling snow released some of the fear coursing through him.

"She's coming with me!" DeBaccian yelled again, desperation in his voice now.

Nate released the safety on his gun. "She is not."

One more step and he was close enough to fire. He was poised to hit DeBaccian at point-blank range. One shot and it was all over. His finger tightened on the trigger.

Vivian shifted and blocked his shot. He pulled his finger away as she twisted and kicked until she could open her mouth. She kicked back hard, caught DeBaccian on the knee and sank her teeth into his arm.

DeBaccian howled with rage more than pain. He dropped her. Vivian hit the ground on all fours, but before DeBaccian reclaimed his hold, he aimed at Nate's head.

"Freeze! Police!" The voice wasn't familiar. Not to Nate.

DeBaccian spun, looked behind him, gun raised.

A shot rang out. Then another. And a third. Vivian remained crouched on the ground, shivering hard.

DeBaccian dropped to his knees, pitched forward. Landed face down in the snow.

"Vivian." Nate ran to her, had her up and off the ground and in his arms in seconds. He swore, he cursed, he held her as tightly as he could as she shivered so hard she practically vibrated out of his hold.

"Okay?" Fletcher came over with a spare coat and boots from his vehicle for Vivian, then dropped a hand on Nate's shoulder as Max passed right by.

"Yeah," Nate whispered as Vivian nodded against his throat. "You're okay, right, Viv?" He pressed his lips to the top of her head, gratitude and relief flooding through him when she offered a choking whimper. "Is he dead?" Nate yelled at Max as his brother nudged a booted foot under DeBaccian's shoulder and shoved him onto his back.

DeBaccian groaned.

"Not nearly." Max bent down, ripped open DeBaccian's jacket. "He was wearing a vest. Fletcher, your deputy." He pointed to the staggering Jeff Bricks, who had a hand clutched against the back of his head as he made his way toward them.

"Son of a… He clocked me from behind." Bricks spat out the words as Fletcher grabbed him by the shoulders to keep him on his feet. "When I woke up, I swear I thought he was on fire."

"He was," Vivian murmured against Nate's neck. "I put oil on the stove and lit it in his face."

Nate couldn't stop himself. He laughed even as he held her tighter. "Watching all those murder mysteries finally paid off. It's over, Viv." Nate didn't think he could hold her any tighter. "It's all over."

"No," she said as he bent down and slipped an arm under her knees, swept her high into his arms. "It's just beginning." She pressed her lips to his. "I love you, Nate. I needed to tell you that, you know, in case something else happens."

"Nothing else is going to happen." He started walking back to the house. "I'm not going to let anything else happen to you. Ever. You hear me?"

"I hear you. Did you hear me?"

"Yes." For now, he left the fear, the anger and the cleanup behind with his brothers. "I love you, too." He'd always thought when he uttered the words they would come with a question, or with doubt. Or, at the very least, uncertainty. Instead he knew, without any hesitancy, that this thing with Vivian was one-hundred-percent right. "I want to take you out on a date. To celebrate everything," he told her. "How does that sound?"

"Madariaga's?" she asked as he rounded the walkway up to the porch.

"Where we first met?"

She looked up at him, a smile spreading across her lush, perfect lips. "Where else?"

Chapter 16

Nate pulled open the door to Madariaga's just as a gust of wind and snow blew in ahead of him. He took a moment to stomp his feet and shake his head free of the weather.

"You're late."

"Yeah, I know." Nate offered Seb a quick smile as the bartender took the box containing Vivian's Christmas present off his hands. "She been here long?"

"Long enough you'll be glad you got her a gift."

"Awesome." Nate removed his coat, hung it up and slid a finger under his suddenly too tight collar. The flurry of activity that had taken place in the days following Marty DeBaccian's apprehension put the recent snowstorms to shame. But finally, the last piece had been placed, and he was officially on vacation.

"You want your usual?"

"Club soda?" Nate laughed. "Nah. Tonight we're celebrating. Scotch, on the rocks, please, Seb."

The bartender nodded. "You've got it."

"You weren't worried, were you?" Nate said as he slipped up behind a seated Vivian and brushed his lips against her cheek.

"Me? Worry?" She covered the hand he rested on her shoulder and squeezed. "I figured you'd call if you couldn't make it." She didn't look worried. But she did look nervous. Beautiful in an embroidered blue-and-white dress that made her look like a Grecian princess. "You look…" Her smile radiated the warmth of the dining room. "Wow, Detective. You need to wear a suit more often. Everything okay?"

"I'm going to give you the short version." He sat, smoothed his tie down his chest. "Because I don't want to spend tonight debriefing you."

She reached over, slipped her fingers through his. "Well, that's too bad." Her smile lit up her eyes. "I was kind of hoping to be debriefed."

That comment went straight to his groin. "Noted. DeBaccian cut a deal."

Her brow furrowed. "What kind of deal?"

"The kind that guarantees he'll be in prison for life. He turned state's evidence on multiple organized crime figures. In exchange, he gets a new identity and a private cell in a federal prison in Colorado."

"Well, good for him. And us." She lifted her glass of red wine as his drink arrived. They clinked in a toast. "How'd your Colton conference this afternoon go?"

"Colton conference," Nate mused. "I was thinking it was more of a summit, but yeah." He nodded. "It went well, I think. Chase said to thank you for putting their security system through the paces. He and Sloan are going to be making some changes after what happened with the power outage."

"You ever figure out how DeBaccian did that?" Vivian asked.

"He stole a glass repair van and got in with the construction crew. Early enough he gained access to the office and all the information he needed. He already knew what house you were in, thanks to that tracking email."

"Your ferret friend owes me a new computer," she grumbled. "But after the holidays is fine."

He wasn't the only one taking some time off. She'd put her clients on notice and said she'd be back in touch after the New Year. As for Nate, after the holidays, he planned to do a deep dive into his mother's reported connection to Markus Acker and his so-called church. He was not going to let Jessie ruin another holiday for him. "I'll get it taken care of," he told her. "So, about that summit, er, conference—"

"Before I forget." She held up a finger. "I stopped at the hospital today to visit Dean Wexler."

"Did you?"

"I did. He's going to be okay." She looked at him, narrowed her eyes. "You already knew."

"Lizzy told me this afternoon. Did Wexler tell you he's going to plead guilty to the robberies?"

"He did. And he apologized for putting me in danger." She ran her index finger around the rim of her wine glass. "I think he's had a change of heart when it comes to a criminal lifestyle."

"One can hope." But Nate wouldn't bet money on it. "So." He cleared his throat. "I have some, well, family news."

"Okay." She leaned her arms on the table and looked into his eyes.

"We've been invited to Christmas Eve dinner at the ranch in Owl Creek."

"We?" she teased.

"Well, Sarah and I have. And you have, too, but hopefully you'll be coming with me. As my date." He tightened his fingers on hers. "Does that sound like something you'd like to do? I know the holidays aren't the easiest thing for you."

"One thing almost dying does for you is help release the past." Her black hair glinted in the candlelight of the votive flickering on their table. "One of my happiest childhood memories is that Christmas I spent with Lizzy on the ranch. It only seems fitting our first Christmas together happen there as well. That's my long way of saying yes." Her smile was full and generous. "I would love to go with you."

He had no words. But he did have a gift. He looked over to the bar, caught Seb's eye and signaled to him. "Then we should seal this plan with a gift."

"Not a kiss?" She pouted. "You're really striking out tonight, Detective."

Maybe he was. But not for long.

"What's this?" Vivian asked as Seb appeared with the rather messily wrapped package topped with a big red bow. She accepted it with both hands, shot him a look. "Nate, what did you do?"

"It's why I was late. Ruby called at the last minute. I hadn't planned to do this until Christmas Day, then the whole invitation to the ranch happened and… I'm babbling."

"Happens to the best of us. Can I?"

"If you don't, we won't have anyplace to eat." The box took up a good part of the table.

"Okay." She smiled at the box, tears glistening in her

eyes. "Other than from Lizzy, I haven't gotten a present for Christmas in a really long time." She rested her hands on the top of the box. "Thank you, Nate. Oh!" She started when the lid jumped. "What on earth…?" She popped open the lid, peered inside. "Oh. Oh, Nate." She reached in and pulled out the little black kitten. "Oh, he's— He?" Nate nodded. "He's beautiful."

Nate put the box on the floor as she cuddled the kitten against her chest. The tiny gold bell around his neck tinkled as the cat gave Vivian a good sniff, then licked her chin. "Ruby picked him out for you. He was the last in a litter and the only black one. She said they don't get adopted as often and are often lost." He inclined his head, reveling in the joy on her face. Tears streamed down her cheeks. "I thought you might appreciate that."

She shook her head, leaned out of her chair enough to brush a kiss across his lips. "You are the best thing I could have ever hoped for."

"Yeah?" He reached out, tapped the kitten on the top of his head. "You think?"

"I don't think," she murmured. "I know."

Epilogue

"You ready?"

Nate looked down at Vivian's hand, clasped around his. He'd needed a moment, after the drive to the Colton ranch, to get his bearings. It was one thing to have met most of his brothers and sisters in town or in Boise. It was another to be stepping foot on their land, into their home.

But it was time. He reached out and took hold of Sarah's hand. He could feel his own nerves in his sister's grasp, heard her nervous breathing as he tugged her close. He met her eyes and, for a moment, was transported back to that night he'd told her the truth about their father. Their family. Their brothers and sisters.

Back then, this day hadn't seemed possible. All the fresh pine garlands decorated with gold bells and bright red bows. The various trees decorated with lights and ornaments and the wrapping around the water vessels for the wildlife and ranch animals to drink out of. The snowcapped fences stretched to and fro, framing the picture-perfect setting in an image he didn't think he'd ever forget.

"We're ready, yeah?" he asked his sister. Sarah nodded.

The three of them walked up the path, hand in hand.

The closer they got, the louder the laughter and celebration sounded on the other side of the door.

Taking the stairs up, Nate's heart pounded.

He nearly stepped back when the front door burst open.

"Finally!" Lizzy leaped out and caught him in a huge hug. "We were wondering when you'd get here."

"I like to be on time," he said, glancing at his watch. "You said—"

"Yeah, yeah. Did you bring Jinx?"

"We left the kitten well tended to at Eddie's," Nate said.

"My neighbor," Vivian said. "He's declared himself an honorary grandfather."

"Fabulous." Lizzy beamed at Vivian, then turned her smile on Sarah, who, for the first time since getting out of the car, looked as if she might be changing her mind about coming. "Sarah. It's nice to see you again. I'm Lizzy."

"Yes, I remember. Oh." She found herself on the receiving end of another hug. "Thank you for inviting us."

"Of course. You're family, after all. No place else you should be. Come in." She stepped back inside and waved them in.

"They're here!" Lizzy yelled into the house as Ajay stepped out from where he stood with Chase and Wade.

"Forgive her," Ajay said as he closed the door behind them. "She started the eggnog at breakfast."

"Did not!" Lizzy called over her shoulder.

"Vivian." Buck Colton, standing slightly shorter than Nate, approached, held out his arms to her. "I feel like you should still be a little girl. Welcome back to the ranch."

"Thank you." Vivian shifted uneasy eyes to Nate. "Thank you for including us."

"Of course," Buck said easily. "You're family." He turned his attention to Nate and Sarah. "You're always welcome here."

It was on the tip of Nate's tongue to ask if Buck was sure, but he could see, with the lively humor and good intentions shining in Buck's green eyes, that he meant what he said.

"Jenny, Nate and Sarah are here." Buck stepped back, held out his hand. "I'm not sure you were properly introduced the first time we met."

Nate, still holding his sister's hand, felt it tighten around his. He knew immediately what she was thinking because he was, too. She was their mother's twin, but whatever resemblance they might have borne to one another no longer existed. Where Jessie was all harsh angles and anger, Jenny Colton radiated a warmth and maternal generosity that reached out and enveloped them.

This was, Nate realized, the moment he'd been most dreading. "I'm—" He was what? Sorry for actions he'd had no part in? Sorry for existing? Sorry for causing her and Buck pain he couldn't begin to fathom. Vivian leaned against him, wrapped her arms around his and gave him a gentle nudge. "Merry Christmas," he said instead.

Jenny lifted a hand to his cheek, then to Sarah's. She smiled. "Merry Christmas."

"Does this mean we can finally eat?" Max hollered and earned a combination of cheers and jeers. He hoisted four-year-old Justin, Greg and Briony's adopted little boy, over his head as Lucy Colton, only a year older, jumped up and down as she clung to her mother Hannah's hand.

"Let's get you something to drink, yeah?" Jenny pulled them farther into the room just as Frannie walked up a couple of stairs, turned and clinked her spoon against her wine glass. Her beaded white dress flared around her knees, and her blond hair had been sharpened into its usual bob.

"Before everyone goes nose down in the turkey…" She looked down, held out her hand and drew a man up beside her. "Dante and I have a bit of a surprise for all of you."

"No more surprises, please!" Lizzy called over the din. "We've had enough for the year."

"Well, then," Frannie said, then waited for quiet. "This should bring this year to a perfect close. Since we weren't sure when we could get the entire family together again, we figured we might as well make this day, a day when we're *all* here—" she toasted Nate and Sarah "—even more special. So…"

"We're getting married," Dante said, as if tired of waiting for her to get to the point. "Today." He glanced at his watch. "Right now, as a matter of fact."

It was impossible not to get caught up in the joyous cheers that erupted through the room.

"No one saw this coming?" Nate asked Vivian, who shrugged.

"And thank you to Hannah," Frannie yelled to get the family quieted down again. "We couldn't have pulled this off without her, especially since we had to have a cake!"

Hannah did a little curtsey, which her daughter copied. "Always happy to help with a wedding that isn't mine."

That earned another round of laughter.

"What do you say, Reverend Bostick?" Dante called to a middle-aged man wearing an ugly Rudolph sweater. "You ready to do this?"

"Me? Now?" Reverend Bostick seemed to choke on his eggnog as his eyes went wide.

"We're ready if you are," Frannie confirmed.

"Well, all right, then." The reverend patted his chest for his glasses. "I think I can wing this. Merry Christmas, indeed."

Ruby and Lizzy came over to draw Sarah away while Nate and Vivian made their way to a pair of chairs scooted together. Nate ran his hand down his tie, and when he looked at Vivian, he saw her beaming at him. She rested her hand over his.

"You know what this is, don't you?" she whispered.

"What?" He pressed a kiss to her lips.

"The best Christmas ever."

He pulled her close, tucked her head under his chin and watched his family swarm and settle and sigh. "I think you're right," he agreed. "You're absolutely right."

* * * * *